Shadows
OF THE
Mind

BOOK TWO

Shadows OF THE mind

BY OWEN CLOUGH

weka
ficton

WEKA FICTION
owencloughbooks.com

Cover design by Tania Hassounia of Drawer Full of Giants.

National Library of New Zealand Cataloguing-in-Publication Data

ISBN Paperback: 978-0-473-45407-4
ISBN eBook: 978-0-473-43410-6

Published in New Zealand

A catalogue record for this book is available
from the National Library of New Zealand.
Kei te pātengi raraunga o Te Puna Mātauranga o
Aotearoa te whakarārangi o tēnei pukapuka.

This book is dedicated to

My wife Kaye for the support she has given me over the years of my writing, for without her support this book and future books would never get off the ground.

Author's Note

This is a work of fiction. All persons, places, things, and events in this story are a product of the author's imagination, and any similarity to real people, places, events and organisations are coincidental. Although some mention is made of historical events, they are there to enhance authenticity and are not intended to be fact or to describe or portray any real world person, tactics, beliefs or policies.

"Yesterday is gone. Tomorrow has not yet come. We have only today. Let us begin."

— Mother Teresa

Acknowledgements

I would never have got to this stage if it was not for my wife Kaye, who tirelessly edited every chapter, correcting grammar, changing the flow of sentences to make the book flow and making it that much more comfortable too read. Without her, I would be a lost soul in the woods. I love you to bits.

My daughter Tania with all her talent as an illustrator, designing the cover of the book in keeping the same look like the first novel. Also, her help creating the business cards and banner to promote my books and everything I get stuck with on the computer she is there for me.

My Granddaughter Sofia for her continuing help with my web page updating it with reviews and in general keeping it fresh. I'm so lucky to have talented woman in my family.

To my son Brent who read the fight scenes from the next book to give me his thoughts, he was a Black Belt 3rd Dan at karate and was the definitely go-to person.

A very special thanks to Paula and Terry Grundy, hard working proofreader duo from Canada, who in my opinion put the icing on the cake and now are good friends

Fraser Newman from Atlantis Books who's help was immense with getting this book up too publishing format. I cannot thank him enough for steering me in the right direction.

To all those so numerous to mention my sincere and grateful thanks.

CHAPTER ONE

1863 HMS Esk, Tasman Sea

I was born on the 18th May 1863, at the age of thirty years old or thereabouts. Nobody has a clue, but they reckoned that was how old I was when I regained consciousness.

My birth place was aboard HMS Esk a three-masted coal-fired steamship, pounding across the Tasman Sea to Australia from New Zealand. My parents are unknown, so is my birthplace but they think it could be Scotland. The weird thing is even the army had no idea who I am; they figured I was an officer, so they took that at face value. Then the nurse explained, according to the document in my pack my name was Lieutenant Samuel Mack.

When I looked at myself in a mirror, I noticed that I was big in build, broad in the shoulders and a little over two metres tall. When I mentioned the word 'metres' to my companions, all I got was, 'None of that froggy stuff here Lieutenant, you are about 6ft 5 inches tall'. I didn't understand what they meant, but I seemed to tower over everyone. Anyway, I had just been born so there will be a lot of things I'll have to learn. My face has an open smile with healthy teeth, my eyes are blue but showing a bit of tension, and there are dark circles around them. Both my face and arms are as brown as a berry, surprisingly my chest, back and legs are as well. Everyone who noticed thought this was a bit unusual as nobody takes their shirt off in public or even to show their legs, so how on earth I got this colour, I have no idea. I also have been told I've lost a bit of weight, but apparently, this was typical for a person in my condition.

I am sturdy with large hands, no doubt this goes with my size, I have no idea really, but that sounded okay to me. At this point in time, I was unsteady on my feet. It had nothing to do with the ship I was on, it was because they said I had been shot three times in the head, and it would take time for my balance to return. When I walked or tried to, I hung onto the railings or supported myself against the walls of the ship, anything that was stable. Luckily it didn't happen very often as I had this angel with me most of the time, who assisted me and made my life as comfortable as possible. I didn't mention my hair colouring, as my head was completely wrapped in bandages and I hadn't seen it then. I am clean shaven though I noticed the bristles on my face are whitish, and when I looked down at the family jewels, there's the same white there as well. I thought as I'm newborn that will darken up when I'm older.

Like all births, it was painful, not for the mother this time, but for me. I awoke to excruciating pain in my head; my eyes were full of water as I screwed up my face in agony. The nurse was there like a shot with some pain killer; eventually, the pain eased to the point that I could take an interest in my surroundings. When I was coherent, the nurse›s first question was, ‹Do you know your name?› I frowned and thought, how do people who are just born are aware of their name, ‹I have no idea,› I replied. So that was when she opened my pack and found the document with my name on it. They now call me Sam.

She commented that I had been in and out of wakefulness over the three days since we had left New Zealand and that this was the first time I was fully awake. I was surprised, but I told her what was more important to me at that moment, and that was that I was hungry and could eat a horse. She clapped her hands, 'Oh, wonderful that's the best news I have heard from you.' And off she went to get some tucker for me. When I had mentioned 'tucker', she did not know what I meant, so I guess I must come from somewhere they speak English a bit differently. At that moment, though, all I could think about was food, and in she walked with lamb stew, thick white bread and tonnes of butter to wipe the plate with, and an enormous tankard of ale. I gather this was extremely irregular on a Royal Navy Ship, a tot of rum, yes, but booze, no! She had arranged for the ale as there were twenty of us wounded on board and beer helped with the pain and the healing.

She watched me eat and gradually over the following couple of days my strength slowly returned, well, I could stand and waddle a bit, and my headaches eased. On the day we arrived in Sydney Town, I was allowed to go up on deck to watch the city come into view. The crew started to think I was a bit funny in the old noggin. Because the first thing I said was, 'Where the hell is the Harbour Bridge and the Opera House.' I sure got some funny looks, but they let it go as I had a head wound and most likely daft.

We slipped into Botany Bay and wove our way through all the other ships. Then this tall bloke, well not as tall as me, and skinny with it, walked up to stand beside me. He introduced himself as Governor Grey; I had no idea who he was. He told me he was pleased to see I was on the mend and thanked me for saving the Wattle family in Auckland, the night the Maori attacked the city. He carried on telling me Auckland would eventually become the Capital of the Southern Hemisphere. Then he went on to say, that he had recommended me for the New Zealand Cross. As he turned to look at the Wharf, he commanded, 'I want to emphasise that under no circumstance will the Auckland attack be mentioned. If anyone wishes to know the place where you were wounded, it was on the border with the Waikato.' He turned back to me, and with piercing grey eyes he added. 'Do you understand lieutenant?' I was immediately on my guard, 'Of course,' I stated. ' You won't have to worry about me, as I have no recollection of anything you are talking about, I don't even know who I am.' His face softened, 'I'm sorry to hear that, when you leave here you will be going home, and you will be able to recuperate with family. Good luck,' he said as he turned away, and that was the last I ever saw of the bloke.

Going home to family, well, that's good, but who are they? It was all a bit much for me as I slowly wobbled back to my bunk. When Bella my nurse came in I asked, 'Where is home?' She looked at me with those big green eyes and replied, 'Scotland. We think you come from Edinburgh.' 'Oh,' I said, frowning, 'how did you work that out?' 'Well, your friends told me you came from Dunedin, and that's Gallic for Edinburgh so putting two and two together, that's your destination. There is a city in New Zealand called Dunedin, but we think you are from the United Kingdom. You would have joined the army in Scotland, so there is a better chance of finding family there. Don't you worry, Sam, you are not just going to be dropped off there and left to your own devices, oh no. There is a military hospital there where you will go first to be assessed, and then if that works out, we will try and find your family. If we cannot, we will climb over that barrier later. I will never leave you alone, on that you have my word,' she informed me.

She paused, 'The Captain told me you had won the New Zealand Cross, that is wonderful, it will be awarded to you shortly after we get home.' 'I can't remember a thing, so to get something you have no idea about, has no meaning. Those friends I had, what were their names?' I asked. 'Ah, there was Captain Kidder, his first name was Robert or Bob, but I heard his friend call him Brill, whatever that means. Then there was a Lieutenant Lang his first name was Shane, but I did hear the Captain call him Grunt, once again, whatever that means.' Something pulled at my heart strings, Grunt, Brill, no it had gone. 'Strange names,' I stated,

'I thought for a moment, it might have meant something, just a flicker, but no I can't remember.' 'Then,' she continued, 'the Maori Sergeant, who was killed by the rebels at the same time as leaving you wounded, was Wiremu Hohepa, his body lay on top of you.' No bells rang for me with that information either; I frowned. 'Memory will come back slowly Sam, don't you push it. You just need to relax, do not think too hard about everything it will come back naturally, remember patience is all you need,' she kindly added. 'Yeah I reckon, something came back when I saw Sydney, but why would I say that, it's silly. I wondered where the Sydney Harbour Bridge was and the Opera House, so where did that come from?' 'Don't you worry Sam, the mind can play funny tricks on you, and this is one of those times. Until you have fully recovered, it might happen quite frequently. In the meantime let us keep a journal. I want you to write everything down each day that you don't understand, and then at the end of the day, we will go over it together. Something might trigger a response.' 'That's a good idea Bella I will do that,' I gushed.

All this time I had not met or spoken to the other officers that were wounded, but when I did, that was the moment that I realised that I didn't have a Scottish accent. Some of the fellas I could hardly understand, but the boys from Edinburgh, at least I could get by talking to them. Though, now and again I had to stop them and ask them to speak slowly. Then I thought to myself did I really come from Scotland. I gather the name Mack was a common name, but I did not feel right with it. Still, it was early days, hell I only was born a week or so ago.

I should at this time tell you a little bit about my angel, her name was Bella Wrightson. She was from Herefordshire in the UK, but wherever she came from she was the bee's knees as far as I was concerned. She was the most attentive and attractive person in the whole wide world. She stood about 1.58 metres, or as I was told 5ft 2, small and capable not just in personality but physically strong as well. I gather from what I have overheard from some others, she was not like a lot of women, she wasn't afraid to state her views. Her hair was a rich auburn colour that flowed in waves down past her shoulders when you could see it unpinned. But as a nurse, she always had it tucked in underneath her nurse's cap. Her complexion was not peaches and cream as you might have expected. She was lightly tanned, working in the field, and exposed to the sun each day she had this healthy glow about her perfectly round face and arms. Her eyes were emerald green with long lashes, and when she looked at you, they made me melt. I have looked into those eyes many times as she leant over me, changing my head bandages and even shaving me, her touch was so light. She had a small upturned nose with a full mouth and perfect white teeth, and then when she smiled the world smiled with her. She also had this infectious laugh, which she used to good effect. She was simply stunning, and everyone loved her from the Captain to the cabin boy, and I loved her the most. Fortunately, she was with me more than with the other patients, I was so lucky as there were four nurses on the ship. I think I was her pet project and so got a lot of her attention. She was a bit unorthodox in her ways, showing her arms and not having as many layers of clothing under her skirt. She said it was because it wasn't practical having so many layers on, on such a hot sticky day. I think the other nurses were a bit shocked, but Bella was never perturbed. If she had had a dog collar around my neck I would have been quite willing to follow her around like a wee puppy; she was my strength and confidence.

Once we had discharged our passenger in Sydney, we revittled and within two days we were heading out of Sydney Harbour for the trip north to Scotland. It would take about 30 days, maybe a little more. Having wounded on board Captain Hamilton was asked if any adverse weather were approaching to drop speed, and where appropriate call into a convenient port for fresh food. The Captain explained we had to skirt around the bottom of Australia then out into the Indian Ocean until we rounded the Cape of Good Hope. We would call into Cape Town for fresh food and coal before heading up the African coast, then on to the United Kingdom. So it's a long haul. The Suez, the Captain, later informed me, still had five or six years of construction until it was finished. What a difference that was going to make, not having to go around the Cape every time. It would cut weeks off the trip to India, Asia, Australia and New Zealand.

Each day, I got stronger and fitter, and Bella was always there looking after me until she finally said, 'I think it is time for the bandages around your head to come off permanently.' They had been off before of course, when she changed them, and my head, right from the beginning had been shaved. So to have the bandages off permanently was the big one and I was quite nervous. I worried about it as I had no idea what I was going to look like, and the bandages were like a security blanket for me. So I must admit that I was quite apprehensive. The big day arrived, and all the nurses came to watch and gave me encouragement. Bella slowly unwound the bandages from my head. Gradually they came off till at last, my head was clear. I watched everyone looking at me. 'My, my,' Dorothy, one of the nurses said, 'look at the colour of his hair.' 'What the heck is wrong?' I whimpered like a baby. 'Now there is nothing wrong, Sam, it is just that your hair has turned white, well steel grey actually. When you let it cover your ears you are going to be a splendid looking gentleman,' she smiled at me. 'The colour of your hair and that tan will make you irresistible to the ladies.' I heard the other nurses giggle, 'That is a bit forward Bella.' 'True,' she laughed. She came in close to inspect my head. 'Oh, that is so good ladies, the wounds have healed up well. The scars are under your hairline Sam so you will not see them. Your friend that sewed you up was a good physician; it is a shame he did not come with us; he could give a few of our doctors a lesson or two.' She handed me a mirror; I looked at myself. 'What was I like before?' I asked no one in particular. 'You were a redhead Sam, a good old Scottish redhead, now it is silver, I like this so much better, it gives you a certain sophistication. I believe, and this is only my point of view, but the head trauma you had has somehow affected your hair colour, well, all over,' she smiled. I look at all the nurses; they had all bathed me at various times when I was out of it, and they had seen me in my birthday suit, so they knew what they were talking about. 'You have me at a disadvantage ladies,' I replied. 'Not having any of you in the same situation, I will have to take your word for it.' The girls laughed, 'I tell you, Sam, if anyone heard us talking about this subject they would march us all off to the matron. Are we not lucky there's no matron on the ship?' 'Amen,' the nurses voiced together. 'I do believe though Sam as you have gone prematurely grey, I would abstain from growing a beard. You are too young for a grey beard, that would age you, but the colour of your hair now makes you unique.' Bella affirmed.

CHAPTER TWO

The first hurdle was over. So I started my journal, I was a redhead, and I put that down. I also wrote I was easy going with my speech, which wasn't usual. I always treated the nurses as equals, sometimes receiving unnecessary frowns for my effort from some of the officers. Even though these girls were all loved by the wounded, some of the blokes spoke down to them, and that pissed me off no end. So that went down in the journal as well. Another thing that Bella use to smile at, I shortened everyone's name. I never used rank, even with the Captain, and when I found out his name I called him it all the time. The girls got used to me calling them by their Christian names and so did a lot of the army and marine blokes. A couple of the army captains were a bit put off, but I couldn't have cared less. All the matelots on board when I found out their names got called by their first names as well and I used mate, all the time; it seemed natural to do so. With me being wounded in the head, I imagine they thought it was the injury talking. Deep down within me, I knew this is how I was, and if this is all that was left of my former self I was not going to let it go at all.

One bright sunny morning, about ten days out of Sydney with still a way to go to Cape Town, Bella came in and said, 'How is the journal coming?' 'Good,' I replied, 'but nothing hits me between the eyes though kiddo.' She looked at me, 'Write that down Sam, kiddo, what does that mean?' 'I think a form of expression. The kid in this case, is not a goat but a child, and used in an expression

9

of love, familiarity, it could be a junior family member.' She looked at me, 'That is so good Sammy.' She had tears in her eyes, 'The brain has still retained the things that you say and express, oh we are getting there slowly.' 'What you just said to me Bella, Sammy, it has a mother or sister feel, as though family used to say it as an endearment, it feels comfortable.' I looked into her eyes; she looked back, 'You might be right there Sam, endearment is certainly something I would call it. I find you enchanting and honestly the longer I am with you, the more I'm impressed. You are educated, but nothing like what I have come across before. You know such a lot of different things. What you say sometimes we may not understand, but whatever you say, it is said with conviction. So you are not silly Sammy dear. But,' she hesitated, 'before you get carried away with all of your attention and talk of love, I want you well. You never know, I may even succumb to your charms, but in the meantime, I want to see you walk around this ship unaided. To eat your meals without your hand shaking, to build up the muscles in your arms and legs again to what I imagine they were before you were shot. Then, Sam, I will fall under your spell because you are a fine looking man, and I believe in my heart of hearts I am not going to let you go. Do you think that is too bold for a woman in my position?' She was looking at me seriously. I just sat there with my mouth open. 'Come on Sam say something, there are flying fish around this part of the world, and I'm sure one would fly in if you don't shut your mouth.' 'My God Bella, I just don't know what to say, did my heart do a flip. You are the best thing that ever happened to me. Though I only have a memory for just over a fortnight. I grin every time I see you I just want to grab you, is that wrong? I keep getting this feeling that I should do it regardless, where I come from it might be the accepted thing to do, everyone here is very conservative.' She came closer; checking behind to make sure no one was around. 'Yes, we do what is socially correct, but Sammy if you want to grab me now and again, I don't think I would mind. All I'm worried about is you getting well, and if you are too excited, well that might affect your recovery. Medicine is improving, but we have a long way to go.' She leant over and placed her sweet lips on mine, gently holding my head and kissed me deeply. As she pulled back, she smiled, 'I think Mr Mack that we will stop now as you never know how things will turn out if we kept that up.' 'I think I remember how it goes from there Bella. That part of my brain is still intact.' 'Well, that's alright then, as a well brought up Victorian lady we won't talk about that,' she laughed. 'I think we should examine your bag today.'

I hadn't looked at my pack since I had been on the ship. Well, I looked only at the outside of it, and Bella had found the document sitting on the top when she opened it, but that was it. 'Right, get off the bed and we will spread all the contents there then we will go through them together. If you recognise anything, it goes into your journal. I think about 30 minutes of this, then a walk around the deck. You have to get your strength back if you want to chase me.' 'There is not another incentive in the world that would make me recover,' I replied. She was serious for a moment. 'Well, when you have recovered, and once we are back in the British Isles we will have to have a down to earth discussion. There are things about me that I haven't told you and won't until you have been discharged fit from the army assessment hospital in Scotland. It is no good trying to get it out of me until we are home. Now in the meantime, let us look at what is here in the bag, which incidentally is unusual in its self.' she added. 'No, it's a pack Bella, I can carry up to 50 kilogram's in that.' '50 what?' 'Oh, sorry I only know a little bit about imperial I mainly think in metric.' 'Write that down Sammy, don't do a thing until that is down. How many pounds, is that I wonder?' she said. 'I have no idea, but it's a heavy load.' 'Wait a minute, the second lieutenant is good with numbers

I'll go and ask him.' Five minutes later she was back, 'write this down, about 110 pounds. Sammy that is my weight! You carry that on your back?' 'Well, that's what came into my head when I thought about it. But where did I do that? It's a bugger, ops sorry Bella.' 'No, don't worry about it. I know you are big and strong, but to carry a bag on your back the same weight as me, you must be a very able-bodied man Sammy, and I do like my men strong,' she smiled. 'Every time you smile I just go weak at the knees.' 'Well, we cannot have that, here sit on this stool. The pack' she said, 'this is interesting, it has lots of pockets.' 'Yep, it's good for tramping.' 'Oh, Sam another word, what is that?' Writing it down I stopped and looked up at her. 'Ah, hiking, walking in the bush, a ramble,' I replied. 'Fantastic,' she exclaimed clapping her hands, 'look how far we have got already, and we haven't even opened the bag yet, I mean pack,' she corrected.

'Look at the time, let's just take one thing out now then we will start properly tomorrow.' She dived into it like a Santa sack and came out with a harmonica. She looked at it and inquired, 'Do you play this?' Frowning, 'Yes, I think I do.' 'Before I give it to you, do you know the make of it?' I thought for a moment, 'Yeah, it should be a Hohner, it's German made and best in the world, I think. ' So I wrote that down, I may be able to play the harmonica, and it dawned on me that I knew everything about it. 'Do you want to hear a song?' I asked. 'Can you remember any Sam?' She looked worried about me you could see it in her eyes. 'I'm okay Bella. I truly am. To prove it here is a number that has been around for a few years.' I started to play Amazing Grace. I felt great; it seemed to lift my spirits, and I played and played for nearly an hour. There were people standing three deep in the doorway, and my small cabin was chocker. In the end, I was quite tired, and everyone was ushered out of the room, all clapping and smiling. Bella looked at me, 'Sammy that music was fantastic. You have certainly a talent, but for now, it is rest for you. You need some time off now until dinner time. After dinner, we will have a slow stroll around the deck and then an early night, you need your rest. As I have heard you numerous times say, is that okay?' I smiled and replied, 'Yeah, good as gold boss.' 'Oh, more words, don't worry Sam I'll write them down for you. What do they mean?' 'Good as gold means everything is fine. The person in charge Bella, like the Captain, is the boss of the ship, or if you work for someone the person above you is the boss, like your matron.' 'Oh, that is marvellous we have already filled up a whole page today. Okay, time for lie down before dinner and I will be back to take you to the galley." She leant over and kissed me lightly, 'Sleep my handsome man,' she whispered as I dropped off to sleep.

Right on the button, she was there to take me up to the mess deck. I was regularly eating now, and the chief, cook and bottle washer was doing his damnedest to see how much he could fill me before I burst. He kept winning, even though I have a big appetite. After dinner, everyone took out their pipes and tobacco, and once again I said something that turned heads. ' Fellas, smoking that rubbish is only going to kill you; It causes cancer of the lungs, mouth and a lot of other places as well.' The standard reply was Och Mon; it's your head wound. But Bella was thoughtful, 'How do you know that Sam?' she asked, 'I don't know Bella, but I think where I come from, they are encouraging people not to smoke. I think when you look at it logically it's worse than people think, hang on I'll show you.' I turned around to Angus, an ensign who took a full shotgun blast as some Maori rushed passed him losing his lower arm below his elbow in the process. But I can't remember a thing about any attack at all. 'Would you like to do an experiment with me, mate?' 'Is it going to hurt?' he answered with a grin. 'No, not at all, has anyone got some cloth, preferably white muslin would be good?' 'I'll get some,' Bella said, as she jumped up and was soon

13

back with a piece. I then ripped a strip off and turned to Angus, 'Right mate, I want you to smoke normally and blow out over this cloth, every time you exhale put it up to your mouth.' I had a few taking an interest now, including the surgeon. Good old Angus did about half a dozen exhales and passed me the cloth. The brown mark of nicotine was there for all to see. Bella took a look and frowned, and then we passed it around, till it got to the surgeon. He looked at me, 'That's what's going into their lungs Alistair,' I explained, 'in a few years it will cause emphysema, cancer and death. It's a bugger of a way to die. Ops sorry Bella.' I muttered. Alistair looked at the cloth again, came over and asked Angus to open his mouth. 'Well, I can see what you had for dinner.' He plonked himself down next to Bella and me, 'Well, I could see the discolouring of his teeth, I have heard about this disease, of course, but I have never really thought about it. How do you know about it, Sam?' 'I have no idea it drives me mad sometimes. I wish I did, but there is nothing to look back on as a reference. I just come out with these things, but, in this case, you can see the muck they have inhaled into their lungs. It cannot be good for you.' 'You are right, but other physicians say how beneficial it is to persons well being.' I grinned, 'Well this is one bloke who is not putting that stuff anywhere near his mouth.' 'Time for your walk Sam,' Bella encouraged. Turning to the surgeon 'I don't want him over taxed Major.' 'No you are right dear girl, take the wee fellow for a walk, he needs it, he ate half the ship's stores,' he laughed. We heard chuckles behind us, as headed up to the poop deck.

We had been lucky with the weather. It was now the end of autumn, and by now the southern ocean should be rough. For us, it was soft and smooth. Bella took my arm as we strolled around the deck. 'You amaze me Sam, that experiment in the galley it proves a point, this is what all smokers inhale into their lungs. It makes you think, it most definitely does. Now you have a few more additions for your journal. Then an early night for you, my wee chap,' she smiled looking up at me. She only came up to my armpit, held my arm and supported me down to my quarters, we must looked odd together. She took out the journal and wrote in all the things that had happened that night. We went over it together with heads close, as the candle light was dim. As I read nothing seemed familiar, not even a hint of recognition came to me. My mind was a complete blank. But, as Bella explained things take time, and I had to have patience. She kissed me good night and gently shut the door. With the roll of the ship and the slap of the sails, I drifted off to sleep.

CHAPTER THREE

Southland, New Zealand 2019

My name is Robert Kydd or 'Bob' as everyone calls me. It's been four years since I came back through the mist from the Waikato of 1863. In all that time I've often thought about my two mates who didn't return with me. I wasn't as concerned about my mate Shane; he'd married and stayed back in the past. I knew what happened to him and his family from that period, because I had Shane's diary from 1923 or at least a copy of it. He had kept it methodically up to that year, to pass on details of his life to his twentieth-century family, which was then copied and passed on to me. This diary had helped his family of today to heal and to come to terms with him disappearing into New Zealand's distant past. The diary had been handed down over the years through the family, until it had finally arrived in the hands of Tui. She was the eldest child of her generation; the eldest had always been the diary's custodian. Shane had instructed that it wasn't to be opened until my name popped up sometime after 2014; then it was to be copied and delivered to me. The original would stay with the family so they could then read the actual story of the life of their ancestors Shane and Tui Lang.

So, the Tui of today arrived at my door not long after I had returned from the past. She had to wait longer than predicted, as I didn't arrive back until nearly two years after leaving even though I'd only been in the past a few months. I had lost over a year somehow on the trip home. She came across my name in an article in *The Southland Times*, a small story titled 'Back from the Dead,' about a bloke who lost his memory for 22 months. Well, that was the official rubbish the government had told me to say. Anyway, when Tui saw it, she turned up at my place, fulfilling her ancestors' wishes after 150 years.

When I returned to the twenty-first century, the three of us, Shane, Sam and I, had been presumed dead, and there had even been memorial services for us all. We were gone burgers. Naturally, when I turned up out of the blue, the shit really hit the fan. Then of course, the government got on the job and threatened me with the Official Secrets Act you can't go letting people think that time travel is possible. I was held for nearly three months while they considered what to do with me. Eventually, they let me go home with a warning of you'll be put away for a long time if you talk about your experiences to anyone;. They had told my family and my friends parents' this cock-and-bull story about how my mates fell into a hot pool. They even said I'd hit my head,, lost my memory, and had been a John Doe until a week before they sent me home. That was pack of lies also. I wasn't going to keep quiet about that, so I told our families the full story of what had happened to us all. I explained to them how the three of us blokes disappeared back into the past from February 2014, to the beginning of the New Zealand Wars of 1863. The problem was, my mates didn't return with me when I arrived home in 2015. It took me all day to tell the family what happened when I was eventually released by the police.

While attempting to return to our time through the mist, a couple of Maori blokes took a dislike to me and filled me full of lead. I was wounded three times from the musket balls in my arm, leg and side. It took me ages to come right. Besides that, after spending ten months in that era, it had left me a complete mess mentally. Luckily, Tui was a nurse, and with her help I was nurtured back to normal. We become very close in a short period of time, fell in love, and married. It was inevitable on my part as I had loved the Tui of the past, but she was Shane's wife. I was so lucky to have had another chance, because my Tui of today was so very like her ancestor, with the same personality and looks. It was strange to marry my best mate's third great-granddaughter, but then, the whole story was weird. She had had no idea about the history of her family and was quite overcome when it came out. My family and hers are very close now, as are Shane's mum, dad and sisters. We all get along well together. They lost a son and brother when we went back into the past but gained three generations of family. Shane had eight children back in the nineteenth century, and now his parents have truckloads of family. The family of today call them 'The Greats.' All the living generations look on Shane's folks as unique. Not many people in the world can say their third and fourth great-grandparents are alive and well. In Shane's families' case, that is the truth. The only thing different was Shane's name. He went under the name 'Lang,' not Langford, to remain incognito in 1863. If anyone comes out to our place, I have a wedding photo of him and his wife Tui, taken at Otahuhu in 1863. I took the photo myself with my slimline Nokia, and those pictures of that time survived, though my solar power unit died in the end.

But, I do worry about my other mate Sam as he's a different kettle of fish. Bugger, I really do wish I knew what happened to him, I feel so guilty that I never followed him to Scotland when I had the chance. But I'm not a good sailor; I get sick as a dog in any sort of boat. In fact, to be honest it gave me the shits at the thought of travelling all that way by sailing ship to the UK. I've been racked with guilt ever since I returned. He's my mate, and I let him down when he needed me. For my own peace of mind, I have to do this. So it's time to find him. Of course, it's not just for my sake as I have to keep my promise to his parents and his sister Mary. After saying that, I've still held out hope that his memory would return, and with luck he will manage to return to our time, and make it home. In the meantime, I have to do something.

I'd taken a while to get started on this journey because life had slowed down the search. I had married, then went back to school and finished my degree in history. From there, I received my teacher's degree, and then we had two children. But now it was time to begin the search for him. Shane had written in his diary that in 1901 through to 1902, he and Tui went to the United Kingdom to try to find Sam. They had spent a long time scouring the country, but hadn't any luck. All they knew was that Sam had arrived in Edinburgh on the HMS *Esk*, with twenty other wounded soldiers from the New Zealand wars, and with him was a nurse, Bella Wrightson. They both seemed to disappear off the face of the earth, and as hard as Shane and Tui had searched, Sam was never found. Well, I hoped I could get further with the search. There's a heck of a lot of information on the net now and more coming on every day so I was going to give it my best shot. I had the money as I had bought my army pay of 40 pounds back from the past. A dealer valued the old money at practically 600,000 dollars current cash. So I budgeted 60,000 dollars towards my research. I took leave without pay for a year from Southland Boys High School in Invercargill, where I'm a history teacher and rugby coach. I intend to look after our two children while Tui goes back to Invercargill Hospital as a charge nurse. With help from my mum caring for the kids, I could put aside about four to five hours a day for research, and if I had to go anywhere, mum was my backup. I had been in touch with Sam's parents and explained what I was about to do, and they said they would put up 50,000 dollars and more if I needed to travel extensively. I didn't quibble about this, as they needed to be involved every step of the way. They had also come into a lot of money. Sam's Army pay from 1863 had been sitting in a vault in the ANZ bank in Dunedin for over 150 years. When Shane and Tui took off to Dunedin in the South Island of New Zealand, they took Sam's pay with them, and deposited it in the bank vault when they couldn't find him. The money in notes and coins was in mint condition, and they had received close to 800,000 dollars for the collection. To them, it was Sam's money, to be used to find their boy. They wanted closure and money was no object.

Sam had been shot three times in the head when the Maori attacked Auckland in May of 1863, about six weeks before the real war started in July. You'll never find that bit of history in any of our history books. It was denied by the government of the time. Governor Grey put a 'D' notice on all correspondence, claiming instead that Auckland had a massive fire that affected the commercial area of the city. It was true to a point but there was no mention of the caused the fires so most of it was bullshit. The Maori attacked and stormed up Queen Street burning and shooting everything in sight. I was there trying to protect a pubload of people with Shane. Sam and a relation of mine, Wiremu Hohepa, my third great uncle by marriage whom I had come across back then, had run across the road to the Wattles shop to protect Wiremu's boss's family. In the fighting Wiremu was shot and killed. I felt a deep personal loss when I found Wiremu lying there. His body had covered Sam and had protected him. However Sam was wounded in the head and ended up on the HMS *Esk*, a steam corvette used as a hospital ship for wounded officers. The ship wasn't meant to leave Auckland at all, but it did. That threw Shane, Tui and I into a frenzy. They told us Sam was being sent home to Dunedin, as he had a Scottish name, so they thought he was a Scot. The ship left for Dunedin NZ, or so we thought, but It wasn't until it had gone that I found out that Dunedin was Gaelic for Edinburgh, and that was where he went, to the bloody UK. Because of his head wounds, Sam was suffering from amnesia. When he came to, he would have had no idea who he was. The day before the boat left, Sam was just starting to show signs of awareness from the coma after a week of being out of it. We were there with him when he opened his eyes, and he didn't know who we were. Shane and I, as you can imagine, were a tad upset. There was an attentive nurse with him though, doing her best to make him comfortable. So thinking he had gone to Dunedin, New Zealand, Shane and Tui had arranged for the army to book their passage down south. They left the next morning, heading south to Dunedin to catch up with him on the *Esk*, taking Sam's pay with them. Like all good plans, it turned to custard. I never saw Shane and Tui again and neither did I see Sam. I spent months in the bush waiting for a letter from Shane, but nothing came. It wasn't until I read Shane's diary 150 years later, that I found out the reason, the mail ship had sunk in Cook Strait in a southerly blow. So now, it was all up to me to find Sam.

I've been interested in history all my life, and I'm a skilled researcher of genealogy, but this was going to be a real test to see if I could find him. I was hoping my expertise on the subject would be a huge help. He would be 36 now, in our years. Over there in the United Kingdom, where he was sent, he would have been dead for over 100 years. But he might have married, in that case. If I'm lucky we may even find his third great-grandchildren, as we did with Shane's family. How did I feel about all this? I was still hoping he would knock on my door, with his pack on his back and rifle in hand. I would love to see his huge smile framed by his red hair all over the place, ready to play rugby like we used to. That was in my heart. Realistically though, I knew I would be happy to find out anything about him. I just hoped he'd had a happy life, that he was loved, and also that his appreciation of the outdoors stayed with him the rest of his life. I had, over the years, scanned old Scottish newspapers for any mention of a Samuel McInnes or a Samuel Mack. He went under the name Mack back in 1863, as we all used different surnames as a security blanket. Up until now, I hadn't found a thing, though not all old newspapers were up on the net. Anyway, I had just kept playing around, but now I was going to get serious.

CHAPTER FOUR

Southland New Zealand 2019

The first thing I did was write down everything I knew about Sam, not just his name or names, but his personality, his likes and dislikes. Music was a big part of his life, and of course with his love of music, he could play quite a few musical instruments. So I would look into that aspect. He was a greenie, a conservationist, and back in the nineteenth century not much was happening in that area. I wonder if he'd done something in that line. He was a superb shot and an excellent tracker, so realistically, I think he would have been involved in something to do with the bush or forestry. I'm sure that would have been a pull for him if he had survived as a leopard can't change his spots. One thing I did think to look at and not many people knew about this, was that he was a bit of an entrepreneur. I've seen him in the past make a big deal or two over some little thing. For instance, he had taken a photo of the bush and sold it to someone in a magazine. Then, on making the deal, he added, 'If you pass it on or resell it I'll take 2 percent.' You wouldn't think he was like that to look at him, but he had a nice little nest egg tucked away. Now his photos are all over New Zealand, and they are still bringing in royalties to his sister's trust account. So there was a lot about the bloke that I can look into in my search. If he survived, he must have left a trail. Even if his memory never came back, his personality, I think, would have persevered. I felt confident that I would find something. Also, I will look for anything out of the ordinary, regarding the era. Say, if someone came up with a drawing of something that didn't fit in the nineteenth century, I would look at that. It might not be Sam, but he could have influenced someone.

First, though, I had to get a handle on his family names. Not just his surname, but also the females in his family, their maiden names, nicknames and pet names. My first job was to interview his parents and get as much information as I could. I wanted places of birth, marriages and deaths anything about the people in his family where they lived and where they died. If Sam had memory loss all his life, he might still have had flashes of the names of his immediate family. He might not have remembered the family, but their names, might have made him feel comfortable. If this was the case, there's a good chance of him using that name for any of his children.. This research wasn't just a matter of looking it up on the computer and in five minutes getting the answers. Oh no, this was going deep into everything about Sam, including his relationship to food. He was an enthusiastic gourmet after all, he just loved his tucker. He had an enormous appetite and could polish off big meals. So that was another trait to look out for, along with the way he spoke. He had a Kiwi accent and he was a pretty casual bloke. Everyone was called mate, or when Sam communicated with friends or met someone new, he always liked to call people by their first name. That would stand out as someone might mention that in passing or in conversation, or maybe in a diary. He was a big bugger, slightly over 2 metres tall, and that had to stand out. He wouldn't be able to buy clothes off the rack as they would need to be tailored made especially for him including his shoes and boots. He was a redhead, and a big, redheaded man with a red beard must have been very distinctive. So I had a lot to go on even before I started. Nothing set in concrete of course, but it was a start.

I had also met the nurse when she came over to the Wattle's shop to check on Sam while he was convalescing there. She suggested taking him out to the HMS *Esk* for better accommodation and fresh air. I had the nurse's name: Bella Wrightson. She was from Herefordshire, so that should be easy to trace or so I hoped. Bella had trained as a nurse at the Nightingale Hospital London, so I should be able to find those records. Description, now I'm racking my brain. She was short, about 1.5 metres and her hair was auburn I think; well, I couldn't see much of it as it was mostly tucked under her cap. Green eyes yes they were mesmerising. Thinking back, she was good looking, and for that era she particularly stood out, as she was a determined, independent young lady who didn't suffer fools gladly. Age-wise, I think she was between 23 to 29 years old, so I was looking for a birth date between about 1834 and 1844 in Herefordshire or surrounding districts. I like to round it up to ten years when I am researching

Then, of course, there was the ship, the HMS *Esk*. I will endeavour to find the records from the Royal Navy, and if I get lucky, locate the crew list for the trip back to Scotland from New Zealand in 1863. I might even find the injured list. Someone from this list might have written a diary, or there might be something in the records or in the ship's log about someone on board or an occurrence that happened. I needed to find out the route the ship took back to the UK. Did they call into another port on the way home? Did anything out of the ordinary happen? I knew the boat went to Sydney with Governor Grey on board. He was the man who insisted that the vessel just up and leave, without going through the standard procedures. They left at a moment's notice, about eight days after the attack on Auckland. I gather it was to raise a loan for the rebuild of the city. There was a lot of fire damage. I was there, so I knew this as a fact. I must check to see if any of the crew left anything behind in New Zealand when the ship returned. It had been on station in the Bay of Plenty at the Battle of Gate Pa. Were any matelots wounded and then convalesced in the area? They might have left diaries of their time on the *Esk*. So I had loads to go on with, even before I started searching further afield. I needed to put all the information I had into folders as references. That information would be the starting point, and I would need to sieve through it methodically. Well, that's a week's work in itself, I thought.

I wanted to do the easiest things first, and that included going up to Dunedin to see Sam's parents, Wayne and Mary, and of course, his sister Mary. People forget the kids sometimes. I've found if you sit with them quietly and talk softly about family, it's amazing what they remember. They are looking at life through children's eyes, and they will remember the fun times. Mary is now going on seventeen. She was eleven when Sam disappeared, but I'm sure she'll remember something that even I didn't know about my mate. I gave Wayne a call. He was retired now, as was Mary, but he still kept a few of his clients on from his accountant days. He told me it was to keep him busy. Mary, their daughter, was a change-of-life child, and growing up into an attractive young lady. She had been Tui's flower girl at our wedding, and we treated her like a niece. She would come down during the school breaks to stay with us and catch up with my folks as well. Her ambition is to be a doctor. With Tui being a nurse, it's given her all the encouragement she needs. Wayne suggested to come up for the weekend and to bring the kids. However if Tui was working, and it was okay with her, just bring the kids anyway, though they would like to catch up with us all. Tui was a charge nurse and her shifts weren't too bad, but she did do a few weekends, and on this occasion she was working. 'Take the children, Bobby,' she suggested. 'They always like going up to Dunedin. Young Mary just dotes on them. She has them trailing her wherever she goes, and besides, it's only overnight.' So it was arranged to drive up Saturday and come home Sunday afternoon. I had all my questions worked out by the end of the week, and I was looking forward to squeezing them dry of all the information I needed about their family. It was about a two-and-a-half-hour drive north to their home. They wanted me to be there for lunch, so I left about nine thirty. They lived on Hanson Street, Portobello, on the hill overlooking Lamlash Bay. A quiet area on a no-exit road, with plenty of space for the kids to play outside, and Mary usually walked them down to the beach. As we pull up outside their gate, Mary came out like a shot. 'G'day Bob, come on kids, I have the paints all set up.' As she picked up my wee fella Shane, his big sister Libby grabbed the shoes that he'd kicked off and followed Mary inside, talking nineteen to the dozen. Wayne had also come out to greet us. 'Well, Bob, that's the last you'll see of them until we have dinner. Mary has food for them all set up in the rumpus room.' I had to grin. I wish she lived with us; a built-in au pair.

Mary senior had a light lunch ready for the three of us. I had taken out my folders, and while munching on a sandwich, I explained, 'This is going to take a while, but I need it to get an overall background on the family.' Then I started to ask question after question. They were very patient with me, answering as best as they could. I commenced with the family name of McInnes, Wayne's parents, and their places of birth and death and so on. Wayne's dad Alexander was born in Riverton in 1932. His mum Joyce was born in Invercargill in 1934; her maiden name was Selkirk. So it went on for each generation until I got back to 1842, on both sides of the family. We had gone right back to Angus and Stewart McInnes. This was Wayne's second great-grandfather, and my mate Sam's third. Angus's siblings were Stewart and Mary. The whole family had come out to New Zealand in 1848. When my mates and I had been back in the past, we had met Angus's younger brother Stewart in the Waikato of 1863. He was born in 1845, and his sister Mary was born in 1841. Mary married Thomas Fenton; they adopted a couple of boys whose father was killed in an ambush on the Great South Road. The boy's father was with my mates and me, along with Stewart, on the road from Papatoetoe to Otahuhu that day. So I knew a bit about Stewart, and therefore, Sam's family. All of us blokes, were close to Stewart. He was, after all, Sam's third great-uncle. He fought alongside us, and it was at his suggestion that the children of the teamster who was shot and killed with us that day, should go with him to Dunedin, where his sister Mary became their mother. He was a good bloke and Sam was proud to be his relation. This bloke never hesitated about the children, and the men at the redoubt at Otahuhu raised over 20 pounds to help them out. It left me with a pleasant memory amid an awful bloody episode in our time back there. I now had filled in the very long list I had come with. Sam took after his mum's family in size. All her menfolk were big men, but he had the Scottish red hair from his dad's side. Wayne was a big bloke to me, but not as huge as Sam. I added all the women's maiden names, their parents' names and any other information I had gleaned from Sam's folks, until I had exhausted myself, and them as well. After the marathon questioning, I sighed, 'Let's call it quits for now and have a drink.'

We sat and had a couple of beers, and chatted about Sam in general, and about all the little things that parents know. Then we doubled over with laughter when talking about Sam's eating habits. 'He cost us a fortune,' they said, with sad nostalgia. After a while, a satisfied feeling washed over me. This has been a good start on my journey to finding my mate; it's been great reminiscing with people who knew him so well, and now I had a lot of material to go on with.

The little ones needed to be down by six after an early meal, as they were awake early every morning. Young Mary and I bathed them, and afterwards with them wrapped up in towels and smelling fragrant of baby powder we popped on their jammies, then put them into bed. That's when we were rewarded with lots of hugs and kisses, the little monkeys doing their very best to keep awake as long as possible. I suddenly felt sad; I will miss all this if I have to travel away on the hunt for my mate, but it's something I really need to do. Turning the light out, I whispered, 'I'll be sleeping in the room next door, see you both in the morning.' I pulled the door to, then we went down to the dining room for dinner.

Mary asked in a quiet voice, 'Bob, do you remember when I was about 10, I brought Sam that silver pin with a New Zealand fern on one side and a small Kiwi on the other, with my pocket money? I gave it to Sam for his birthday; he always carried that with him. Oh, it wasn't expensive, but I wonder if he would have kept it. He took it everywhere, as it reminded him of home.' 'Mary, I do kiddo, I do. You just jogged my memory. He always had it in the small top pocket of his pack, wrapped in a light, waterproof wrapper. Let me write that down, it might be significant in the future. I'd forgotten about that; he never took it out of his bag. He did tell me whenever he was away he would look at it. He would read the wee message you wrote, and it would remind him of home. Especially when he was overseas in the Army, so I gather that must have been in Afghanistan.' Mary continued, 'We all know how he liked his food, and he was always in the kitchen trying out new recipes when he was home. I remember once he was writing down a recipe for a homemade steak sauce he had made, and the reason I remember is that he asked me to help him stir it to keep it from burning. I think it was a standard sauce, but he'd added Kiwifruit as well as orange peel, and it gave it quite a different flavour.' 'I didn't know that, Mary. I'll write that down as well; you never know with Sam he might have bought a restaurant.' We had a laugh. 'NAH!' we said together, 'he would have eaten the profits.' That was our Sam. It was good to talk about him without breaking down and nice to remember what and who he was. His personality has to have survived, I thought. He was full of life, and loved it to bits. He must have left something of himself that survived to this day. So any wee piece of information went into the journal. It was coming together nicely. I had all their family history, or at least as much as they could remember. So I was thrilled, although whatever way you looked at it, this was going to take time. It's always hard when you are looking for someone who might have had a name change. I would still have a look, of course, at the family name. If he was using his real name, then the question is why he never tried to get home or leave some message that would have turned up in our time. I didn't hold out much hope of him using it, but you have to look. I had lots of place names now for my research, and a host of family names. A mate of mine created a computer program for me. I can search a name or a series of names and it will search each page that's up on your screen. Then it will place them into a file with the information and a link back to it. That means it comes up with a flag so I can check it out straight away. It's a smart wee program, especially when you get pages of words in the old newspapers. It'll be a great tool to use. So when I get home, all this information will go into the computer and everything will be at my fingertips.

For the rest of the evening and Sunday morning, we just talked about old times, looking at photos of Sam as a boy. My heart went out to them. It's not easy to never know what happened to your child, and it made me more determined than ever to find something. Anything was better than nothing. When Shane and Tui went over to the UK in early twentieth century, nearly 40 years had passed since Sam arrived on the *Esk*. Records would most likely have been moved into storage. The doctor in charge of the hospital probably would have retired, moved on or died; the nurses would have married most likely and had children and grandchildren of their own by then. So it would have been quite hard for them to find anyone who could remember or even recognise Sam. But, and it is a big but, you don't disappear unless you want to. If Sam never recovered his memory, he would have carried on his life generally in the open, he wouldn't have hidden, and he would, I believe, have been the usual good old Sam. That's what I was counting on, and in my case, I was going to find him. No excuses, it's just good old-fashioned sleuthing.

CHAPTER FIVE

HMS Esk 1863

We were now fully into the ship's onboard routine, and as the days drifted by, I grew in strength to the point that I took great pleasure in climbing the rigging up into the crow's nest. Even though the Esk was a steam-powered Corvette, the Admiralty didn't like the idea of running the engines, so only cranked it up as we neared the port, and again on leaving. I thought the whole idea stupid, and I pointed this out to the captain. 'If you have the power, you should be using it.' He agreed, but his hands were tied. So it was a much longer trip than they first informed us. Under sail, she would do about nine to ten knots, but it increased to seventeen under steam. Ultimately, it was about a 40 day trip from Sydney to Cape Town, with another thirty days to the United Kingdom. In that time, I got to really appreciate Bella's company. Of course, she knew all about me, as the lady was there when I was born in May of this year.

I have continued to be methodical in my journal writing, and the day we emptied the pack onto my bed, I spent the whole time writing furiously. The first things we inspected were the camouflage pants, shirt and jacket. Bella found them extraordinary; she said the styling was odd, and she'd not ever seen anything resembling the material that these were made of. Bella was intrigued by the outside labels on the clothes and thought them unusual. I wondered at that. Everything I recall was labelled, so that snippet

31

of information went into my journal. The tags on the inside neck informed us they were made in Canterbury. 'Well, at least that place is familiar,' she remarked. We put them all to one side. We then glanced at the tent with the aluminium poles, and the boots and gaiters. But what took her fancy were my sets of thermals. She felt the cosiness of them and gushed, 'These are so lovely and warm Sam, and look they're also made in Canterbury. When we get home we will have to find out who made them; these are so warm and practical.' Next, she saw the shorts and tee-shirts, and frowned, 'Did you wear these?' she asked as she held them in the air for inspection. Then she continued, 'Well I guess you must have, I can see the practicability of it. What are they called?' she added. 'Shorts, Bella,' I answered, then I grabbed my journal and wrote down 'shorts.' 'What an original name' she said, smiling, 'we don't wear them back home and this shirt?' 'It's a tee-shirt,' I told her. Out came the quill once again. 'It does look a bit like a letter T, doesn't it?' She said with a grin. Suddenly I felt overwhelmed, and moaned, 'How can I remember about this stuff, but not about my past? Oh, I know this is part of my past, but how do I know all these things? It's so hard to understand.' She touched my arm and gave me a smile with genuine warmth in her eyes. My heart skipped a beat. Wow! I think things were becoming even more complicated than I thought, I closed my eyes. I can't deal with it right now. We turned back to what was next on the bed; the gas stove. 'What on earth is it?' I told her and she replied, 'who makes these things and why aren't they for sale back home?' The waterproof matches went down a treat; then we came to the iPhone. 'What is this?' she said, picking it up and frowning. 'That's an iPhone,' I replied. 'Oh! But what does it do?' 'Well,' I explained, 'you can call and talk to other people all over the world who have a phone as well.' She was incredulous, 'That's a bit far-fetched,' she accused. 'No, it's true,' I assured her. 'That's incredible, I can't possibly believe that.' I held the phone up and pointed. 'See, it's an Apple, that's the name of the company that makes them in the States. Look, it's also a camera.' 'No! Now you're really trying to pull the wool over my eyes. That's impossible cameras are big things with tripods and lots of equipment. This can't be a camera.' 'Hang on a minute Bella, I'll see if there's any life left in it. It hasn't been switched on for a while and it might not work.' I pushed the button at the bottom of the screen and the phone switched on. Bella jumped back with surprise, 'What happened? What's it doing?' she looked terrified. 'Don't worry Bella. Everything is okay, it's just looking for a signal. There appears to be none around. I'll see if I can open my photos. I clicked on the icon, and up they came. I quickly leafed through them and felt crestfallen as I didn't recognise any of them I hesitated, and then turned to Bella. 'Come over and take a look at the photos.'

She put her head on my shoulder nervously, but soon leaned forward in awe of what she saw, forgetting her past denial. 'Sam, this is utterly incredible, these photographs are in colour.' 'Do you recognise anyone Bella?' I whispered, 'because I sure as hell don't.' I was confused, I knew what I was doing, yet I didn't understand any of it. 'This is a photo of a wedding, who are these people, Bella, do you know them?' 'Yes, I met three of them. That is Shane and his new wife Tui, I met them in Auckland when they were taking care of you. That other man is Bob. See, they have the same clothes that you have. Oh, that's the Maori Sergeant who was killed, they called him Bill. I don't know the others. That red-headed man next to Bob he looks a lot like you, don't you think? Do you recognise anyone at all, Sam?' 'No I don't, not even a flicker. But I've just had a thought. The phone is going to close down soon; it needs electricity to charge the battery, and there isn't any here on board. Do you have any in England?' 'Electricity?' she asked with a puzzled frown.' 'Yeah electricity. See this cord? You plug it into a socket, and it charges the battery.' 'There is nothing like that in England Sam.' I felt crestfallen. I didn't know how long the battery would hold out and then it started to beep. 'Oh bugger, it's dying. Once it does, I won't be able to see the photos again.' Suddenly the image disappeared.

We both stared at the black screen. Deep inside me, there was a hollow in the pit of my stomach. How did I know those blokes? Were we close? I wondered. I felt a profound sense of loss. I gazed up at Bella with watery eyes. She grabbed me and hugged me tightly, her eyes leaking as well. 'Your memory will come back Sammy, it really will. Just believe this is only the start. Have faith and don't let go.' She kissed me on my forehead. 'Time for a nice cup of tea for us both, my wee chappie,' she said cheerfully. 'I am truly astounded Sam; I have in all my life never seen such things. I don't understand them; it's quite beyond me. But you cannot get away from the fact that they are sitting on your bed. It certainly is a complete mystery to me.' She went out to inquire about the tea, and I sat there staring at the bed, feeling empty.

Why do I know so much about all this gear? As Bella had said, she had never seen anything like these things on my bed before, so where had all this stuff come from, as it appears not to come from around here? In fact, most of it doesn't fit at all into the real world, nor do I for that matter. Where was I from? I kept coming back to it. My mind was going around in circles and it made me feel depressed. When Bella returned with a pot of tea and a few hardtack biscuits. I looked up and smiled at her, I always felt better in her company. She handed me a mug, and to soften my biscuit I dunked it into my cup. She laughed when I did that and copied me. 'That compass' I pointed to it 'that's normal isn't it?' I began. 'Of course,' she said. 'But the map.' I took a peek at it. 'The title states it's a map of New Zealand, but the area says it's Tongariro National Park.' 'Yes. Is that a problem? Well!' She stopped, looking uncertain. I waited, then plunged ahead, 'I'll tell you what, when you take the cups back, ask if the navigation officer is free for a few minutes and get him to come down. I'd like him to have a gander.' I browsed at the map after she left.

Ten minutes later, Calum McDonald banged on the door, 'You wanted to see me, Sam?' Yeah mate, take a squiz at this map. 'What?' he replied. 'Sorry, take a look and give me your opinion.' He plopped himself down on the bunk beside me; I had to smile, he was only as tall as Bella. He stared at the map, turned it upside down, then onto its side. 'My god, Sam, where did you get this from?' he asked. 'This map Is of the middle of the North Island of New Zealand. The place hasn't even been explored yet, let alone surveyed. How the bloody hell did you get it? Oops sorry, Bella.' 'It was in my pack mate, but the funny thing about all this is I know and believe I've seen most places on this map. I've been there. Don't ask me how I don't know it's almost so close I could grab it. I just wish I could remember.' Calum focused on the index and read it out loud. 'Topographical maps using the official LINZ's 1:50,000 / Topo 50. Map last updated July 21st, 2012.' He stopped and stared at the date, 'Well that's got to be wrong, it has to be.' 'Yeah.' I said with a frown. He continued, 'But if it is an error, it's a big one, as it's 1863 now. How could that pass the proofreader? Also, the measurement is one centimetre to fifty thousand centimetres; it's not even in imperial.' I scratched my head. 'What do you mean?' 'We use imperial, not the froggy measurements.' 'Well 'I'll be buggered, Calum, that's another problem, I only know metric. It doesn't make sense. Am I European?' 'No Sam, not at all,' he insisted, 'you don't have a European accent. Well for that matter, you don't have an English one either, not from the British Isles that is.' He looked at me. 'Perhaps you have been abroad for quite a while and your accent changed, or maybe with the head wound, that could have changed your way of speaking. Would that be possible Bella?' he turned to her. 'Well, it's certainly a possibility, Calum. But I met his friends in New Zealand, and both of them spoke the same way as Sam. As you say, they might have been away from the mother country for quite a while, which could change the way they talk.'

'Okay', I cut in, 'let's get back to the map. You said yourself this area is yet to be explored, let alone surveyed. It has me baffled, because how come I can tell you the name of every mountain, creek and track?' I sat back on my bunk when another bout of depression hit me; I had the names in my head of all the birds in that area. I could tell them the names, if asked, of all the trees, and where the hot pools were. But, when I came to thinking about how I know, it was still a complete blank. Calum shifted, uncomfortably on the bunk. 'I have no idea, Sam. That map is worth a pretty penny to anyone going out there. But maybe it would be best to keep it quiet and hide it away until you are back home and have had time to think about it all. That date has to be wrong, but the detail of the map is intricate, as though studied from the air, which of course is impossible.' 'A chopper', I exclaimed, jumping up, 'a bloody chopper.' 'What do you mean?' Bella asked with a startled look. 'When Calum mentioned 'from the air,' the word 'chopper' jumped into my head and, the word 'flying.' I must write it down. Suddenly I felt exhausted. 'I don't know, Bella, I guess I should stop. It's all getting a bit much.' She turned to the navigation officer, 'Thank you, Calum, for coming down. I think Sam can do with a break.' 'That's fine lassie, just don't show anyone that map. It will be too unsettling for the public to see.'

Once he had gone, I had my journal out and started to write furiously. I wrote down everything I thought relevant up to this point. There was a worried look on Bella's face and her green eyes filled with tears. 'I'm okay, Bella, don't be upset,' I said gently. 'I'm just doing as you told me. Remember you said when something unusual comes to me, I need to write it down. 'Chopper' and 'flying,' those words felt right why I don't know but I believe I have flown before.' She looked at me, stunned. 'No, I'm not crazy, Bella, I just need to write it down. It was most likely in a dream anyway, but I have this feeling of being high, looking down on this mapped area.' 'Well, as long as you feel alright, that's all right then,' she clucked, wiping her eyes. I think we should stop now, have something to eat, get some fresh air and come back to it another time.' I agreed. It was unnerving getting these ideas in my head without knowing where they come from. We had a good lunch with a sit in the sun, and even though it was cool, it was pleasant.

The southern ocean was being kind to us; we now had been thirty days out of Sydney and experienced only one bad day up till now. Can it last? The time had done wonders for the recuperation of the wounded blokes. The doctor and the nurses were incredible with their care. The leak that came from the Bridge suggested we were to spend about a week in Cape Town to resupply, and also to use our expertise to properly fix a couple of minor things at the docking facility. We were looking forward to it.

After our break, we were back into the pack in my cabin. 'There's mainly the food, and also the biggie, my rifle, left to look at.' I let my thoughts wander a moment, then I picked up my journal and said, 'Dehydrated food, backpack meals, and deserts, etc. but as I was saying, Bella, once again we can't ignore the dates. All are stamped on the rear of the packets, best before 2015 or 2016. They all can't be a proofreading problem?' Bella scratched her head and enquired, 'Do you eat this Sam?' Distracted, I answered, 'Yes, you just pop it into a pot with a bit of water and its food for one. Maybe when we get to Cape Town, we'll have a picnic. I'll take some of this with us to show you, and have a cook up on the stove.' 'That would be interesting,' she smirked, but then perked up and went on, 'in fact, it's a great idea, as it might help your memory doing something that you have done before.' I found some Cadbury's chocolate, so I broke off a piece and gave her half.

'Oh, that is so delicious,' she moaned. 'Well, at least you won't have to worry about it making you fat,' I laughed, 'you can't fatten a thoroughbred.' She grinned. 'You can say the nicest things, Sam.' I returned her smile with tenderness, then turned the packet over. 'Look where it's made. It's written on the packet, Bella: Made in Dunedin the Edinburgh of the South. Heck, do you think I come from there?' She frowned. 'Well your friends said it was your base, but coming from there I'm not sure Sam. They do have a small Scottish garrison there so maybe you were attached to that garrison, it seems more likely this scenario. There's no chocolate production down there. Up until the gold rush, there were only 2000 people living in the city. It's only a small place, mind you; no doubt there will be more now since gold was discovered in Otago.' To this, she added, 'No, I think this is just a play on words. Edinburgh is in the South of Scotland. It's ingenious isn't it?' 'Yeah, you are most likely right,' I admitted. But I still wondered. The wrapping had a date on it that was also 2014. It was so confusing. I felt I was out of step with reality, but Bella kept saying it's the head wound you will come right. I had a journal full of stuff that I couldn't explain. Bella didn't understand most of the information either and had never seen nor heard of anything like it in her life. So, who or what was I in my previous life? I sure had a lot to think about, but I'm glad I didn't have to do it on my own. Thank goodness for Bella.

Then we came to the rifle; there was nothing like it on board this tub. They used the Enfield rifle musket, where you poured the gunpowder into the barrel and jammed down a ball, and then you placed a percussion cap under the firelock. My gun is so completely different to what they've got. It's light, with a short barrel and holds ten rounds of .308 ammo in a magazine. Plus it has a bolt action. I had about 70 rounds with me. I saw it was Japanese made and I instinctively knew how to use it. I also felt that I shouldn't let anyone near it. My instinct told me that it was years ahead of its time. Why I should think like this, I had no idea, but I was beginning to get used to this gut feeling. So I showed Bella the gun, then rewrapped it again, saying, 'When we get home, I'll get this checked out by a manufacturer.' And as usual, the same niggling question popped into my mind where's home?

CHAPTER SIX

HMS Esk 1863

My journal was full, the day was coming to an end, and I had repacked everything into my pack. 'There's another thing I don't understand, Bella that order that came from the governor. When he met me on board, he never once mentioned about the assignment I was on for him, not a thing. You would think he would have said something, as he signed the order, but he didn't look and act as though he had even remotely heard of me. What do you think that was all about?' 'It's a mystery Sammy, it surely is, as he has a remarkable memory for names and faces. Well known for it in fact. I just don't know, but the order is there, and it has his signature. The governor may not have recognised you, because maybe your friend, the Captain, was given the orders and he never got to meet you or Shane,' she concluded. 'That must be it, Bella; I was beginning to think I'm from another world, that I don't fit in. All that's happening around me doesn't feel right. It's hard to explain. I've even got this feeling we should be able to get to the UK in 24 hours, not three months. It's daft kiddo; it can't be done so everyone says so why would I even think like this? It's bloody frustrating. I need to pull myself together.' She studied me, and offered, 'I think you are pushing yourself too hard Sam, so until we get to Cape Town, no worrying about yourself. No, I mean it Sam. Instead, you can put all your energy into thinking about me,' she laughed light-heartedly. 'Well, young lady, it just so happens that's all I do.' She blushed, hardly believing that she had been so forward to have actually said that out loud, but thrilled nevertheless at the reply. 'Just one last thing boss,' I said, 'that other letter we found in the bottom of the pack, the one about my pay. I haven't got a cent...er...um...a penny. According to that letter, I was entitled to one pound a day, so I wonder where all that went. Have I received it, do you know?' 'No, I haven't heard anything. But we must do something about that. When we get to Cape Town, we will go to the army headquarters and sort that all out.' I continued with my misgivings. 'By the time we get there, I would have 50 odd days owing. Even if they give me a percentage of it to start with until we get home to Scotland, I'd be happy.' 'You needn't worry Sam; I'll do all the worrying for you.' 'Thank you,' I said with a weak smile, feeling comforted. 'There's no need to be concerned, we'll make it our priority.' Then she pointed out, 'I must say they certainly weren't very generous with your pay though, Sam. You must have been doing quite dangerous work, and to only receive a pound a day. Even a lot of labourers and farm workers are receiving that sort of money now. It's a sign of the times;-when there is a shortage of labour, wages go up. Of course, not all are so lucky,' she noted, a wave of sadness coming over her as she shook her head. 'Some of the places I have seen and the people. There needs to be change. Too many are living in poverty, and a lot of wealthy people are living off their backs. They own the slums that the poor are living in all over the United Kingdom, and charging too much. Frankly, it's wrong,' she hesitated looking up at him. 'Do you think I'm too opinionated Sam?' 'No, of course not, Bella. You should speak out about what you believe in. I would agree if I knew anything about it, but the UK is just a blank to me also.' 'Well on to better things,' she cheered, 'I have enough money. They have been paying me handsomely, so there is no need to worry on that score. I'll not let

41

you starve.' 'Well that's good,' I replied, feeling quite relieved. 'I haven't really thought about it up until now, and you're right we'll sort it all out when we get into port. I'm looking forward to going ashore for our well-earned break.'

A couple of days out from the Cape of Good Hope, the sea gods decided it was time for a winter blow, and the weather changed abruptly. A southerly wind swept viciously straight out of Antarctica and rapidly grew to gale force. Mountainous waves crashed over the ship as seawater poured through open hatches, drenching decks below, then disappearing out through the scuppers the scene repeating again and again. The captain immediately converted over from sail to steam to make better headway and forbade any passengers from venturing on deck. The hatches were bolted and anything that moved was soon lashed down, including the wounded, to prevent them from falling from their berths. Many of the able-bodied soldiers crept into their bunks, as the rolling and pitching of the ship made it unsafe to move around. Soon there was the sound and smell of vomiting throughout. The Esk slogged onward towards Cape Town.

After two days of being thrown around, we turned towards Cape Point and on into Cape Town. I was pleased that part of the trip was over, but the rain and blustering winds continued, though not as strong as before, and Table Mountain was covered in rolling black thunderclouds. We tied up in the relatively protected area of the wharf that was set aside for the Royal Navy ships. We all gave a collective sigh of relief, and the walking wounded cheered. The first half of the voyage had finished next stop, Scotland. But the thought of that made me apprehensive.At last, the weather cleared up, and a few of us went up on deck to get some long-awaited fresh air. We could still smell the salty fragrance of the sea in the air, along with the fragrance of last summer's flowers. There was also another stronger odour I couldn't name, so I asked a passing sailor who told us that it was the popular Afrikaans sausage called 'boerewors.' The Navy had booked us into a small hotel close to the wharf, for the walking wounded and some of the nurses which were a godsend.

We gained four glorious days of fine weather in port and I felt I needed to stretch my legs. I was starting to feel I was getting back to normal, whatever that was, so we decided to climb to the top of Table Mountain. I persuaded Bella to wear longs, but she wasn't too sure about that. 'It's not the done thing,' she said. 'You have to be practical,' I advised, 'long skirts and all those petticoats are unrealistic for such a walk.' I visited one of the smaller matelots who lent me a pair of trousers. With her shirt tucked in, a woollen jacket and boots on, and a hat pulled down over her ears, she looked like a young bloke. 'Oh,' she said, a little more confident, 'I do feel daring. I hope I don't run into any of the other women.' 'Well, if you do, just turn away. You'll be okay; they won't even recognise you, and it's so much easier to walk in this gear than in women's clothing.' I grabbed my pack already weighed down with the food I had, along with my stove and a couple of water bottles. Then we headed out on our big adventure

We hired a cart on the wharf to take us to the start of Kloof Neck Road, as the trail wound its way up right to the top from there. We climbed up onto the simple cart, excited that we could have this quiet day together, away from the hotel and Bella's responsibilities. As we travelled along the track, still muddy after all the rain, we took the time to have a good look at our surroundings. The Dutch Colonial Architect was stunning so different from what we were accustomed to. The whitewash buildings were squat with flat roofs and raised verandas which, according to our driver, were called 'stoeps.' The track wasn't an easy tramp, and after being cooped up on a ship for over a month, my calf muscles were screaming. I had not done that much exercise on board, except climbing the mast and doing a few laps of the ship each day, so we took our time.

We stopped frequently to observe the view as we climbed well, that was my excuse anyway. It took us just over three hours when we finally arrived at the top. I had trouble catching my breath, but Bella took it in her stride. 'What a magnificent view,' she said as she took in the panoramic seascape, hardly breathless at all. 'You know, it's been marvellous without all of my usual women's clothing to hamper me. I wish I could do this in England, though of course, it would be utterly scandalous. But if I was disguised, who would know?' she added with a wicked grin.

Now that we had arrived at the top, I realised just how unfit I was and decided I must get this sorted. I should be able to improve my workout even back on board the Esk. We found a cracker place to plonk ourselves down to admire the fantastic view of the city and could see Robben Island behind it. To our rear, we had an unimpeded view over to False Bay. It was fantastic to be out in the open and unconfined. This was me. It felt so exhilarating, so right. Even though I was stuffed, the climb had made me feel alive once again. The temperature felt like a pleasant twenty odd degrees Celsius, but I knew, once the sun dropped in the evening, it could go as low as minus five I was told by one of the hotel guests. I set up the stove and small gas bottle, then with Bella watching me, I lit it with the waterproof matches. She clapped her hands like a little child. 'That's marvellous,' she kept saying. I had my small pots arranged and dropped two dehydrated dinners into one pot, then added a bit of water and brought it to the boil. I let it simmer for a couple of minutes, and then popped half into the other pot and handed it over. 'Okay, Bella try this.' She was tentative at first, but as soon as the food was in her mouth, she looked up, astonished. 'This is lovely Sammy.' Afterwards we shared the rest of my rations, including the choccy biscuits that had melted, but still tasted okay. There wasn't much point hanging on to them. I informed Bella that we were about 1100 metres above sea level. 'What's that in feet?' she asked.

'Ah heck, it's been a while since I did maths, but I've been converting most days since I've been on the Esk. I think it's about three to one, so I'd say about 3300 feet.' 'My goodness,' she declared,' it's nearly as high as Ben Nevis in Wales I think that's about 1000 feet higher. Gosh, I'm pretty pleased with myself climbing up here.' 'You did well Bella, I'm the one out of condition. Oh, this is the life!' I stood and spread my arms out wide, feeling the breeze tugging through my hair. 'I feel invigorated, with the feeling of freedom these open spaces give me. Deep inside me I knew this is who I am.'

We never saw another person on the mountain all day. I scouted around while Bella was sittinggazing at the view with a cup of tea in her hand. 'Get a load of this Bella,' I yelled. She came over to have a look. 'That lizard with the green and blue head, I don't think I have seen one like that before. I've been seeing animal footprints all over the place; I'm not sure what they were. The spoor shows they have four toes. Man, I wish I could stay and really get to know this place.' Time ticked by, and soon Bella announced, 'We need to get back, Sam, it's the middle of the afternoon and sunset is about 6 pm.' So with regret, I gathered up all our rubbish, and slowly we headed back down to sea level. Coming out of a gully, I spotted an animal a bit like a large guinea pig, well not just one, but a mob of them. One let out a kind of trill, then they all dived for cover. 'Wow! I wonder what type of animal that is they made the spoor I'd seen,' I pointed out to Bella. 'It looked like a rat to me,' she answered with a shudder. 'No, too big, it must have been about 50 centimetres tall.' 'It looked more like eighteen inches to me,' she said with delight at knowing the right measurement. 'I scratched my head and grinned, 'I'm glad you knew that, because I would have had trouble converting centimetres to inches; that sort of conversion has got me stumped.' 'Oh Sam, you come out with the most delightful words. What's cricket got to do with it? Anyway, I think I get your meaning,' she said with a laugh.

As we came out into the open, I saw movement way above me. 'Taihoa Bella!' I hollered. She stopped dead, turning to face me with a puzzled look. I pointed up towards a powerfully built leopard perched high up on a rocky bluff, its tawny coat glistening in the late afternoon sun. 'My god, see that it must be the best-looking cat I've ever seen. What a country,' I said in awe. 'He was looking right at us, then turned away.' 'You amaze me, Sam. Most men would want to kill that leopard for a trophy you are just the opposite.' 'I guess I'm starting to realise this about myself, Bella. There's a part of me, something touched my heart, that tells me we need to take care of our wildlife. If we don't, they won't be around for the next generation.' 'Well that makes sense,' she answered. 'What was that that you yelled at me before, Sammy? It stopped me, but what were those words? I didn't recognise them.' 'Ah, I think it means 'stop' in Maori, or 'don't hurry.' I spoke it without thinking, another word for my journal. 'Come on kiddo, let's keep walking; we have a way to go yet.' I held out my hand, she placed hers in mine, and our eyes met. My heart suddenly started pounding, and it wasn't from exertion. We looked at each other, without saying a word, both realising what had just happened. My grin spread from ear to ear, and the look on her face told me all I needed to know.

All at once I felt over the moon. I reckon I could fly, and without a chopper. Possibilities crowded my mind: of a world, I had never thought had existed before, a place where you could spend your life with someone who loved you as much as you loved them. Not having the words to say what was in my heart, I just smiled and took her hand tenderly, placing it in the crook of my arm and covering it with mine as we turned toward home. As we neared the end of the track, we came across a lone baboon. We stopped and watched it scamper over the rocks away from us. Then as we moved on a bit further, something caught my eye in the crevasse of a rocky outcrop. I bent to pick it up. 'Well blow me down,' I exclaimed, 'look at this, Bella a porcupine quill.' I handed it to her. 'This is a reminder of a wonderful day with the most beautiful woman in South Africa.' How did I know about porcupines?, I thought.

'Oh, Sammy,' she marvelled and stood on her tiptoes to kiss me. I lifted her up and hugged her tight. 'My god, woman, I love you.' 'Mmmm, I love you too,' she claimed, with a smile spread across her face. Then the funny side hit me and I laughed. 'If anyone could see us now, it would be around the town like a forest fire 'I saw two men kissing on the edge of Table Mountain.' The last part of the tramp was an easy walk, with a Sunbird flying over us. The plumage was the colour of the rainbow blues, greens and yellows. 'That bird must be a sign,' Bella gushed, 'it rounds off the end of a beautiful day.' I looked at her. God, she was beautiful, and she loves me. We picked up a cart that took us back to the small dockside hotel where we were staying. We snuck in quietly as we didn't want anyone to see the way Bella was dressed, and she shot upstairs for a bath and to change. With only one bath in the establishment, I went outside to a barrel full of cold water. I stripped off my clothes, washed the day's grime away, then headed back inside to dress before dinner.

I was out in the dining hall when I heard the door open to the owner's area of the hotel; I turned and saw a piano. Something just hit me, and I felt drawn toward it. I knocked on the door. 'Dinner,' Mrs Sommerfield (the piano's owner) announced to me, 'will be in 30 minutes, lieutenant.' 'Oh no, nothing like that, madam.' I stammered, 'I see you have a piano, would it be possible just to take a look?' She studied me. 'Can you play?' 'I think so,' I said, 'sorry to be so vague. I had a head wound from the New Zealand war and lost my memory, but I think I can play. Can I try?' I added hopefully. 'Yes, of course, you can, I'm just off to the kitchen, I'll leave the door open.' I sat down and lifted the cover; I felt a tear in my eye. I played a 'C,' then ran my fingers over the keys. Into my mind popped Beethoven Moonlight Sonata 3rd movement, written in 1801. I started to play. It was a sad sonata, but this was the way I felt with my memory loss, and to my mind, it sounded great. I got completely involved with the music and forgot myself. I just whacked it out oblivious to whoever was gawking at me until everyone from the whole hotel were in the room. That's when I looked up. Bella had tears running down her face when I came to the finale, and the room just erupted. Bella threw herself at me and exclaimed, 'Sammy you're a pianist I knew you were different, you have such a talent!' We both had tears streaming down our face. People were smiling and clapping. Then Mrs Sommerfield broke in with, 'Come now ladies and gentlemen, dinner is to be served in the dining hall,' and the place emptied.

Bella and I stared into each other's eyes. 'You have a vocation, Sam. You must have been a pianist, to play like that. You could go anywhere in Europe, and play for Kings and Queens with this gift you have.' What a day; what a breakthrough. I felt fantastic. 'Come on, let's celebrate with a bottle of Cape wine with our dinner.' As we entered the dining hall, everyone rose and clapped as we sat down at our table. There was a bottle of Cape white chilled in a bucket of ice waiting for us. 'That is from all from all of us,' the gentleman next to me said. 'It was quite a moving rendition, well done.'

CHAPTER SEVEN

HMS Esk 1863

We left Cape Town in a southerly blow, with the wind at our back. The *Esk* ploughed through the swells, spreading the waves aside like a knife through butter, and shaking herself at the top of each new wave which invariably swelled under her. We headed up the African coast en route to our final destination, Scotland. The navigation officer informed me the doldrums would not affect us as we would convert to steam, cutting the time down to reach our destination by a few weeks. So with luck, we could be home in about 30 days. There wouldn't be much rest for the crew there though, since they were ordered to head straight back to New Zealand after their week off. They had to be on station in the Bay of Plenty area before the end of the year. The ship's crew were informed that this would be the next big engagement in New Zealand. It's odd, I thought the first campaign had hardly started now they're talking about another. Years later, I heard that our captain, Captain Hamilton was killed in action, at Gate Pa, near Tauranga in 1864. He would have been sorely missed, as he's a nice bloke and an exceptional navy captain.

I was uneasy as we headed north, and spent quiet moments trying to think if I could remember anything Scottish. Would I recognise any places or streets? Would I know anyone? But nothing came to me. The idea of Scotland felt quite foreign to me. My journal was quite thick now, and Bella had said to give it a rest for a while and do something else maybe take an interest in the ship. She suggested I get involved with its day-to-day running, and if I were to get in the way, the crew would tell me. So I increased my jogging around the deck, much to the amusement of all concerned, then spent time with the lookouts up in the crow's nest and the topsails. The swaying of the ship up that high was vastly accentuated. When in the troughs, my stomach dropped down into my boots. But it was fun, especially when I found that feeling of being alive again.

I also enjoyed time in the engine room to a point. I found the smell of oil and coal dust filled my nostrils, making it difficult to breathe. This was dirty work. I certainly wouldn't like to work in these conditions as the stokers and engineers did, day in and day out. However, this was modern technology and we were stuck with it, though I still felt it was old fashioned. I got a thrill out of watching when they kicked the steam engine over, getting it ready for when it was needed. I observed the engineers as they greased and oiled the engine, and the stokers, stripped to the waist doing all of the heavy work, just to make sure it had a head of steam. All of their faces were black and dripping with their own sweat. I helped in the sickbay with the other wounded, asking them how they received their wounds, so got to know the boys reasonably well. It is when I found out that Governor Grey had told everyone in Auckland in no uncertain terms that if they mentioned the attack on the city, the weight of the government would come down on their heads. The captain had passed this on to the crew at a meeting, and as far as the army and navy were concerned, we were all wounded on the border with the Waikato, kilometres away from Auckland. You had to laugh, even though I could not remember a thing, that all these blokes had to lie through their teeth for the rest of their lives because of that order. How unpleasant to live with a lie like that, I thought.

I played my harmonica every few nights or so for a bit of entertainment, and someone lent me a mandolin, which I found I could play as well. Fortunately, I also discovered that I had a good voice, but the songs I sang, nobody had ever heard of before. Whatever way you looked at it, we still all enjoyed those nights out on the deck. Singing, playing music and yarning.

As we sailed closer to the equator, the nights became warmer, so we spent more time out on deck. We watched the flying fish and tried to catch them with nets, and on some occasions we did. The porpoises were a joy to watch, sitting on our bow for hours at a time, though some bloke thought they would make a good meal and wanted to shoot one. But I told him in no uncertain terms, if anyone took a potshot at them, I would personally break every bone in their hands. I must have looked menacing, as no one took up the challenge.

Then it was decided to have a shooting contest. I didn't use my rifle; I kept that wrapped up and concealed in my cabin. I still had this weird feeling that it was way ahead of the times, and felt it was important to keep it hidden. So after watching the first group shoot, I eventually got to my turn with one of their rifles. I was the last to fire. An empty barrel had been thrown off the ship, with a line attached to it. After each turn they would drag it in, bung up the holes, repaint a white mark on it, and chuck it back over. So by the time it came to my turn, I had watched how they loaded, cocked and fired the Enfield. It was surprising. This rifle didn't sit naturally in my hands like mine did, but when I sighted down the barrel, I was relaxed and felt in my element. The barrel bobbed around in perfect blue water at the rear of the ship, as I fired off six shots at various distances; the last was a good 700-odd metres, which I was told was about 850 yards or thereabouts. When they brought the barrel on board, each shot was nicely spaced in a cluster in the middle of the white dot. No one else had six hits, let alone evenly spaced. I was given two tots of rum that night and was the talk of the ship for the next few days. They called me Deadeye Dick. Anyway, it did break the tedium of the shipboard routine.

I could not get enough of being with Bella; she was a butterfly in full colour, flitting here, there and everywhere. She still hadn't told me a thing about herself, only that she was 25 years old, and had completed her nurses training at the Florence Nightingale Hospital. She was an independent woman and had a sister Amelia, aged 18. She reiterated that when the time was right, she would explain everything. 'Nothing's wrong, Sammy, I just need to get us as you keep saying "sorted," before we move on to the next stage.' So I had to be content with that.

The days dragged into weeks, and slowly we headed into the northern latitudes. The Northern Hemisphere summer was in full swing as we approach the British Isles and we stood out on deck as we passed Dartmoor. The smell of the land whiffed out to meet us, with a hint of perfume from flowers, cut hay and grass. I could make out the nicely laid out green pastures as we headed into the English Channel. We scooted around Dover, heading up into the North Sea and on towards O'Leith, Edinburgh's port, 29 days after leaving Cape Town.

The captain stated, 'I will have to explain to their Lordships about the large amount of coal I used on this trip. But that's by the by ; we have arrived home, and the young officers can now complete their recuperation with their families. I'm still not so sure about you, Sam,' he said. 'Don't you worry about me, Robert,' I replied with a grin on my face, 'I have Bella, and everything else pales in comparison.' It amused me to watch any of the top officers when I called them by their first name; a kind of sickly grin came over their face.

As we approached the harbour entrance, we converted over to steam power for the last haul into the dock at Port O'Leith. I went up on deck as we berthed, and the stench from pumped bilge water rose up to greet me. The activity around the wharf was chaotic. There were ships of every description either tied up and unloading or doing repairs. At the same time, others were loading, leaving their moorings and heading out to sea. I had hoped if I saw the seaport it would feel familiar. After all, if I lived in Edinburgh, I must have been here before. But there was nothing that I recognised. I felt crushed. It was all alien to me and nothing felt real. I didn't belong here, and that worried me. Bella was standing next to me, looking up at my face. 'Anything Sammy? Can you see anything at all to trigger your memory?' 'No, nothing Bella,' I uttered, 'not a bloody thing.' 'Don't worry,' she replied full of optimism, 'early days yet.' Once the ship was tied up, army personnel were waiting to take the wounded off to the military hospital. All the sailors stood by the gang plank and clapped as the causalities were carried or helped off by the orderlies. When it came to my turn, I put both my hands up to stop them, and said, 'I'm not sick and I'm not going into hospital. I'll make arrangements myself to visit the medical board, but I'm not unwell, and it's a waste of a bed to have me there.'

Naturally I was ordered to see the head surgeon to be assessed. Colonel Archibald Mcrea took one look at me and said, 'My dear chap, if all my patients were as fit as you, I would be out of a job. I see the problem is your lack of memory has anything returned yet?' 'No,' I replied abruptly, 'nothing.' Bella explained that all of my personal memory had gone family, friends, places I had been, and now the country of my birth. 'Even though Sam has the Scottish name of Mack, his accent is not right, and his two friends spoke like him also. So it's a mystery. In the meantime, I thought we could be out and about trying to jog his memory along by experiencing ordinary life.' 'I entirely agree young lady, and you will be with him?' 'Oh yes, Colonel all the time. There is another point to bring up, the question of his pay.' She passed a document to him, given to her by his friends back in New Zealand. He gazed at it with a slight frown, 'I'll see to it; we cannot have the lieutenant living like a pauper now, can we. Do you have a place in mind where I can contact either of you?' Bella thought for a minute, 'Would the Waterloo Hotel be convenient?' He raised his eyebrows, saying, 'That is an expensive place.' 'Don't worry Colonel, that will not be a problem,' she advised. 'Right then, well, that is settled. Turning to me he said, 'I'll have your remuneration deposited into the Bank of Scotland when it comes through; I'll send you a letter to let you know, or call around if I have the time. In the meantime Lieutenant, you cannot serve with a loss of memory, so I think a discharge is the only option. You can take it from me, from this very moment you are out of the army. Now you are in good hands with your nurse, and I can see that you're nearly back to full health. Your memory may return, but I have known cases where it hasn't, so be prepared for that. If this is the case, make a new life for yourself and do not dwell on what might have been, it will only cause you heartache in the future.' He glanced over my records. 'You have been awarded the New Zealand Cross,' he noted, looking up at me, 'and cited for a Victoria Cross. But the powers that be downgraded it to a military cross, because at the time, it was not an official engagement. That doesn't hold water with me I'm afraid,' he frowned. 'Anyway in your case, it will help with your gratuity. Well-deserved, Lieutenant a brave man by all accounts, and it is my pleasure to meet you.' He stood up and shook my hand. 'So off you go, and I'll get everything to you at the Waterloo. It might take a week, but I'll push it along. We work different here in Scotland; we are all family.'

So off we went. I could not get my head around any of it. Bella, her eyes gleaming, said, 'A New Zealand Cross and a Military Cross Sammy, that's fantastic news.' 'Yeah,' I muttered, 'but it means nothing to me. I can't remember a darn thing about that attack on Auckland; it's so frustrating.' 'Look I'm here for you, so you are not alone Sam. Let's always talk things over please never shut me out. We will get through this together,' she said with conviction. 'I think,' she continued, 'we will get ourselves settled into the Waterloo and then tomorrow we will take a cab around town to see if there are any landmarks that you can recognise. If this doesn't work, we will put an ad in the local newspaper. That might get results.' Bella thought for a minute, 'I believe the ad should be a priority, so we will do that tomorrow and if there are no results from that, we will rethink our plans again. In the meantime, call that cab, Sam. It is unladylike for me to whistle one up,' she added with a grin.

Bella just seemed to fit right into this city. Me, I was like a duck out of water, but I was only too happy to have her take the lead. It was a pleasure to leave the noise and smell of the wharf area where we had spoken with Dr Mcrea at the medical assessment office. It smelt like dead fish mixed with oil and coal so it was with a sigh of relief on our part when the cabby took off towards town. By the time we arrived in Princess Street, we could breathe properly again well, to a point the smell of a large city with bad drainage, soot and smoke lingered in the air.

The Hotel Waterloo opened in 1816 or thereabouts, according to Bella. She had stayed here before, but didn't go on to explain why. I was just happy looking around to see if any landmarks rang any bells. But it was just a blank; it was as if I was sightseeing in this city for the first time. I enjoyed it though; I have to admit. 'There is one thing I've been meaning to bring up, Bella,' I voiced. 'These are all the clothes I have. I need some more before these up and walk off my back, and you won't want to know me. Apparently these had been bought back in Auckland.' She turned with a grin, her eyes sparkling as she said, 'Oh Sammy, what a funny thing to say. Look, that's never going to happen. I want to be close to you all of the time no matter what you're wearing, and honestly, it is only my upbringing that's stopping me from throwing myself at you. We'll have to have separate rooms though; walls have ears and a young woman going into a hotel with a young gentleman, well tongues will wag, and in my position I cannot allow that. So we must be very discrete.' 'What do you mean your position?' I questioned. 'All in good time,' she smiled and continued, 'just believe in me Sam, I need to work some things out, and then I will explain. I must cable my parents when we arrive at the hotel, just to let them know I have returned safely back into the country. I've been away quite a while, and they were not happy when I left. You see, Sammy, I have a mind of my own, and it's going to take a big, strong man to control me.' She laughed as she swung on my arm and looked up at me. 'I think you just might be that man. Now all I have to do is convince my father. If he disagrees, then I'm afraid you will have to carry me off in your arms, because no matter what he says, you're the man I want.' 'I will piggyback you to the ends of the earth Bella; you are my heart.' I could see she was delighted with that, so I gave her a lingering kiss. The cab we were in was a private, closed-in box-type, and my mind turned to the possibilities that offered. But when the cab swung into Waterloo Place, it jammed Bella up against me, so when it came out of the corner, she moved away discretely and brushed herself down. 'Oh Sam, we must be careful we could get caught, but if it's any consolation, I don't really want to stop. Oh dear, that's so forward of me. I cannot help myself, but we must refrain; my conscience won't allow it. Please be patient.' 'Bella, I don't want to do anything you would feel sorry about tomorrow. I don't mind waiting; you're worth it. I will just go and have a cold shower... um... bath.' An impish grin curled up the corner of her mouth. 'Well, it won't be too long, it really won't. I want to be with you as much as you wish to be with me.' The horse slowed, and we came to a halt. Bella adjusted her skirts and ran her hand through her hair, which had fallen loose when I held her. My god, I was speechless, she was so beautiful. She turned to me. 'Okay. I love that word okay,' she said and smiled. 'Well Sam, this is it.' The cab door opened and a porter bowed to us. Another porter rushed over and took our bags, but I kept my rifle close; I was still a bit paranoid over that rifle. We followed them inside.

CHAPTER EIGHT

Edinburgh 1863

The Waterloo was the biggest hotel in Scotland, an impressive Georgian style building made of sandstone, and standing four stories. Surprisingly, the main door wasn't that grand, but when you walked inside, you were blown away. The lobby was enormous, with luxurious seating and coffee tables, and a double wooden staircase curling up to the next floor. The hotel sported three dining rooms, a coffee room, and one hell of a big ballroom. There were 50 bedrooms all told each with plumbing, toilets and baths. You had to be impressed. Bella headed over to the large front desk to check in. The front desk was manned entirely by blokes, and that surprised me. I immediately wondered why they didn't have the usual women receptionists. The clerk looked up and saw Bella. 'My Lady,' he whispered quietly. I hardly registered what he said; Victorian manners were sometimes over the top. Then it came to me why did I think like that I'm Victorian also, aren't I? I missed what she answered, but the next thing I knew, there were four blokes grabbing all our stuff and showing us up to our rooms. They opened the door to Bella's room, and on entering, she turned to the porter and said, 'I have a cable to be sent; will you please wait while I write it.' She turned to me and promised, 'I'll see you in a few minutes Sam; I will just send that message to my parents. Give me five minutes.'

I was shown into the room next door. It was a big, stylish room, with a double bed, lounge chairs, and a writing desk. There was also a separate bathroom with a toilet, and the words "Thomas Crapper" displayed on the porcelain, jumped out at me. A big grin lit up my face. I then stopped, frowned and looked at it. Why? What is it about those words? Scratching my head, I glanced out through the large bay window, lost in thought, but turned quickly back to the room when I heard a movement. The porters were still there. A tip, that's what they're waiting for. I felt uncomfortable suddenly, as I realised I'd never tipped before. Why was that, I wondered. Oh bugger. Shit, I'm like a fish out of water. 'Sorry fellas, wasn't thinking. Oh, hang on a minute I have some money left over from Cape Town.' I had been advanced ten pounds at the Cape. So I rummaged in my pack and came up with some coins, a florin, a couple of sixpenny pieces, four threepenny bits and some pennies. I wondered how much to give them, so I handed over a shilling. 'Threepence each, will that be Okay?' I queried. 'Er Okay? What does that mean sir?' It means is threepence each, alright,' I answered. 'That is suitable sir,' the tallest one replied. 'Okay saves a lot of words,' I explained to them with a grin. 'I gather you are not from around here sir?' the porter observed. 'What's your name young fella?' I asked. 'James sir,' came back the reply. 'Well James, I don't know where I'm from. I was shot in the head three times and I've lost my memory. If I say unusual things, don't worry, I dare say it will all come back to me sometime. 'Well sir, you don't have a Scottish accent. I don't think you are from here; your accent is entirely new to me, well, to all of us.' The others muttered. 'But maybe we could help? Do you know your surname, if I'm not too bold sir?' James inquired. 'Well, according to the documents I have, it's Mack. My first name is Sam or Samuel. Maybe you can ask your mates and your families if someone might have a missing relation.' 'Are you Navy, sir?' 'No, Army.' 'Och, with you using the word "mate," I presumed.' 'Sorry James, I use it all the time. I also call everyone by their first name, and I gather that's not the done thing either, but I just don't think I'm a formal sort of bloke.' 'Bloke sir?' he asked, looking lost. 'Yeah. Oh sorry, I mean, "man,' I corrected. James grinned. 'I can see you will have a few problems with people here sir, we are not familiar with informal speech. We will put the word out for you though. If there is anything we can do to help, just call upon one of the porters, sir.' 'Thank you James.' I shook his hand, and as they went out, I shook hands with the others as well. Cool, I thought, I had now met a few young fellas who would ask around for me. Someone must know about a lieutenant from the army looking for his family. Something might come up, fingers crossed. It was an unusual conversation though. I really had to listen, as their accent was quite broad. You would think if I come from here it wouldn't be a problem.

I wandered out and knocked gently on Bella's door; she opened it with a smile. 'Settled in Sammy?' I stepped past her and walked into the room. 'We must, for appearance sake, not be caught flitting between our rooms,' she said, looking a bit uncomfortable. 'I have to be so careful now that I'm back in the United Kingdom.' 'Heck, Bella I don't want you to be embarrassed; that's the last thing I'd want. I'm still trying to get my head around all this. But I have the impression that this sort of place we are staying in, is a bit too posh for me; I feel I don't fit in.' She took my hand, 'It's alright, Sam my love. We won't do a thing to embarrass either of us. We just need to be careful wagging tongues and all that.' She drew me further into the room; it was even more plush than mine. The room was feminine in nature, lavishly appointed with flowery wallpaper, lace curtains, and vases of flowers everywhere. 'Sit down, Sam. Would you like a drink? I have some lime, or maybe something stronger? 'No, lime would be welcome.' She proceeded to pour two glasses, added ice, and passed one to me, then sat down in the opposite chair and placed hers on the table beside her. She smoothed out her full skirt and looked up at me. I could see she had something serious on her mind. 'Do you love me Sam?' she asked. I came out of my seat and knelt in front of her; even kneeling, I was eye level. 'You don't have to ask that Bella, you are my life. I would not be me without you; we are one in heart and spirit. I don't think I have ever felt like this about another person, and that is from a place deep inside of me. Even with my memory loss, I feel this is true.' She reached over, pulled me towards her, then kissed me deeply. 'I love you, Sammy, with all my heart. So if we are to be together, there's going to be a battle with my parents, I'm afraid. Be prepared for a fight, but don't worry, we will win through. I'm sure when they get to know you, they will love you too. But the first months might be a bit unpleasant for both of us. I hope I'm not putting you off?' she looked concerned. 'Of course not, Bella. After what we've been though, it will be a breeze.' I grinned, saying, 'nothing like a good fight and Bella I would take on the whole Commonwealth for you.' 'Don't you mean Empire?' 'No, I feel Commonwealth is right, but let's say Empire for now. Another muse for the journal,' I said, smiling.

'Well, my love, I have sent my resignation to the nursing hospital. I cannot be a nurse at the moment; I'll need all of my energies for you, and even more for my parents. So that is done and dusted.' 'Good,' I praised, 'you have ticked that box.' 'You had better explain that one,' she laughed. 'Well, it's like you have all these things to do, and when you have finished one, you can put that aside tick the box. 'Sammy, you are a darling with your sayings and I just love it. I'm just not sure how other people will relate, though. Anyway, I'm positive people will come around once they get to know you. We went through nearly three months on board a ship, and everyone enjoyed your company; you are so easy to get along with. She paused, looking serious, then continued, 'Right, my love, now I want to explain I have told a few lies about myself to you, and I need to tell you the truth before we go any further. Don't say anything. Let me tell you my story, and you can then make up your mind one way or the other.' I was about to cut in, and she leant across and put her finger on my lips. 'Later,' she said, 'let me finish first.' In my position, I'm supposed to conform to my station, to be a lady and all that goes with it. It's assumed I'd marry someone that my parents might arrange for me, to have children and be the dutiful wife. But, I am a strong willed woman, Sammy. I have an independent streak. So a few years ago I went against what was expected, and decided I was going to be a nurse. When I told my parents, they were so angry, they said that I was letting the family name down. There were many tears from my mother and lots of yelling. Even my younger sister couldn't understand. I told her I was going away for a while and not to worry. So I left home, after writing a letter explaining my actions for them to read. I placed it on the mantelpiece in the dining room, then took the coach from my hometown and went to London. I completed my nurse's course and from there was sent out to Dunedin in New Zealand. There I helped in a cholera outbreak, and travelled up to Auckland just before the Maori attack.' Bella smiled and continued on, 'But as you know, we are not allowed to refer to the attack on Auckland; we're only supposed to mention the fires. Anyway, I helped with the wounded on all sides Maori, settlers and army. Then the *Esk* came into port. The matron, with the advice of the navy, decided they would settle all the Scottish wounded on board, to help alleviate the conditions in Albert Barracks. This was when I heard about you, so we brought you on board to join the wounded. The second night, Governor Grey arrived unexpectedly and we immediately pulled up anchor heading west and you know the rest.' Taking a big breath, she sighed, looking a bit soulful. 'Now back when I received my training, I had to give

62

them my name and all the usual details. But as my name is well-known in higher circles, I changed it. I'm sorry my love, but my name is not Bella Wrightson, and I'm not from Herefordshire,' she admitted, looking at me doubtfully. I jumped in, 'It's not going to change my feelings, Bella, not at all.' 'Thank goodness for that,' she continued with a smile. 'My name is Isabella Downett Gale; I'm from Shropshire, not far from the town of Shrewsbury. The name Wrightson is my mother's maiden name. "Well that's not so bad Bella; I like the name.' 'Well,' she muttered, 'Downett is my great grandmother's maiden name. Her husband, my great-grandfather,' she continued, looking at me intently, 'was Richard Edward Gale, the First Earl of Shadymore.' She stopped to let that sink in. It didn't at first; I just looked at her with this look of, 'well yeah, so what.' Until slowly, the penny dropped. 'Earl!' I spluttered. 'Will it make a difference Sammy?' she queried, her face full of concern. I looked at her. 'Well not to me,' I said, grinning, 'but your old man might not take to kindly to me.' She laughed out loud. 'Oh Sam, you do make me laugh with your words. I would love to see his face if he heard you call him that!' 'So, your dad is an Earl?' 'Dad?' she said with a frown. 'Yeah, father.' 'You amaze me. Yes he is, and my...?' 'Mum,' I jumped in. 'Oh, I like that as well. Mother is the Countess of Shadymore.' I looked up at her intently, waiting on her next words. 'So what does that make you?' I asked, holding my breath. 'I'm Lady Isabella Downett Gale.' 'You don't have the "Shadymore" after your name?' 'No, that's only for the Earl and Earl's wife.' 'And your sister?' 'She is Lady Amelia Margaret Gale."You have no brothers?' 'Yes, I had two, but both died young. As you can imagine, my parents are pretty upset that there is no male to pass the title on to. But I don't want to go into that now. How do you feel about it all, Sammy? It is a big responsibility marrying into title people. I have had a lot of young men keen to marry me in the past, and a lot of it was because of my parents' money and title. You are so different to the men I have been introduced to; you want to marry me for me, for love. Even if I were a parlourmaid, you would marry me, and that is the way it should be. So I'm not what you expected, and there are things we will have to talk through. But Sammy my love, before we leave this room, I want you to know that I want to be your wife. My father will have to accept you, and if not, we will make a place of our own without them. Oh I love my parents don't think otherwise. The things I have seen over these past few years, the places I have been to and the work that I have done, has changed me. We are only here a short time on this earth; we must make the most of our lives with someone we love. I will give up all the prestige and money to be with you.' She sat back with a concerned look on her face. I know this is a big revelation for you, my love. Are you able to cope with it?' I looked at her and grinned. 'Bella, I couldn't care a toss even if you were penniless; all I know is that I love you and want to be with you. I will marry you tomorrow, just you say the word. I have no idea what it's like to be from a titled family, or for that matter, from any family. But there's no need to worry; I'll do my best to make them like me. I have no idea what I can do to earn a living though to support you, but I think we should worry about that later on.' 'Oh Sammy, you will not have to worry about money.' 'That's all fine and well Bella, but if you're my wife, then I need to be worthy. I can't live off you or your dad's money; I will need to pay my own way. Anyway, that's not important right now, what is important is that first you'll have to teach me how to act among titled people, or I'll feel like a duck out of water.' Her face softened with love as she said, 'I'm not ever going to change you Sam what would be the point in that? I fell in love with a big, easy going man, who's gentle with bit of a tough streak, a lover of life, and I certainly do not want to change that, not anytime soon. So, my love, be yourself and people will just have to get used to it, or it's their loss.'

I picked Bella up and kissed her passionately. 'Let's get married! I'll sort out a ring as soon as I get my back pay; we must find a church and something needs to be done about my name.' I shook my head, and with a worried frown, continued, 'I don't like the name "Mack," Bella. It eats away at me, so do you mind if I find a name that'll suit me? Anyway, "Mrs Mack" doesn't suit you, either.' She laughed merrily, happy now that the secret she was keeping was at last out in the open. 'Let's both give it some thought, Sammy. Maybe something will hit us. I don't really care what my name is, as long as it's not Bottompaddock.' I grinned and said, 'I think Bella, you might have a pretty good-looking bottom.' I could see her cheeks flush with a touch of pink. 'Sammy,' she said, hugging me, 'when the time is right, you will be the first man to see it.' I could feel tears on my neck as she hugged me tight.

We spent the rest of the day planning. Tomorrow we would walk and cab around town, hoping to see anything familiar to jog my memory. Then we would place an ad in the local paper describing myself to the population, with the hope that any of my family would come forward. Colonel Mcrea had explained that most of my records had gone missing. Quite unusual, but these things do happen. So before I had left the hospital, he filled in his forms with as much as I knew, and added a birthdate of the 1st of May 1833, as he thought I looked about thirty. 'We have to put something down for the records,' he told me, 'and you have to have a point of reference as well.' So I'll add my approximate age to the advertisement. Next on our list was to check out if there's going to be a legal problem with changing my name when the time comes. After that we would have to wait for any replies from the newspaper. In the meantime, both of us needed clothes, so some shopping was on the cards as well. I had to explain that word to Bella. 'Look, don't worry about money, Sam. I will supply all we need for the moment, and when you get your pay, you can pay me back then, if that's what you want,' she added. She knew I wouldn't accept it any other way. So now we had a plan. As it was getting close to dinner time, she checked the hall to see if anyone was around, When it was clear, we both snuck out like naughty teenagers and went down for dinner.

CHAPTER NINE

Edinburgh 1863

The morning was overcast with drizzle as we left our bedrooms and met outside in the hallway to walk down for breakfast. 'I think a cab to start with after we have eaten,' Bella suggested. We looked out the large bay windows at the street below watching the light rain trickle down the panes. Walking down the staircase, Bella held my arm tightly. 'Did you sleep well, Sam?' she asked. 'Yep, I did,' I replied, 'though I still felt unsteady, as if I was still on board the *Esk*. But I did have a dream, and for the first time in a while, it was about us, now.' She stopped and looked up at me, and whispered, 'Can you tell me about it?' I smiled. 'Bella, it was a bit on the erotic side, and I'm sure that's a thing I can't talk about to a fine young woman like you,' I whispered back. She pulled back from me and looked at me with anticipation. 'Was it an exciting dream, Sammy?' 'Well, I would most certainly say so, Bella', I replied and smirked. My eyes softened, and I looked at her with tenderness. 'Heck, kiddo, I love you.' She tightened her grip on my arm. 'And I you, Sammy.'

We had breakfast in a splendid, opulent, dining hall decked out with chandeliers, fancy cherubs around the cornices, and thick carpet. The waiters and waitresses, dressed in full service uniforms, glided pass our table so smoothly; it looked as though they were floating above the floor. This place was undoubtedly upmarket, and I worried about the cost. I mentioned this to Bella, but she replied with a grin, 'It is a little bit Sam, but my father has an account here, so I'm using it. I haven't cost him a penny in the last few years, so I'm going to indulge myself until we can find out about your family. So please, Sam, it's not charity don't think of it like that think of it as payment due.' 'Sam, there is one other thing I meant to tell you; my father gives me an allowance each year of a thousand pounds.' 'Okay, if you say so, but that is yours.' I had no idea how much this was as I still thought in dollars, and a thousand didn't seem that much. 'No, Sam, it is ours. You will be entitled to it once we marry, but we will talk on this later.'

'Talking about money,' I groaned, 'what about the clothes we need, Bella? I haven't been paid yet, and I'm in dire of need of some clothes, as are you.' 'Yes, well, that can easily be arranged as I can order and buy anything I want; all I do is mention my name, and the account will come here. When it does, I will pay it through my bank. This is how everything works for our family. You can pay it back to me once your cheque comes through from the army. My father set up my account years ago. The main thing is to not abuse it, and always pay on time. So you don't need to worry. And you're right about me needing clothes,' she added with a grin, 'I have to get something practical to wear. Frankly, I do not want to wear any formal dresses. A couple of simple day dresses with shorter sleeves would be better, some shoes to go with them, and maybe a couple of nice hats.' She lent forward and covering her mouth, whispered 'and of course, underclothes.' I looked at her, surprised. What a woman! She had it sorted, so I was happy to go with the flow. 'Okay,' I grinned, then asked, 'what about me? I must be honest Bella. These clothes I pulled at my trousers they just don't feel comfortable. I think I'm more used to jeans, or shorts, and open neck shirts.' 'Jeans, Sam, what are they?' She looked confused. 'They're durable, casual pants made of denim.' 'I have never heard of them, Sammy.

That's another word for your journal.' 'Yes I must remember that. I guess I will have to conform for the moment then,' I grumbled. 'So what do you think I'll need?' 'Well, a walking-out suit, and an evening suit, shoes, a couple of pairs of socks, at least three shirts, and underclothes,' she added with a whisper. 'That should see us through till we get home to my parents' place. You might end up with more socks there as when father gets mad he throws them at me. He's not a violent man; so this is about as far as he goes. His bark is far worse than his bite, thank goodness.' She laughed, and continued, 'You could even get a full wardrobe out of him because he will be a little out of sorts when we turn up married.' I frowned. 'Don't you think we should leave getting married until we see them, and then have a large wedding with your folks and all your family?' 'Oh no.' Sammy shaking her head, and quite adamant, admitted, 'He will do all in his power to come between us. No. That's not an option at all. We will get married before we arrive and then he has to accept you. Grudgingly at first I suspect, but we will eventually wear him down. My mother will cry a lot, but it's a falsehood. She is as strong as I am. We are much alike, so it's all put on. She will come around as well, it will just take a little bit of time. So, all in all, Sammy, we'll present a united front. Now, on the other hand, my sister will love you; she is my heart. I have written to her every week over the last few years, so she knows how I feel. I cannot believe that she is eighteen years old I am so looking forward to seeing her. Anyway, I will be Mrs Samuel someone, and they really will have to like it. If it doesn't work out well, then we can start afresh.' I looked at her and marvelled, 'Is it normal, Bella, for a woman to be like you, with such strong convictions?' 'No, it's not, Sam. I cannot and do not want to be a woman dictated to and controlled by a man. I need to be my own person, and that is no disrespect to you, not at all, it's just me. I sometimes think I was born out of time.' 'Well, that might be the case for me as well; it's a no-brainer.' 'Oh, Sam,' she giggled, 'what does that mean?' 'There's no question about it, it's just right. You know I believe marriage is a partnership and we are equal, so I'm all for you being assertive. Anyway, that's what I love about you, it's your personality and strength.' We held hands and glanced lovingly at each other. 'Let's find you a name that suits you,' she suggested. 'Then, let's get married. I don't want to wait any longer than necessary.' 'Right, kiddo, let's find you a ring.'

With that, we rose from our table, walked outside, and hailed a hansom cab. I approached the driver. 'G'day mate, how much for the day?' 'Och mon, that's a pretty penny are you serious, sir?' 'Yep, mate, I am.' 'I'm not sure quite what you mean, but five shillings for the day would be a fair price.' I had nine pounds in my pocket, mainly in coins; this was the leftover of the advanced pay I had received in South Africa. It was so bloody heavy just sitting in my pocket, so I was glad to reduce the weight of it. 'Ok,' I said, 'you have a deal half now, half when we get back.' I handed him two shillings and six pence in coin and announced, 'We need a jeweller, a women's shop and a men's shop. Now I want decent and reasonably priced establishments; also we need to go to the newspaper office.' 'I know just the places, sir.' He jumped down from the rear of the cab and opened the door for Bella and me. We snuggled up close together though it was a short ride, and soon pulled up outside a store with Cavenish Jewellers of Hanover St since 1796, displayed.

This shop didn't look like it sold anything at a reasonable price to me. 'We need an engagement ring,' I declared to Bella as we stepped down onto the footpath. She looked up at me, 'Sam, we are betrothed; there is no need for a ring just yet. All we need, is a wedding band.' 'Are you really sure, Bella?' I asked, uncertain. 'Of course, Sammy. When we have more time, you can do that if you wish. It is more important to have a wedding band for now.' We walked into the shop which was small but well lit with candlelight. There was a counter at one end that curved around both sides in a horseshoe shape. A slightly built balding man stood next to it, surrounded by his merchandise. His glasses were perched right on the end of his long nose, and I stopped to wonder how the hell they didn't fall off. I had to grin. He stepped forward and was most polite and courteous. I had to give it to him; his attentiveness was awesome. However, I only got every third word of what he said, but Bella understood well enough. He showed us a tray of wedding bands and stepped aside for us to admire the designs. We whispered in low voices, deciding on the ones she liked the best. 'Oh, look at this lovely keeper ring; it is so beautiful,' she gushed. I leant over, having a good look. 'What's a keeper ring?' I asked. 'It's a promise to marry ring, or a commitment ring.' 'Ah, it's an engagement ring,' I exclaimed. 'I have never heard of a keeper ring, and yes that is nice a green emerald to go with your eyes. Will it fit?' I asked. Mr Cavenish, the manager, was over like a shot. He took the ring out of the glass case and placed it on a small pillow that displayed the ring's perfection; he then stepped back. So I picked up the ring and slipped it on her finger. It was a little loose and the manager explained, 'That will be easy to fix, sir.' But Bella reminded me, 'This keeper ring is more attractive than the rest, Sammy, but we only came to buy a wedding band.' 'No kiddo, I think this is a ring you should have. We have made a commitment to each other, and you can wear that right now.' She had a tear in her eye as we examined the wedding bands. We soon found a charming one that she liked, with two small diamonds embedded in the band. I asked the manager, 'Can I have an engraving inscribed on the inside?' 'I am only too happy to do that for you, sir,' he replied with enthusiasm. 'Okay, I would like it to read, "Love always, Sam." Is that doable?' '"Doable," sir what is that?' 'Well, can you engrave it.' 'Not a problem, sir, it will only take thirty minutes.' 'What do you think, Bella?' 'This is beautiful, Sam.' 'One more thing, Mr Cavenish; see that chunky, gold band there. Will it fit on my finger, do you think?" Will this be for you, sir? I have not sold a man's wedding ring for years.' He took it out of the case and placed it on the pillow. I picked it up and tried it on, it was a good fit. 'This will be just right.' 'I'm so pleased you are happy with it, sir.' I agreed. 'Right, what is the cost?' He took out his pencil. I watched him jotting fast on a piece of paper, muttering to himself. Then he officially announced his calculations. 'The keeper ring; it is a lovely piece with the emerald setting. Now that will be two pounds three shillings. The gentleman's wedding ring is created in Welsh gold; it is a very hard gold and the best in the world, and it is one guinea. The young lady's wedding ring is one pound fifteen shillings; I have given you a discount on that as you have purchased the man's ring as well. That brings the total balance to four pounds nineteen shillings.' 'Right,' I acknowledged, 'what about the engraving?' 'There is no charge for that, sir.' 'That's admirable of you,' I replied, quite pleased with the purchase. I paid for the rings with more of the loose change in my pocket. He looked up at me, then to Bella. 'Where are you staying?' he asked. 'The Waterloo,' she replied. He took out his pencil and asked, 'Your name, sir?' 'Samuel Mack,' I muttered, 'and the young lady is Lady Isabella Downett Gale.' He wrote down the information and looked up, saying, 'Leave the Lady Isabella's wedding ring with me for the engraving, and I'll deliver it to you at the end of the week, if that is convenient, sir?' 'That's very kind of you, Mr Cavenish.' I turned back to Bella, dropped to one knee and asked, 'Bella, will you marry me?' She threw herself at me, much to the shock of Mr Cavenish. 'Yes,' she cried. I kissed her and slipped the ring on her finger. Mr Cavendish murmured, 'If you give me a few minutes, I will fix the ring for you.' Bella took it off her finger and handed it back to him. We spent the waiting time smiling at each other until he returned. He gave me the ring, and I placed it back on her finger; it fitted perfectly. We thanked him, and finished with, 'see you at the end of the week.' I put my wedding ring in its box safely away in my pocket, and we walked out to the cab.

As I stepped up into the hansom, I stopped and asked the driver, 'What is your name, mate? I cannot go on all day saying, hey you.' 'Rory Kerr, sir,' he replied. 'Mine is Sam. Pleased to meet you, Rory.' I think he was a bit taken aback. 'Okay, a ladies' shop next, Rory.' 'I have one in mind, sir, Kennington and Jenner on Princess Street. Your young lady will be able to buy everything she needs there.' We plodded around to Princess Street. When I saw the building, I thought it looked like a department store, at least that's the word that came into my mind. Bella stepped out and admired the building. Then she smiled and said, 'I forgot about this shop; it has been a while since I have been in Scotland. This will do nicely. Sammy, do you want to come with me? I could be a couple of hours, and it is women's clothing you might get a bit bored waiting around. Or, you could have a look for an acceptable church for us and see if they could fit us in, maybe four weeks from now? If we don't have your family name by then, we never will. You could put an advertisement in the paper for us. So why don't you go into the newspaper office. Here is my card to show them. Just describe yourself and explain your story. We need to get that in, the sooner the better.' 'That's a good idea, Bella.' I looked at my wristwatch. 'I see you are wearing it now, Sam.' 'Yeah, it feels familiar to wear it.' 'Good', she replied. 'Well it's ten a.m,' I stated, looking at my watch, 'so let's say I meet you back here at midday. We can find somewhere nice for lunch, and then we will do my clothes thingy.' She laughed and agreed. 'Fine Sam, see you in a couple of hours then.' 'Thingy,' I heard her uttering under her breath with a giggle as she walked inside the building. I looked at Rory. 'Okay, mate, we need to go to the newspaper office.' 'That will be the *Edinburgh Times,* sir, in St Andrews Square.' 'Fine,' I answered as I jumped aboard. He moved off towards the newspaper office; we must have been doing about three kilometres an hour. I felt that we should be able to go a great deal faster. Soon Rory pulled up outside this big stone building with three massive columns out the front. As I strolled through the main doors, I immediately got confused. The large entrance was well-appointed, but there was no signage to explain where to go. I looked around the foyer feeling like a fish out of water, when this bloke came up to me and asked if he could help. 'Yes please.' I grinned with relief. 'I'm out of my depth here. I need to place an ad in the newspaper for at least a week. Who should I see?' 'What is an ad, sir?' he asked with a puzzled look on his face. 'Oh, I mean an advertisement.' 'Oh, of course, sir, come this way.' I followed him up this bloody great staircase to the next floor and along a carpeted hallway to an office. He knocked once, entered, then beckoned me in.

At the counter a young man sat writing, and he looked up as we came in. My escort turned to me and said, 'The clerk will help you, sir.' Then he returned downstairs. 'What can I do for you, sir?' the clerk asked. 'I have a delicate advertisement to put in your paper,' I replied, then explained what I wanted. 'That will be no problem, sir; I'll get on to that right away. We will need someone to write a good description of you. One moment please.' He went to a long, black tube hanging from the ceiling, blew into it, got a response and then asked for the artist to come up. 'He will be here in a minute, sir. He's just the man for the job,' he promised. I stood dumbfounded. For some unknown reason, watching him with his tube, I wanted to laugh out loud. I don't know why, but I couldn't believe it shit, people really used those things, was my first thought. I had presumed this to be a modern business.

The artist soon turned up, and he sat me down. He studied me intensely, then started writing. I jumped in quickly with, 'Before you put my hair colour down, it used to be red. I was shot in the head and it turned this colour afterwards.' 'How extraordinary, I will mention that, sir.' It took him about forty-five minutes, then he passed it over to me to check. 'This is excellent; you have me down pat.' "Pat, "sir?'' 'Uh you have all of my characteristics correct.' I was starting to get pissed off at having to explain every word I used. With Bella, I was tolerant, naturally, but to every other person I came across, it was getting up my nose. Where did these words and visions come from? Having to explain to all and sundry was a pain in the bum. 'Where can we send the account to, sir?' he asked. 'The Waterloo Hotel, Lady Isabella Gale,' I said as I gave him Bella's card. 'That is first rate, thank you. I do hope, sir, your memory returns soon.' 'Thank you, so do I; it's uncomfortable not knowing my past.' 'This will be run in every edition for the next week. We hope you get some results, sir, our paper is sent all over Scotland. But if you don't think me presumptuous, sir, I'd say as you are a big man surely someone would know you.' 'Thanks mate, fingers crossed,' I said hopefully. I wasn't going to explain that one, so I left quickly.

CHAPTER TEN

Edinburgh 1863

Back out on the street I saw Rory leaning against the coach having a ciggy. 'Right mate,' I voiced, 'we still have time to find a church.' 'Sir, on the other side of this Square is St Andrews and St George, a combined Church of Scotland. It is big though, sir, but I would recommend it.' 'Let's take a gander then,' I suggested as I started to climb aboard.' He looked confused. I ignored it and asked,

'Um, what about the men's shop, Rory?' 'Well sir, there is a nice wee outfitter out at Portobello called Selkirks, with good prices, so I think you will get a good deal there.' I looked at him startled; the names Portobello and Selkirk jerked in my memory. Suddenly I felt excited for some reason, but why? What was it with those names? Shit, I thought there has to be a reason for it. But I couldn't identify it. I closed my eyes. Yes, there was something. An albatross came to mind it was there and gone before I could put a finger on it. I sat back thinking, I did like the name Selkirk though; it seemed familiar somehow. Was this a memory? Anyway it felt comforting, like home. Then it hit me; that's what I'll call myself; it'll be my new name: Samuel Selkirk. It had a certain ring to it and it felt "family." A stirring of excitement returned; the name felt right. Maybe this could even be my actual name. If not, my real name might come back to me later. Anyway, my awareness of how happy I felt inside, combined with the goosebumps up my spine, convinced me there had to be some kind of personal connection. Whether it was my actual last name, I couldn't say. It might even be a family name, or a name I was familiar with whatever I was going to claim it as my own. I was thrilled. What a milestone! I called out to the driver, 'Okay, Rory, let's go over to the church.'

The horse cab trotted around the town square, coming to a stop outside a massive church with four great marble columns bordering two heavy wooden doors. It looked very grand. There seemed to be stone pillars everywhere in this town. A small notice board to the side displayed times of the services on Sunday along with the minister's name, The Reverend Duncan Macintosh. I slowly climbed the stairs to the entrance; the big double doors stood open. I walked inside and wandered down the central aisle towards the font. My footsteps on the tiled floor caused a bloke in a black robe to look up. He was kneeling and had been cleaning what looked like a small chalice. He shifted his weight to favour his left leg, then stood up straight. He was tall, at about 1.8 metres that's a little less than six feet with broad shoulders, big hands and a pleasant face. Age wise I'd say he'd be close to fifty. He looked more like a farmer than a padre. 'How can I help you, young man?' I'm the Reverand Duncan he informed me as he ushered me towards a pew to sit down. I explained what Bella and I wanted to do, and ended up going over my life story again. When I had finished, he looked at me. 'I can understand the need to find yourself, Sam.' It was so good to talk to a person without so many "Sir's" impeding the conversation. At last I'd found someone who was down to earth. 'I can marry you; that is no problem, but under what name? We have to, by law, have a name.' 'Well Duncan, I think I have one,' I said, and went on to explain what had just happened when the Selkirk name came up. 'But I must ask,' I continued, 'is it legal for me to use this name? Or do I have to change it in a court of law?' 'No, you can use any name. Once it is on a marriage certificate it is your legal name, so that's not a problem. Of course I would like to meet the young lady in question as well, Sam. Maybe you would like to come to service on Sunday, bring Bella along, and I will officially read the bands. What say we book in your wedding for Saturday the 29th of August that's four weeks away. That would give you time to find out who you really are; then you could invite any of the family to the celebrations. We could also include some of your friends from the *Esk*, that is, those who could leave the hospital for an hour or two.' He rose and disappeared into his office to pick up his diary. Returning, he asked, 'Now what is Bella's full name?' I told him and he looked startled. 'The Earl's daughter?' 'Yes,' I smiled, 'is that going to be a problem?' 'Not for me it isn't,' he chuckled, 'but I can see rough water ahead for a wee while, for you both.' Standing up, he shut his diary with a snap. 'I will look forward to seeing you and meeting Bella on Sunday.'

Well that's another job I could tick off. As it was close to midday, I jumped back into the cab, and we drove around to the store. Bella wasn't in sight, so I hopped out and yarned to Rory. 'Since we are still close to the hotel, mate, I think we should have lunch there. What do you say?' 'That will be capital, sir,' 'Sam is my name, mate,' I replied. 'I could not call you by your first name, sir; you are my client,' he answered stiffly. So, 'Sir' it remained. Bella came out of the four-story building, with several porters carrying many boxes. I thought she had brought the entire store. She looked very happy, proclaiming, 'It has been a long time since I did any shopping, Sammy. I know it looks a lot, but I had nothing to wear.' We placed all the boxes inside the cab, leaving us just enough room for the two of us to jam ourselves in. We headed back to the Waterloo and I suggested lunch before it was my turn to buy clothes. On arriving back, a couple of porters ran down the stairs, collected all the boxes and hurried them off to her room. I turned to Rory. 'Would you like to join us for lunch?' He looked shocked, and sputtered, 'But sir, I'm not adequately dressed for the Waterloo; thank you all the same. No, I'll have a bite at a tavern and pick you up at thirty minutes after one.'

I couldn't wait to tell Bella about the Selkirk name. She was thrilled to bits. 'This is a big breakthrough Sam. When those two names jumped into your mind, did you feel anything else?' 'Well, I know this sounds silly, Bella, but I did. When the name "Portobello" was mentioned, I instantly had a vision of an albatross.' I stopped for a second, frowning. 'Yes, it was an albatross. Now what the heck is that all about?' She thought for a minute. 'Could it mean freedom in your case, Sam to be free of worry? It came to you at the same time as the name Selkirk. Now having a name, the vision popped into your head as a message to accept your fate and be free of the past.' I looked at her, agreeing, 'You could be right Bella. I felt excited to think that name might mean something. 'Oh, I would like to find my family, but I feel more content now than I have over the last few months. Yes, I think you could be right.' She squeezed my hand. 'Mrs Selkirk sounds nice.' 'I placed the ad in the paper, and it will run for seven days. Then I saw the Padre at the St Andrew and St George Church. A nice bloke, he has booked us in for Saturday the 29th, though he would like to see us at the Sunday service.' She grinned, 'Don't they just love to get their claws into you? But never mind, that is fine. I now have a dress I can use for the wedding. I thought about it and decided to fix it up myself. I will need someone to walk me down the aisle though now who can I get?' 'Well, why not ask Colonel Mcrea from the hospital. I can go and have a yarn with him. Well, we both can. I can also pop up to the infirmary to see if Angus McDonald will be my best man. I got on well with him.' 'Yes, he is a lovely young man. It's going to be hard for him with only one arm,' she confided. 'Yeah, but he is educated Bella;

he's an architect. Why the heck he ever joined the army, I will never know. I think he will be okay. So I'll go to see him. Does this please you?' 'Of course Sammy, all those boys were good men after I stopped a few of them thinking they were above the rest of us,' she laughed. 'But, what about lunch? I'm quite hungry. I believe a celebration meal is called for; it has been a good day so far.'

Rory was waiting when we finished lunch. 'It is about an hour's drive; I thought it would be worth it for you, sir. I have listened to your plight, and this will give you a bit of a look-see of the town, out to the coast from a different road you came in on. We will go via Queens Drive and St Margaret's Loch and then take the London/ Portobello Road. We will be at Selkirks at thirty minutes after two, or a bit sooner.' It was a pleasant drive, the day had turned fine, and the Loch was blue. Ladies with their parasols walked around at leisure along with young mothers and their growing children. Yeah, it felt nice. Nice, but not home, wherever home was. It just didn't feel right in my mind. The street was cobbled, the houses close knit, the smoke. soot and horse dung, that is until we hit the Portobello Road, all hard-packed clay and country fields. and the air smelt fresher. On a wet day, it would have been a hard slog. Forty-five minutes later, we come to a stop outside the shop.

The name on the front, in bold lettering said, "Selkirks of Portobello." I stepped down, then turned to help Bella. Thanking Rory, we went inside. It was a medium sized shop with a wooden-framed bay window in the front. The deeper you walked down towards the back, the darker it got, with only candles lighting the way. A small, wizened old bloke with a broad nose and long white beard, with ringlets on either side of his skull cap, looked up as the doorbell jingled when we entered. He was Jewish how the hell did Selkirk come into the name? He was very bent over as he moved towards us with the aid of a walking stick. 'How can I help you, madam and sir?' 'Well,' I replied, 'I need clothes.' Turning to

Bella, I asked, 'What do I need again?' 'He will need an evening suit, a walking out suit for day wear, socks, shoes, ties, and three shirts.' then she whispered 'drawers' going read in her cheeks. The old man looked up at me and said, 'I will have to have them all made to measure for such a big man like you. Excuse me, I will get my sons to help.' Two young blokes came out with measuring tapes, pencil and paper, then got to work measuring me up. It felt familiar somehow, as though I had done this before and not so long ago, but that thought soon disappeared like most others I had, so I couldn't put my finger on it.

It took about half an hour for them to measure me. One bloke also measured my feet for shoes. When they showed me their underwear section, Bella had walked around the back of the shop no doubt to save her embarrassment about talking about unmentionables. All they had to show me were these long johns thick, woollen underwear with a string to hold them up on your waist. I thought that's rubbish, no way. 'No mate,' I said. 'Can I have a pencil and paper please?' Then I drew what I thought felt right; boxer shorts with elastic around the waist. He looked at my drawing and shook his head. 'Elastic,' he said, 'is quite new. It might be a problem sourcing this, but my son will know about it as he is quite modern. Hmm I have never thought about this before, and to have it on the waist hmm this is exciting.' He looked up from my drawing. 'Yes,' I replied,' and much more comfortable.' 'Yes, I can see that. Might I keep the design? It might change the way men wear their underclothes.' 'Sure, Mr Selkirk.' 'Oh no, he said, 'my name is Aharon Hyman.' 'Then why "Selkirk"?' I asked. 'We had a few problems with people accepting us and our religion, so to make things kosher we changed the name of the shop for security reasons.' 'Clever,' I grinned. 'Yes Aharon, you can keep that design, but for the sake of business, for every pair you sell I get five percent.' He came straight back with, 'Two and a half.' I looked him in the eye. 'Okay, and it goes into my account at the Bank of Scotland every quarter under my name.' 'Done,' he said, spitting into his hands and rubbing them together, then sticking his hand out to shake. I took his hand. 'A Gentleman's shake,' I noted, and beamed. He looked up and smiled. Still holding my hand, he replied, 'I don't know where you come from sir, but I know an honest man when I see one. If you have any more designs, just send them to me. We have shops all over the United Kingdom. At least one in every major city around the country, and some in smaller towns as well. We are always looking for different design ideas. Now sir, what is your name?' It was the first time I had used it. 'My name is Samuel Selkirk.' He looked up, and the look on his face was as if I was pulling his leg. 'No, that is my name, Aharon. I would like seven pairs to start with, one for every day of the week. You can also make them in different colours but not white, pink or red I want manly shades.' 'Oh, different colours, oh my, yes. I can see how that would be better, yes. I think that is all I need for now,' he said and grinned. 'Have you a shop in Shrewsbury?' I asked. 'Oh yes,' he affirmed, 'in New Street Frankwell.' 'Under the same name?' I inquired. 'Oh, yes, we don't want to upset the population.' 'Good, then I will send any new ideas that I think of through that outlet. Fantastic, now how much do I owe you?' 'Well,' he said, 'just one moment.' He hummed and muttered, then lifted his head. 'That comes to seven pounds two shillings and ten pence. Now, what we will do, except for the ties and socks, is work on getting everything made to measure for you, including the shoes. I'll have them all delivered to your hotel.' Looking down, he continued, 'Ah, yes, the Waterloo. By midweek, you can pay in full then, does that suit you? No payment until we deliver.' 'Are you sure, Aharon?' I exclaimed, 'That is very kind of you. Will you deliver them yourself?' 'No, one of my sons will, and the arrangement starts today for our partnership.' Just then,

Bella finished her stroll around the shop and joined us. She looked up at me. 'Did I miss something?' she asked. 'I'll tell you in the cab kiddo.' Turning to Aharon, I shook his hand and said, 'Thank you. It's been a pleasure doing business with you.' With that, we strolled out the door.

Rory opened the door of the cab for us. 'Home James,' I instructed, 'and don't spare the horses.' He looked at me with alarm, and Bella burst out laughing. On the way back to the hotel, I told her about the underwear deal. 'I tell you, Bella, you should have seen what they wanted to sell me. To hell with that. I drew up a new design for him. I'll show you what they were like when we get back. But you remember the shorts I have, well they're similar to that, only with lighter material.' 'You are brilliant Sam,' she said as she snuggled up close to me. 'Do you think that could take off with women, Bella?' She went red to the tops of her ears again. 'I'll have to see yours before I can answer that,' she mumbled. The day was fast coming to an end; it had been fairly full on. Looking back, I had proposed, bought the rings, sorted out the ad for the newspaper. Also, the church was organised, Bella had bought her clothes, I had done the same, and I had a finger in the pot with my Jewish mate. But the biggie was I had a last name finally. Boy what a day. I wondered how the deal with Aharon would pan out. I didn't know, but it was a good start. I was sure after looking at the underpants that are available, my design should take off like a rocket. I had used almost all of my money for the payment of the cab and the keeper ring, so I hoped my Army pay would come through earlier than later. At this point, I didn't have enough to pay Aharon, and I was uncertain about asking Bella for a loan. We had an early tea with a glass of wine, and then I escorted Bella to her room. We managed to sneak in a quick kiss before I went off to bed, quite knackered.

CHAPTER ELEVEN

Edinburgh 1863

I had a restless night and rose early. After dressing, I went out for a walk to take in the early sites of the city that was just starting to come alive. I took pleasure in the walk along the streets and watched the citizens heading out to work. I gazed at the cobbled streets with their houses so close together, you couldn't slide your hand in between the gaps. The thoroughfare wasn't empty though as folk were up at dawn. Men pushed carts full of goods to set up for sale, and women sold flowers on the street corner. Young boys rushed past with their long chimney brushes, and housewives were out early, hoping to purchase their food as fresh as possible. It all seemed alien to me somehow, and there was rubbish scattered everywhere with horse droppings on the road. What I did find really distasteful was the underlying stench of blood as it dripped onto the pavement from the meat, which hung on hooks outside the butchers shop. This just didn't seem normal to me, it didn't feel right but why, I kept asking myself why do I feel it's so strange? I expected to see something else. But what? The word 'car' slipped into my mind, then 'truck' and 'van.' I looked up and down the street, but there were no cars here. All I saw were horses and carts, some gigs and handcarts, and a few horse cabs. So why did I think of a car when they didn't even exist nor did the word as far as I knew? I couldn't even visualise what a car, truck or van would look like, I only had the words. Looking down at the ground, the word 'tarseal' jumped into my mind. What the hell does that mean? All the roads are cobblestone, which later changes to clay as you head out towards the edge of town. It confused me, and I didn't like it.

As I walked on down Princess Street, I looked up when I heard a horse and cart come trundling down the road, full to the brim with the daily papers. The newspapers were being delivered to the paperboys. A bloke standing in the back chucked the bundles off the cart to the ground near a waiting boy. They didn't stop, but plodded on down the road to the next kid. The boy picked up the bale, cut the twine and was ready for business. Before you knew it, there were callers on each corner selling their papers. One young fellow yelled out, 'General Cameron bogs down in the New Zealand War.' The paper was the *Edinburgh Times*, so I bought one with a penny to check out the ad that I'd placed, and to see if it would jog my memory about New Zealand. I folded it under my arm as I walked slowly back to the Waterloo. It was still quiet as I went into the reading lounge and sat down. A waiter came over to ask if I'd like a tea or coffee. 'Tea thanks, mate white please.' I opened the paper to read the article on the war, but nothing in the newspaper triggered any memories. Then I searched for my ad. It was on the third page and much larger than I expected. The main heading was impressive:

Brave Scottish Officer
A brave Scottish officer, fighting for the British Empire against the most vicious foe in New Zealand, is just back from the war and is looking for his family. This officer was shot three times in the head and wounded most severely to the point of having a complete memory loss. He has no recollection of who he is or where he is from. We are asking if you had an officer in your family away at the wars that you have not heard from for quite a while to take note. Is he a member of your family? Found with the officer was the name Lieutenant Samuel

Mack, he is uncertain if this is his name. The officer in question has all his faculties, just no memory of his past. His contact is the Waterloo Hotel in Edinburgh under this said name. Then there was an excellent description of me which closed with: *This gentleman would be hard to miss, a tall, robust man of over six feet five inches. Let us help our own. Ask your friends and neighbours; let us find this officer's family.* Well I was chuffed, if anyone reading this paper saw that, surely this would bring results. Anyway, I hoped so, as long as I didn't get any nutters.

I sat quietly, drinking my tea and let my mind roam back over my morning walk on the streets of Edinburgh. I couldn't understand why strange words just kept popping up into my mind. Why hadn't I seen any of these objects around here? I mean, you don't think of something unless you have either seen it or heard about it before, but that's not the case here. Take this morning, the word 'car' or 'cars,' and then 'truck' and 'van' had slipped into my mind, but I couldn't get an understanding of what these words meant. I knew the names, but why not the physical images. I felt a car didn't have to have a horse to pull it the same with a truck and van but that's where my memory stopped. And yet I had remembered how to use my camera at sea before the batteries went flat. That was another thing that raced through my mind; there was no such thing as a battery, and yet I had them for all to see. My camera looked, and is, completely different from any other camera I had seen here. Come to think about it, everything about me was different. It was even more obvious now that I was settling into the city life. Things just were not right for me. Also I had this feeling of being out of place in this town. My yearning for the mountains and bush was strong; I missed trees and wildlife. I was still brooding like an old hen when Bella glided into the room like a ray of sunshine.

She took one look at me and rushed over, deep concern etched on her face. 'Whatever is the matter, Sammy?' she cried, grabbing hold of my hand. 'What is wrong?' She sat down, and I tried to explain about my morning. 'Bella, I don't understand myself, the feelings of not belonging and names of objects that come up out of nowhere from goodness knows where I'm so messed up. Look, do you really want to marry a bloke who acts so weird and can't remember his past? One who talks about things that are not even on this planet?' I went on to mention the names this morning that had jumped into my head. As she listened, my gaze settled on the steps that rose up to the next floor and announced, 'Escalator.' 'What is that word; do you know, Sammy?' 'I think it's a moving staircase.' I pointed to the stairs. 'You step on the bottom rung, and the moving stairs take you to the top. Saves you walking up them yourself. You see what I mean? I have these random memories and visions that are not of this world or not invented as yet.' She smiled, advising, 'Remember that thought Sam; that would be a marvellous invention. I have heard that they are going to put a lift into this hotel. About ten years ago when lifts were invented, I remember my father, who was in New York at the time, travelled on one. Maybe you are one of those people who can somehow see potential in everything around you. A man of vision, and with that you just need the expertise to fulfil the dream. I tell you what. When we get settled, you might feel better if my father or I introduced you to some young engineers and such like, so as to talk over these ideas with them.' I grinned from ear to ear, saying, 'You do it all the time Bella. You can take any negative and make it into a positive; you are my strength.' 'And, if you think that I'm going to throw out an exceptional man just because unusual words pop up in his head all of the time, you are very much mistaken, Mr Selkirk,' she teased. With that, I felt much better. So I opened the paper for her to see our newspaper ad. 'This is really positive, Sammy. It's splendid; well done. But I think if there is no answer in the next couple of weeks, we will reassess everything. In the meantime, let's organise today and the rest of the week, then go in for breakfast.' 'There was an article in there, about the New Zealand War, Bella. But it didn't trigger anything in my mind. Oh, and another thing there's no chocolate factory here in Edinburgh, so that's another mystery to add to the list as well.

Colonel Mcrea from the army hospital arrived just after breakfast to see us. We had only seen him a couple of days ago, so he was certainly on the ball. Before he began, we thought this was a golden opportunity for us to ask him to be Bella's escort at our wedding. 'This is an immense honour,' he replied and beamed at her, 'I would be only too happy to stand up for you.' 'We will sort out all of the arrangements later,' Bella told him, 'but you were the first on our list. Now, as Sam says, we can tick that box.' We all chuckled. He turned to me, holding out something in his hands, 'Well, Sam, I have your discharge papers it is now official.' He passed them over to me with a smile. 'Also, we will need an address to send you your medals.' 'Oh, send them to my father's estate,' Bella replied, and gave him her card with the address on it. 'Wonderful, we will get that done.' He turned to me and continued, ' Now, I have also got your remuneration organised Sam. I told them in no uncertain terms, I wanted it done and done quickly. But even I am surprised at their speed. It only took two days. Let me tell you, that's impressive. Here is the slip for the bank. Take this with you when you go in; the money is available for you now. They have paid you one hundred pounds in gratuity and another fifty pounds for your war wounds and for your bravery. You won't see that last fifty pounds on any official form; it is given at the discretion of the Commanding Officer here in Scotland. As I know Sir James Ferguson personally, I spoke to him about it. He is in full agreement and felt it his duty to give you that wee bit extra. Especially as in your case, your memory might never return. He felt it was asking a lot of you to bear this loss for all your remaining days, after fighting for Queen and Country. So, Sam, here is one hundred and fifty pounds; just show this to the cashier. They can transfer this to any account in the United Kingdom or you can draw on the monies at any bank in the country.' I was blown away. One hundred and fifty pounds 'Is that a decent amount?' I asked. Bella leant across and whispered, 'A captain of a ship can receive up to one hundred and twenty pounds a year. So you have at least a year and a half of wages Sam, and by that time we will have settled our domestic arrangements.' I was thrilled to pieces. Neat, I thought; I now had the money to pay my way including for the tailor and also to support Bella until we worked out what we were going to do. I then asked the colonel, 'How are the boys off the *Esk*, those who came home with us, coming along? Would a few be able to make it to the wedding do you think?' He thought that about six would be fit enough to come if they had a couple of nurses with them. Angus would be keen to be my best man; I was sure of that. He was a bloody good bloke. Back on the boat, we were always yarning, and he was a good friend. That was my next job, to go and see him. Apparently his parents had been down from Inverness, trying to entice him to go home with them. He's an independent young fella though, and even though he told me that with luck he could be well enough to return home by the end of the August, he had hoped to do something for himself instead. Inverness was too far out of the way for an architect, so when his health and arm were back to full strength, he would be heading back to Edinburgh or Glasgow. He reckoned there was more happening down here and was positive this was the place to be.

'It is an honour, Sam, indeed a rare honour to be asked to stand with you on the day,' he smiled. I was overjoyed that I would have such a good bloke with me when I got married. He told me he expected to be discharged from the army when he left the hospital, and had hoped he could start up his own architectural business, if not maybe acquire employment with a reputable firm. Now I had another tick in the box; I had my best man. My clothes arrived a day later than expected, with a note of apology. They took just a wee bit longer than they had envisioned. The son, Aaron, a nice young fella, explained that the underpants were starting to prove a hit, and I would be pleasantly surprised with my commission at the end of the first quarter. I gave him the name of my bank for my commission, and he left me as a friend. Mr Cavenish arrived on the Friday with the ring. 'Anything at all I can do for you, please get in touch,' he said with a smile. Another box to tick off.

Slowly, things were coming together. Sunday came around and Bella and I walked to the church. It was packed to capacity and we had trouble finding room on a pew. I had not seen so many people all in one room before. Religion was alive and well in Scotland. We sat in the middle row and received a few stares. The sermon was inspiring, rather than of the fire and brimstone sort. At the end of the service The Reverend Duncan McIntosh read out the banns, Once the service was finished the Reverend Macintosh joined us. I introduced him to Bella, we talked about the wedding, then made arrangements to see him next week to finalise everything. We left quite content to have another box well and truly ticked. Up to this point in time, I had not had one reply to the ad not even a whisper and by the time the week ended, no one had come forward. We sat down on the last day it appeared in the paper, and went over our options.

CHAPTER TWELVE

Edinburgh 1863

'Well, Bella, it looks as though I have no family here. Well, not so far anyway. My memory might come back to me later. Even a hint of where I'm from would have been something, but for now it's time to think of us. I know I will keep hoping, but even though there is hope, we still have to get on with life. So, my love, what now?' 'Do you want to wait another three weeks to marry me, Sammy? Or do you believe we should marry sooner rather than later? I have been thinking the sooner the better, really. I don't want my father turning up in Scotland making a fuss; it would be better to have the fuss contained back at home. At least when he rants there, only the servants and the wildlife can hear him. He knows I just close my ears and mind off and walk away,' she grinned. 'Though that makes him even more mad, but eventually he settles back down. He really is a good man and normally very rarely loses his temper.' 'Bella, it would be best if I know a little bit about your parents and your sister, to make it easier to get to know them.' 'Yes you are right. I will explain all about my family to you after we work out our wedding arrangements. But right now this very minute the question is, do we marry earlier than we said? If the minister cannot arrange an earlier date, then we can say our vows at Gretna Green.' 'What is the significance of that?' I asked. 'Well, you just turn up and get married, no questions asked. Not long ago, you could just come across the border from England and get married immediately, as long as you were both over 14 years old. But they have changed the rules, and now you have to be in Scotland 21 days. Though in our case, as you are Scottish, we don't have to worry about that.' 'How far away is Gretna Green from here, Bella?' I inquired. 'I think a few hours by rail, but I'm sure the minister will squeeze us in,' she said with assurance. 'Okay then, let's pop around and see him and see if he can change the date.'

Duncan Macintosh was only too happy to slot us in earlier. 'I cannot have the ceremony on a Saturday as I'm tired up with others, but if a weekday suits you, I would be happy to fit you in.' So it was arranged to have the ceremony on Monday afternoon at two p.m. We had some quick organising to do. I shot around to see the colonel again to make sure he was okay for that time and day. It turned out in our favour and as well as my best man's. I arranged with the hospital for all the blokes from the *Esk* that were up to it, to come to the wedding. Then I managed to get hold of Rory again to pick them all up. He had a couple of mates to help him with their cabs. Next, the colonel suggested he would use his gig for himself and Bella, along with her bridesmaid. He would pick up a ride with his patients for the return journey back to the hotel. Either that, or walk back; it was not far. Bella had asked one of the nurses, Dorothy Temple, to be her bridesmaid. They had been in New Zealand together and were close. She was a bit like Bella, a no-nonsense woman with a heart of gold.

So all we needed to organise now was some afternoon tea for the wedding breakfast. I spoke to the hotel manager, Mr Craig about it, and he assured me that they would arrange everything for us, for about twenty people. I thought that was a bit too many, but when I counted up who would be there, it was about right. Bella had arranged for a seamstress to help her and her bridesmaid with their dresses, and I had my new suit. I sent a letter by cab to the Selkirks, and also to Mr Cavenish, inviting them along. Mr Hyman from Selkirks couldn't come, as he wasn't that well and had in fact been feeling poorly for quite some time. But his three sons would be there, and one of them was married, so his wife would come along too. At last, everything was all arranged. I bet this must have been the quickest wedding breakfast that the hotel had to arrange in quite some time.

We now had the weekend to relax and maybe take in a few sites like Edinburgh Castle. But Bella wanted to spend the time working on her dress with the seamstress and her bridesmaid, so I ended up doing the tourist thing on my lonesome. I enjoyed looking through Edinburgh Castle and climbed up into the turrets, moving along the battlements to stop and look down at the city. I even had a quick squizz at the National Gallery and the Princess Street Gardens. It filled in a good part of Saturday, and I finished it off with a pint at the Royal. The racket in there was confusing, with blokes drinking and shouting above the noise, and the smoke hung in the air from their lit cigarettes, so thick you could hardly see. Their accents were so broad I could barely understand what they were talking about, but I managed and enjoyed their company. I left the hotel in a jovial mood, returning to the Waterloo for dinner and a catch-up with Bella.

The next day she continued with her sewing, but I wasn't left alone, as my best man came round and I gave him the rings, ready for the big day. Then we had a good yarn about his future. He was looking forward to getting back to designing and hoped to work with an architectural firm here in Edinburgh. He wasn't a complete invalid, as the arm that he'd lost was below the elbow. I promised him that we would invite him down to visit us when we got settled. 'That is,' I let him know, 'after I work through the problems I know I will face with Bella's parents.' 'I will look forward to that, Sam,' he said with a smile. Then the conversation returned to the wedding.

After supping a pint of beer, he called for a cab and headed back to the hospital, leaving me to my own devices. He intended to pick me up about one p.m. the next day, and we would take a leisurely stroll up to the church. After that, I met Bella for lunch, during which she told me I wouldn't see her tomorrow until the actual ceremony. Apparently it was bad luck if we did, and it was traditional for the woman to spend the time preparing herself.

Monday was slow to come. By ten a.m. on the day, I was ready and paced up and down not knowing what to do. I was bored out of my tree and extremely edgy. The colonel turned up at midday, and we had a light lunch together. Then Angus arrived and we walked together to the church. The first of the guests started to arrive at one thirty p.m. Angus welcomed those he knew, and introduced himself to all he didn't. The Hymans, the jeweller, and some people who even I didn't know, were there. Even a few of the staff from the hotel turned up, along with some I had met around town and invited over the past few weeks. The boys from the hospital arrived in two cabs with a couple of nurses, smiling and joking as blokes do when we haven't seen each other for a while. We assisted them to the pews at the back. When the Hyman's arrived, they got a few looks understandable I suppose as the sight of Jews in a Methodist church was certainly unusual. The second eldest, Moshe came over and introduced his wife Ayala to me. 'There is a Jewish saying Sam, for your marriage. May your joining together bring you more joy than you can imagine,' he quoted. 'Congratulations!' I thanked them warmly.

At last it was time to move down to the front of the nave. It was about this time I was starting to get more than a little anxious. I hadn't thought too much about it, but now reality was setting in. Shit, am I going to be the right man for her will I be able to support her? What happens when or if my memory comes back, will it change everything? Was I actually married before the head wound?

94

Oh shit! I never even thought of that, but I felt deep down that I wasn't. Was I getting cold feet? I didn't have to question if I loved Bella, as I was besotted and I couldn't imagine being without her.

Angus and I stood waiting together. Standing there in my suit with a worried look on my face, a light film of sweat began to form on my brow. Angus was decked out in his uniform, with his half-arm sleeve pinned to his jacket. The minister came out from the back of the church and smiled at us both. 'Relax Sam,' he grinned, 'this is not a funeral.' Then the organ starting to play the *Wedding March*, I turned to watch this white angel gliding down the aisle, holding on to the colonels' arm. Her white dress, covered in lace with a splash of pearls around the neckline, just brushed the floor. It had a full train that the bridesmaid arranged and a transparent veil that came down to her breasts. She floated toward me, and I could see her beautiful smile through the veil. My god, I was a lucky man; I couldn't keep my eyes off her. All my fears vanished as we turned together towards the minister and the ceremony commenced. 'We are gathered here today in the sight of God and this congregation to join this man and this woman in holy matrimony.' Thirty minutes later we were married; I couldn't believe it and felt quite stunned. This was certainly a game changer. I had made a lifetime commitment. We walked down the aisle arm in arm, smiling at our friends, and the army boys threw rice at us once we stepped outside. The colonel's gig waited at the bottom of the steps as we slowly walked down, with passers by stopping to watch, smiling and clapping. I held Bella's hand lightly as she stepped up into the gig and the vehicle slowly pulled out into the traffic and moved on toward the Waterloo.

The morning room had been set aside for the wedding breakfast, well, afternoon tea actually. It was quite informal and everyone just mingled. Angus did his best man speech well. I had only known him from the *Esk*, but the way he went on, you would have thought we had been friends for years. In any case, we both appreciated his words. By six o'clock it was over, and the last to leave was the colonel with his wife and of course, Angus. As my best man was leaving, he announced, 'If you ever need to design a home, you can contact me through my parents.' At this time he hadn't decided where he was going to settle, so we exchanged addresses. With a final handshake and wave goodbye, the place went quiet.

Just the two of us at last, we sat down to relish the quietness and I poured a glass of wine for us both. 'To us, Bella, may we love each other forever.' We drank our toast and looked into each other's eyes, acknowledging it was time to retire. We left the room and walked up the stairs side by side. 'Which room do you think?' I ventured. 'My room I think, Sammy. It's much more feminine than yours and it smells heavenly, as Dorothy left us a room full of lovely roses.' When we arrived at Bella's door, I opened it, then scooped her up into my arms and carried her across the threshold. Soon after, I kicked the door shut and gently placed her feet on the floor. She put her arms around my neck, pulled me down, and gave me a lingering kiss. Then she moved towards the bed, removed her veil, and placed it on the corner post. I watched her closely; in fact I couldn't keep my eyes off her. 'My god, Bella, you are so beautiful,' I stammered as I went over to her. She looked up at me with those big green eyes. I was mesmerised by them and couldn't look away. 'Oh Sammy,' she cried, throwing herself into my arms, 'I love you so much.' She lifted my hand and placed it on her chest, saying, 'Feel my heart, it's yours can you feel it racing?' Then she reached up and pulled my head down again and smothered me with kisses. 'Sammy, she whispered, 'you will have to be gentle with me, as it is my first time,' I saw a glint of a tear as she looked up into my eyes. 'I'll never hurt you, Bella.' She smiled at me, comforted by my words. 'I wonder if you could help me undo these buttons on my dress, there are so many.' I sat on the bed as she stood with her back to me. I was all fingers and thumbs trying to undo them, but eventually the dress fell to the ground. Next, I helped her loosen the hoop strings and the stays, and then as she stepped away from her clothes she turned to face me. All I could do was gaze at her enthralled. 'Oh hell, Bella I can't believe it you are so perfect, so beautiful.' She moved close to me as I ran my hands down her back to her waist, then cupped her perfect breasts. When she started to undress me, I just about fell off the bed trying to get my pants down, but soon my clothes were scattered around the foot of the bed. 'Sammy,' she murmured as I kissed her mouth, then continued on to kiss her eyes, neck and shoulders. Moving down to her breasts, I stopped to kiss each nipple. I could hear a mewing noise at the back of her throat as I kissed her navel. Then I felt her tense up as I moved further down, but she slowly relaxed as this new sensation filled her with pleasure. She held on to my head and arched her back. 'Sammy, that is exquisite don't stop.' After satisfying her more, I gradually moved over her and gently positioned myself, not wanting to hurt her. There was a small resistance and I felt her gasp, then her hands dug into my back. I gently pushed through, with a sigh of relief. She held me tightly and kissed my forehead, then latched her legs tightly around my waist. 'I'm yours forever, Sammy,' she said as she went over the edge with a smile on her face.

We lay in a glow of tenderness and fulfilment, still in each other's arms as the night wore on. When I eventually did move, Bella hugged me tightly and teased, 'Don't you dare move Mr Selkirk; I like you where you are.' Just then, my leg muscle started to cramp. 'Bella, I have to get up; I have cramp,' I quickly rolled off her, tried to stand up, and nearly fell on my face. I quickly righted myself and stomped around the room getting circulation back into my leg. She rolled over and with a wicked grin said, 'Well, that is a beautiful sight to see, Sammy. You do have a lovely bottom.' 'Hmmm, so do you Bella, and I hope I haven't left any marks on it.' 'I'm sure,' she said with a lecherous grin, 'you could kiss it better.' We didn't get much sleep that night, but eventually we both dropped off. I woke to her green eyes gazing down on me as she leant over watching me sleep. In a low voice she said, 'Sammy, last night was wonderful. Well after the first initial part that is that was a bit uncomfortable. You know, I didn't think I was going to enjoy it like that. Lovemaking in marriage was never explained to any of us. Anyway, I really appreciated it to the point, I think, that I would like some more right now, thank you very much.' She reached under the blankets and placed her hand on my manhood. We forgot about breakfast, and we were late going down for lunch.

CHAPTER THIRTEEN

Edinburgh 1863

Tuesday came round and still no sign of any family coming forward. We discussed how long we should wait and came to an agreement that we would hang on till the end of the week. If we had no contact by then, we would leave our forwarding address with the hotel under my old name of Mack, and also with Colonel Mcrea, at the hospital. We would leave then, regardless; so we headed down to the railway station near Edinburgh Castle to book our train journey.

The station was a grand affair, with marble columns out in the front foyer, a huge tiled floor covered with purple thistles, the emblem of Scotland, and large windows opening up onto the platforms. With its vast domed ceiling, wreathed cherubs, and scrolled ironworks it was a pretty impressive place to visit. We were in luck as well, as there was a new service running from Edinburgh to London via Shrewsbury, making its maiden journey on Friday. So we booked first class seats. Apparently, cabins in the first class section had four seats that converted into a sleeper for a family. As this was the inaugural trip, we would have the cabin to ourselves, so we could pull down the seats if we wanted a snooze. Also another first for the Great Western Rail Service was to have a dining car. Afterwards, we made arrangements for Rory to uplift and transport us to the railhead at nine a.m. for the ten a.m.

departure on Friday. As it was the maiden journey we gathered there was going to be a lot of fanfare, with railway officials, the usual band, and the standard quota of self-important politicians, so by getting there a bit earlier, we should avoid all the razzmatazz.

Bella organised accommodations for us at Nursery Cottage, Shrewsbury. It was owned by her father, along with the nursery. She cabled him to let him know of our arrival time and to break the news of our marriage. The return wire from him was quite tense and straight to the point and included the words 'disappointed with you,' more than once it was only natural, I guess. Bella said not to take it personally. She told me, 'I can weave my father around my little finger, it will just take time, but he will come around. 'She explained to me that he had a plantation of over one thousand acres of managed forestry, of which he was quite proud, so hence, the nursery. Why the nursery was not close to the source, I was not sure, as that's where it would be if it were me. She also told me that two thousand acres of his land was tenant-farmed and around seven thousand acres left as natural forest, that he hoped he would never have to cut, if possible. I noticed she was getting excited to be going home and to catch up with her family. 'Mother will be only too pleased to see me and so will my sister, and whatever Father says can be taken with a grain of salt. He will be relieved, though, that I'm back from distant lands and all in working order. Now don't you worry, we will sort it all out, just don't let him manipulate you into doing something that you are not comfortable with. You are your own man, and we don't need them, remember that, he needs me, more. I don't want to sound callous or mean, but we need to be strong, though the announcement of our marriage would have hurt them. You see, they wanted a big wedding with all the trimmings that a titled family would normally have expected. So Mother will be a little bit put out as well, but Sammy, together we will win out, you mark my words.'

We went back to the hotel dining room and ordered tea, then she got down to business. 'Right, I think it is time to explain who I am and why. Don't be put off by it, Sammy, this is who I am, but if it is too much for you, I can change. After being away for nearly two years, I think I can look after myself and I have proven that. We can make a go of our life without the influence of my father's money and title. I believe you will do your thing, and I will be there to help. If we can climb this hurdle with my parents, though, it will be that much easier. Okay? Love that word, where do I start? Bella asked. 'In the beginning, I suppose, is the best place,' Bella continued. 'The first Earl of Shadymore Richard Edward Gale was born in 1756; he married Margaret Elizabeth Downett in 1786. He was not a man of the land as he held no freehold estate, but he was a man of literature and diplomacy. In 1780, he was sent by King George the third to the American colonies to try and forge a peace agreement with the so-called rebels. 'King George wanted to end the war and was willing to try anything, but all his efforts were in vain, and we lost the American colonies. It did not deter the king, and he continued to favour Richard, making him an earl for his loyalty to the crown. The king knew Richard had no land so he granted this area of Shropshire to him. Incidentally, most people thought he was not getting a good deal out of it, as it was all heavily forested hills and valleys. Kings in the past used this area for hunting, but now it become Shadymore, and Richard was the first earl. He took the grant seriously and managed the forest well. He felled some of the timber in the beginning to sell. With that money he bought pasture land, and as soon as he was able, he reforested the parts that had been logged. The words "a bit before his time," jumped into my mind. Where the hell did that come from? Bella took a breath and continued, 'He continued to increase the land this way to what it is today, and the forest is still there, most of it untouched for hundreds of years. This is

101

what my father inherited. But when I was last at home, I must admit he seemed at a loss with what to do with it all, but that's by the by. That is how we got started. 'My father has twenty tenant farmers now who farm one hundred acres each. I believe he has a good working relationship with them. They pay their lease and he keeps out of their way, or something like that. I feel more could be done, but I don't know what. We have two villages within the property boundary as well, Brittermore and Sledgemore, and there are five villages just outside of our land. I think father was having a problem with poachers, but being such a large property it is very hard to catch them, and for all I know the problem might be solved by now. He does not like to talk about business to women, though it is a different story with Mother,' she said with a hint of sadness. 'More fool him,' I said, 'this is a family estate, everyone should have input.' 'Well, most men don't think like you do, Sammy, you are different, that is for sure."The house,' she went on, 'was started in 1786 and took three years to build. It has been added on to and improved over the years, up to the stage that now all of the bedrooms have a bathroom each with cold, running water and a privy. Two cottages have been added for the groom and the coachman, as they are both married men. And if the gardeners were to get married, my father would have a cottage built for them as well. The house is nestled in three acres of gardens with a large swooping drive and huge oak trees as the border. It has twenty bedrooms on the second and third floors, but I won't go into that, Sam; let it be a surprise for you.

'Needless to say, my father had a staff of fourteen when I was last at home. I don't know how that is going to affect you, but at least you will be aware of what you are heading into. Everyone is always very formal, and I can imagine some wide eyes with open mouths when they hear you speak, so it should be interesting. We will let everything work its own way out, and if you are too uncomfortable with the situation, then we will reassess what we need to do. 'My father also has business dealings with the railways here and in the Americas. My grandfather, the second earl, discovered gold on a hill on the Welsh side of our property. We now have a small gold mine that is not big but it fills the coffers. We also had a couple of small tin mines on the property, but they were in the process of closing when I left. Father has an interest in Hereford cattle and a few pedigree Merino sheep; I think he would like to be more involved with their breeding. Also, we have a couple of purebred racehorses. The businesses are a means to an end, just enough to keep the estate working properly. Some of the other big landowners seem to squander their money, but my father is not like that. There is something you will be pleased to know, Sam. We have a lovely grand piano; I'm sure you will want to get acquainted with that. In fact, I'm looking forward to it. Now, there is a way to my father's heart and that's through classical music. That is why I'm not too worried about both of you getting along. All you need to do is go into the music room and play. I'm sure he will be your friend for life. Well maybe that is expecting a bit too much, so maybe not to start with, but I think you might get my meaning. Anything to do with music, he is happy. We will keep that secret from him until we see the lay of the land, Sammy. We don't want all our eggs in one basket. One of the things you might want to try, Sam, is to learn to ride and also to drive. We are four hours from Shrewsbury, so it is important that you have that ability. How are you feeling now, Sam? I hope you are not too overwhelmed.' 'Nah, Bella, I'll get by. I can do anything I put my mind to, I'm sure, memory loss or not. I don't think I'll go belly-up.' 'What does that mean, Sam?' she asked with a frown. 'I won't give up, toss in the towel, die without trying,' he reassured her. 'Ah, now I understand your meaning, but I have never heard that saying before. Anyway, I have faith in you, Sam, and that is all that matters.' Bella went on to say, 'The coachman is George Cotton, his wife is Mary. He will pick us up at the station and take us to Nursery Cottage and then onto the manor on Saturday morning. He will be the man to ask, for riding and driving lessons; he is an extremely nice and so is his wife. She helps in the big house when needed. They have two boys; time goes so quick, they must be fourteen and sixteen now. They had six children, but unfortunately, they lost four. Also, there is Richard Cook, the groom; he looks after the horses and is a nice man as well. He is married to Ellen and they have four children. I find most people who look after animals are good-natured, don't you think? Well, the ones that I have met are Father has eight hacks as well as four for the coach and there are the racehorses. They are thoroughbreds and are his babies. I think he gets quite good money for their breeding, but once again, Sam, it's men's business apparently. Women are not business inclined, so they say; of course, that is not what I think and never will be. We are just as good as men, we just don't get the opportunity.' She was starting to get riled up. 'I can tell you now Bella, you will have the opportunity with me; two heads are better than one. So anything we do, we do it together, our relationship is equal in everything.' A look of delight crossed her face. 'Well, that is the bones of it Sammy; my father is not as big as you, though he seems tall to me about five feet eight inches. But being with you everyone seems small, and I feel tiny next to you.' 'You are bite-sized and tasty all over,' I said with a gleam in my eye. 'Size or looks don't mean much to me. I would judge, no, that's too harsh a word, I don't believe I like to judge. I prefer to use my intuition concerning a person's personality, regardless of what or how they look. But I do like to take some time to get to know someone before passing any comment. I somehow feel I felt like this before my memory loss.' 'Yes, I realise that Sam, I don't think I have ever heard you say a nasty thing about anyone; you seem to look at their good points first.' 'Yeah, I cannot remember what I was like before, but I think this is part of me. Everyone has some good points, and I feel it's important to look for those first. Where the heck does all this come from Bella? I must be running my thought process on remote. It must have been part of my DNA before the memory loss.'

'DNA, Sam, what's that?' Bella queried. 'We all have it, Bella, it's in our gene pool and it makes us who we are.' Sam tried to explain. 'I don't understand, Sammy. What is our gene pool?' a confused Bella asked. 'It's the characteristics you've taken from your mum's side and your dad's side of the family, and that's what makes you the person you've become. You have the traits of all your ancestors running through your veins. They are your gene pool, but you still have your own personality. Don't ask me how I know this Bella; it just came out.' 'That is a bit daunting to think of right now. But Sammy, your personality is what I saw from the first day you opened your eyes, and you looked up at me. I thought, here is a man who is thoughtful, loving, and caring. I don't think memory loss takes that away from anyone, it is the building blocks of the person.' 'There you go, Bella, you have it in one. That's DNA the building blocks,' Sam happily answered. She looked at me as if a light had been switched on. 'I see, just another terminology,' she replied. Sam added, 'Yes, and I'm pleased I'm like the way I am; it makes it easy to get on with folk, and if you take an interest in the things they do, people warm to you. I take a lot of interest in the things that you do Bella, to the point, I could watch you all day.' 'I hope you don't do that to all the other women you take an interest in,' she teased, then leant over and kissed me. 'Oh Sammy, I'm so lucky to have you.' Bella gushed. 'I feel the same Bella, I don't know how a good looking woman like you would want a big bloke like me, but I don't care, you do, and that is all that matters to me. 'Now I have lost my train of thought telling you about my family,' she reminded me with a smile. 'Yeah, let's get back on track, kiddo. What's your old man like, then? 'Bella laughed, 'Oh, he's going to like that saying. Well, he is a stickler for being on time. He also loves music. He is not an authoritarian at all, but he does like to have his own way. He has big, bushy sideburns, a longish face is slim, and has a pale complexion; By the by, Father will be horrified at the colour of my skin. He is a confident man and doesn't suffer fools gladly, though he is thoughtful and treats his staff well. He can have a big voice if he wants to but is quietly spoken, generally. So that's my father. His horses and music are his greatest love, and he does love his family. 'With me leaving the way I did, he was hurt. He never said it in his letters I received but underneath I know he was. So I want to if he will let me make it up to him. Sam, I think you will both get on in the end, I'm sure of it. I believe you coming home with me and being a part of our family, I will be making it up to him somehow. You see, as he has no sons, I hope he finds in you a lost son. 'I could see tears welling up in her eyes. 'I'll do my best, Bella; you don't have to worry on that score,' I assured her. She kissed me again, 'I know Sammy.'

'Okay, now your mum,' I said. Bella grinned and began. 'Oh. mother has the same personality as me. She gets things done by quietly talking father round. She loves her church, flower arranging, and gardening. She loves to knit and is also an excellent seamstress. She likes to make some of the clothes for the staff as well, uniforms and such. For a countess, this is incredible, as most of the titled gentry that I know have everything done for them. They spend all day talking about nothing, have tea every five minutes, and gossip all day long. Mother is not like that at all and likes to keep busy. She works on the household accounts, as well as keeping father on his toes. She is also a stickler for getting everything paid on time. Yes, she complements Father so well. Mother is my build and height. She has a pale complexion most English do. She has dark blue eyes, a different colour to mine actually which they believe is a throwback from my second great-grandmother. Mother has a round face and dark hair. When I left there was a tinge of grey coming through. I'm sure you will like her, Sammy. I know after the first shock of meeting you, she will like you too.

'Then there is my lovely sister, Amelia. As with me and all of the family, she is slim with brown hair down to her shoulders. She sings and is a good dancer. She loves animals to pieces, to the point of having a small room set aside at the back of the stables to use as an animal hospital. Like me, she can be forthright. Father sometimes rolls his eyes with three strong-willed women in his house, so any male companion will be a blessing. You will love Amelia, Sammy, and I'm sure she will love you as well. So that is your new family, so what are your thoughts, Sammy? A lot more to get used to, what with the staff and all. You will need time to sort it all out. Then, of course, there is the forest, there will be lots of exploring for you in there. I have a feeling that you will be in your element.'

I smiled. 'It's a lot to take in, Bella, such a lot to remember, so little steps first. I need to get to know the family and then the environment and staff. I will then learn to ride, drive, and all that goes with it. Also, I want your opinion on my rifle. We both know it's different, or maybe your dad might have contacts that will help. Once settled, I would like to take it to a rifle specialist, or an experienced rifle manufacturer and see if it is commercially viable to copy. If that's the case, there might be enough in it financially, for us to be completely self-supporting. It would be good to be independent of your folks. I'm sure this would prove to them, if they have concerns, that I didn't marry their daughter just for her money or title. I wouldn't want them to think that. Not that I knew about who you were before I fell head over heels in love with you,' Sam explained. 'If everything goes okay, maybe your dad and I could have a joint agreement with the rifle,' Sam continued. 'I'll play that by ear. Then there are the boxer shorts. 'I have a couple of other ideas which I'd like to talk to you about when we get the chance. I was thinking about the women's underpants idea,' Sam said. 'Yes, you have mentioned that before; I've been thinking about it. Take a look at this dress I'm wearing, there is so much material involved with this design, it makes it so heavy compared to lighter, informal wear. The underpants I use are crotchless as it is easier with all that bulk, but for daily wear at home, yes. Your idea just might prove a good solution. Now, if it were made of silk, I think that would be a positive contribution to female attire within all classes of women.' She smiled, 'I have come a long way to be able to talk about my underclothes freely like this, and without embarrassment.' I laughed, 'Married life does change a person, Bella.' 'Yes,' she said, taking my hand, 'for the better.'

CHAPTER FOURTEEN

Shrewsbury 1863

The week slipped by so fast and before we knew it Friday had arrived. There had been no bites on the newspaper ad, though I was pleasantly surprised when the bill came from the Times with an accompanying note which told us there was no charge, as it was the least they could do for an officer who fought for the queen and her country. I sent a note back thanking them for their generosity.

I was looking forward to the train trip. It felt like I was on holiday, and I hoped that seeing the countryside would trigger memories for me. We were up early, had a light breakfast, and met, Rory, our cab driver standing by his cab for the last time. 'I'm going to miss your smiling face, mate,' I said. 'You have been a good bloke and Bella and I have appreciated your time and effort. 'I tipped him ten shillings and Rory just about fell over. 'Mr Selkirk, that's far too much, sir,' he said. 'No, it's not Rory, you were the first person to help us, and I hope we will catch up with you in the future.' He looked embarrassed by my remark, but by the time we arrived at the station he had recovered and helped us with our luggage. I shook hands with him, and he gave me his card adding, 'If you ever need transport, please get in touch.'

A porter placed our luggage on a barrow, and took it towards the guard's van; we kept our small day bag with us. The station was busy with everyone in a rush attempting to get their first trip prepared before the passengers and the bigwigs arrived. We stepped through the barrier and presented our tickets, and then walked up into the rather luxurious carriage. Inside we found a friendly porter, who took us to our compartment and explained how to pull the seat down if we needed to stretch out, or he would do it for us if we called. 'Just ring this bell, sir,' he said, 'if you need anything at all. Morning Tiffin will be served at eleven a.m. and lunch in the dining car at one p.m.; your table number is six. We expect to arrive at Shrewsbury at eight p.m. We hope you have an enjoyable trip on our inaugural service to London, sir.' The roomy berth was comfortably styled and included everything to make our journey enjoyable. Our sleeper seat was comfy, and on the roof were two large ornamental lights. A small table held a lamp along with a newspaper of the day. Also on the table I noticed an itinerary of where we were going, with hopefully, interesting things to look out for on the trip south. We organised ourselves, sat back, and relaxed. Before long I heard the band start up on the platform, and later the dignitaries started on their speeches. Sometime after that everyone who was anyone had their say. Finally, they climbed aboard. The train driver had finished his preparation for the trip and leaned out of the open cab to check for the guardsman's flag. He noted all was well and gave a long pull of the steam whistle. The train slowly moved forward in a cloud of grey smoke and sparks, and the crowd waved madly as we pulled away from the station. The driver and fireman in the open cab only had the roof over their heads to protect them from the odd spark and also the weather.

At last, we headed across the country towards Glasgow. It seemed all very old hat to me steam. I don't know why, but I had the impression that all of that had been replaced years ago. Are these thoughts going to plague me for all of my life? I found the countryside slightly familiar with trees, green rolling hills, and endless space. But I remembered I saw something similar to this in South Africa, so it might not mean a thing. We crossed many rivers and streams following the contours of the hills as we wove our way south. When we arrived in Glasgow there was another band, and it took even longer this time getting away from the station. But soon the train huffed and puffed and we were on our way to Shrewsbury. She was a powerful, wee beast as she pulled away from Glasgow with her sixteen carriages, dining car, and a guard's van. We were away for the second time and to the start I thought of another chapter in my life.

I enjoyed the trip, as it was awesome to be out in the open away from a large town with all of its associated smells and clutter and into a countryside dotted with farms, lakes and bush. I must admit it did seem to be different to what I thought I was used to, though I was not sure what it was. The country just felt different to me; I couldn't put my finger on it. Why? I wondered. Also, I didn't recognise a lot of the wild animals and bird life I'd seen since I had been in Scotland. Like all things with my memory, I was at a loss. I really needed to change my thinking, this was going to be the norm now I must accept it.

Both of us savored our lunch in the dining car. We had a table for two next to a large window which overlooked the scenery. The carpets were so thick you couldn't hear the waiting staff approach. The meal was delicious with pigeon pie, vegetables, and freshly baked bread along with a glass of French wine. We finished with coffee then we took our leave. After that we spent most of the time by ourselves talking in our compartment, just using the small bell to have the service bring us coffee or tea. As we headed south, Bella leant against me and dropped off to sleep with the gently rocking motion of the train. I sat there mesmerised by the motion, not quite asleep but soon fell into a trance-like state. The train paused briefly in Manchester, before reaching our destination. Shrewsbury Station came into view as we crossed the Severn River.

It was dark now as the early evening was just settling in. Sparks glowed in the big puffs of black smoke above the engine funnel, and the whistle from the cab announced our arrival. We pulled into Shrewsbury to another fanfare of music and dignitaries.

As we left the train we did our best to avoid the fanfare, and when we received our luggage, a short, stocky bloke approached us. 'I'll take those my lady,' he declared with a smile on his face and a twinkle in his eye .'George.' She laughed as she gave him a hug, not the thing I suspect a lady normally would do with the hired help, but Bella was not your normal titled lady. 'Sam,' she said, turning to me, 'I want you to meet the best coachman in England, George Cotton. George, this is my new husband, Samuel Selkirk.' He looked me over for a few seconds, and I studied him. 'G'day George,' I said, 'Thanks for meeting us here, mate; I'll give you a hand with this stuff, too much for one bloke to carry.' His eyes went wide and then he smiled. 'I've always believed,' he said, shaking my hand, 'that when Lady Isabella married, she would marry someone quite different than all of us, and I see she has done just that. Lovely to meet you, sir,' he said. 'Not sir, George Sam,' I gently corrected him. 'Hmm, I'll need to think about that one.' He grinned. 'But you are right; there are a few cases, and a hand is what I need.' So the three of us carried them out over the railway concourse to the coach as there wasn't a baggage barrow to be seen or a porter for that matter. George pulled down the luggage holder on the back of the coach and we tied the cases on. A thought came to mind no bungee cords? He turned back to us and announced, 'Mrs Moore has a light meal for you at the cottage, so we will head over there now. 'We piled into the coach and within twenty minutes had arrived at the door. We had a small overnight bag so we didn't have to unload the gig. George said he would pick us up tomorrow about ten a.m. if that suited us. He took the coach and horse around to the stable at the rear of the house as we went inside.

Nursery Cottage was a large, double-storied white house built in 1800. It was built in the Tudor architecture style with a slatted roof and bay windows. It had five bedrooms and picturesque gardens backing on to the tree nursery. Mrs Moore, a short and stocky older woman with an open face and brown complexion, was there to greet us. She must have worked a manual job all her life as her hands were very rough. 'It's just lovely to see you again, Lady Isabella,' she gushed. She led us up the magnificent oak stairway to our room. There was an old-fashioned, four-poster bed with a washbasin on a nightstand and a fireplace. Through a door next to the wardrobe was a new privy, and at the end of the hall was a full bathroom. New gas lamps had been fitted to make the house more modern, bringing it right up to date. Mrs Moore was of Welsh descent and had quite a broad accent, so I did have a bit of trouble understanding her, but Bella could communicate quite well with her, and they chatted away. We set our bag down and went down for a late meal. I thought it was going to be a light meal, but it was lamb and veggies with passion fruit pie and coffee. Even I found it hard to eat it all, and that was saying something. Mrs Moore served then informed us that she would come back and clear the dishes away when we'd finished. We didn't see her again until the next morning when we came down for breakfast. So, all in all, we were left to our own devices. The bed was cosy, and the journey must have caught up with us since we dropped off to sleep in each other's arms.

We woke to the dawn chorus outside the window. This, I thought, lying in bed with my arm around Bella, was the day; the moment of truth when I get to meet my new parents-in-law. How will they react? I seemed to make an impression on George, so I hoped that was a good sign. Bella had said just to be myself, and don't try to change or please someone for the sake of just pleasing them. Will I pass the test? I was still apprehensive, but I suppose that was only natural. I went downstairs and outside for a quick look around while Bella was getting dressed. I found George out the back hitching the horse to the coach. I went over and watched. 'Can I help you, sir?' he asked .'George... mate... please; this "sir" stuff might go down okay with people you work for, but heck, mate, with just the two of us, it's first names, okay? Okay means alright, and you will hear me say it a lot.' 'Well, as you are mentioning it, I'm happy to call you Sam,' he replied. 'That's good. George, I need your expertise. I have no idea how to ride or drive a horse and cart. You see I lost my memory in the New Zealand war, shot in the head. I'm not sure if I have ever ridden or driven in my life. I don't think I can; it seems alien to me somehow. So would you teach me?"Of course... Sam,' he uttered my name hesitantly, as though he was unsure at calling me that 'it would be a pleasure.' 'Thank you, mate. Well, that's a start. Between you, me and the gatepost, I'm a bit nervous about meeting the earl, today. I don't think I'm into this title stuff, but Bella has told me to just be myself, but I don't want to embarrass her. 'George looked at me. 'Sam, I have only met you for a few hours last night, and just now. In that time I have the impression you will fit in fine. Oh, the earl will be a bit standoffish to start with, and he was quite angry when Lady Isabella joined the Nightingales. But getting married without his lordship's knowledge, well he was outraged. Look, I am good at observing someone's nature and I believe you will fit in with the family. The way you speak is strange, but you have a friendly personality, so I'm sure you will get on with all the staff. Just don't insist on expecting them to call you by your first name, especially around other people. It is extremely uncommon for us to do that, and it will embarrass them. If you want them to when no one else is around, well that's another matter. Mind you, only some of them will though, as it is a bit bizarre, and you will never change them. If you keep that in mind, you will do fine. You must remember you are the earl's son-in-law so it is usual for us to call you sir. As long as you keep that in mind, most of the staff will never call you Sam. We older staff members just might. Perhaps they might find it easier if you ask, but I doubt it. 'Well,' he said, looking up as Bella came out with the overnight bag, 'we are ready to go.' We said thank you to Mrs Moore and climbed into the open carriage. She waved out calling 'hwyl fawr am y tro.' 'What did she say?' I asked, looking a bit baffled. 'She is saying goodbye for now.' Bella grinned. 'It is a difficult language to get your tongue around.'

The four-wheeler carriage was a different one from last night, it was bigger and there was room enough for four passengers. George sat up higher than us in the front. He had transferred all our bags over onto the tray on the back and had covered them with a tarp. We plodded out of the cottage gate heading onto the Shrewsbury Road, to begin my day of reckoning. We were lucky as the day was beautiful, and being in an open carriage, we had a good view all around. I found the houses and buildings with the Tudor architecture quite attractive, so it made the trip interesting. The Shrewsbury Castle dominated the town as we turned our back on the city. If things work out, this will be my hometown. We headed south to Shadymore.

CHAPTER FIFTEEN

Southland, New Zealand 2019

I had established my plan of action as I sat down with a full list of things to do. I booted up the computer, and one of the first things I took care of was to join the Rootsweb New Zealand list. This was an excellent list for anyone researching genealogy. By adding your name to the list, it can help you immensely. You just ask questions; all the list members will see them, and if you are lucky, you will receive answers quite quickly. I also joined the Hereford, and the Scottish lists, plus the Royal Navy, Scottish Regiments, and Edinburgh lists. Then I continued on with the surname lists of McInnes, Mack and Wright son. This was the simplest beginning I could think of. I flicked off emails to these listings explaining who I was looking for, and if anyone had come across those names in their research.

I sent an email to the New Zealand Society of Genealogy, asking for information on the *Esk* in New Zealand waters. I was pleased to get that away early as well. The next thing I did was start to look at the birth, death, and marriage index of both England and Wales. I was looking for the birth of Bella Wrightson. Their records began in late 1837, so any time before that; I would have to go through parish records and that can be hard work. Anyway that search was a dead end as nothing came up. So I tried Isabel or Isabella, and I got a few more hits this time but none in Herefordshire. Of course that meant nothing; people were travelling around a lot at this time as rail was coming into its own, and people often were born in one place and registered in another.

I spent three days on names Bella could have been registered under with little result. I did find six names of births fairly close to the dates I was looking for, though I must admit, I didn't hold out much luck. In this game, you have to try everything. I connected with a lady in Wales who said she would just pop into the nearest General Records office in Southport for me and buy any certificate I wanted. It's essential to attempt to get the right person you are researching, if not this method could become quite expensive. So in the end I bought six certificates, which cost me fifty-four pounds. I transferred the money into her account, plus of course, her costs. When she picked up the documents, she scanned them straight away then emailed the copy to me, and later posted the originals by snail mail. So I got the certificates in digital form the next day, by my time. In this case the certificates I received were a dead end, as none of them were the woman I was looking for. I checked each name on the 1841 census and continued right through until 1871. I knew that Bella had joined the Nightingale Hospital in 1861, but she was not on the census for that year. Out of the six there was only one possibility. But in the end, I found her married in 1862 and by checking the 1871 census I found she was married with three children living in London. Bugger, wrong person. So that was another dead end. The other five didn't fit the bill either; I was now at my first brick wall. So I flicked off another email to the Hereford list explaining my dilemma and hoped that someone could relay any information about this woman. I then moved on to the marriage certificates. I found a few, but no marriages of a Mack, McInnes, or a Wrightson, so at this stage of the research she was just another anonymous nurse. I tried deaths as well, and all the ages were wrong by at least ten years. I estimated her age when I met her in Auckland, at about twenty-three to twenty-six years, which gave me a birth and search date of between 1837 to 1840. But most of the likely deaths I had come across were born before 1830. So if she had died in the United Kingdom, she would have had to have been registered under a married name, either that or had left the country. After a week of searching her name, I was no further advanced. So I changed tack and decided to check the Nightingale Hospital records. I especially looked at the New Zealand files, as she worked here in 1863.

Bingo! I had a hit. In November 1862, there was a cholera outbreak in Dunedin. The old records, now online, told me that there had been thirty-four deaths to every thousand with many barely surviving. All known cases attended by the nurses were quarantined at the hospital in the Octagon Hospital. The data listed names of patients who had died, and at the very end were the names of the nurses who had helped stem the epidemic. There in black and white was Bella Wrightson, with half a dozen other nurses who had all arrived together on the sailing ship, *Ben Nevis*, from Graves End. It was the first bit of positive news that I had found. I was over the moon. How it would assist me in my search, I didn't know, but at least I now had a small paper trail. Proof that she had been here alright and that I wasn't mistaken. It was time now to see if there was anything in the local newspaper in November 1862. I went on to *Papers Past*, a digitised register for old newspapers. I looked up the *Otago Witness*, then added the dates I wanted in the search box, along with Bella's name and the Nightingale name. About a hundred pages came up from my inquiry. I trolled through the information and found that the nurses had worked hard to contain the cholera, and it had taken about four months to get on top of it. First they had introduced the idea of boiling the tap water for domestic use, then with help from public pressure, the authorities started to clean up the filthy streets and to move the privies well away from the fresh water wells. Soon the disease slipped away, and the nurses paraded with honour outside the Octagon Hospital. Included with the article was a very grainy photo of them all, taken on the steps. I found in one newspaper, a piece about the dedication of two nurses, Bella Wrightson, and Dorothy Temple, who went into the dirtiest shanties to help people with no regard for their own health. Wow, I thought, she had a friend. Well I hoped it was a friend. This might enable me to find Bella through this woman, coming in through the back door, so to speak. This could be progress at last. Of course it wasn't much, but nevertheless it was a step forward.

I sat back and rubbed my hair. Bugger me; I need a beer. I had examined this stuff for hours, and it was a time for a rest. I made a sandwich, grabbed my beer and went out to sit on my wee knoll overlooking the sea. I needed to clear my head. As I sat in quietness I felt a bit melancholy. After all of that work ploughing through the archives and old newspapers, I didn't really have much after a week or so. But I did have another name, so that's a boost of sorts, barely, but it was something. I returned inside and noticed the time, it was one p.m., and I had another couple of hours before I would have to pick up the kids from Mum's place. I dropped our daughter, Libby, at school each morning, and took our youngest, Shane, around to Mum's most days when it was possible. She looked after him for us and then picked Libby up after school. That gave me around five hours a day for research with no stoppages for small children. I wouldn't make it any longer than that as I needed to spend time with the kids, and afterwards I would make dinner for Tui, especially if she had had a rough day at work. Everything was working out okay; I was lucky. Over the next few hours I decided to see if I could find anything on this girl, Dorothy. I did a Google search on her name, but nothing of relevance came up. I looked through *Roots Web*, still nothing. I had to leave it there then as it was time to pick up the kids.

The next day I was on the job again trying to find Dorothy. I checked marriages in the births, deaths and marriages' register in the UK, and came across a Dorothy Temple married to Charles Waters in 1869 in Manchester. I then checked the 1871 census, and it had her occupation as a nurse. A breakthrough! So she was still working as a nurse two years after she married. I checked all of the censuses up to 1911. In that time she had had three children and lost two. She had moved addresses a couple of times also. Then in 1891 she became a widow. According to the census after that, she lived by herself but a couple of visitors were noted, a C of Shadymore and an E of Shadymore. I'm blowed if I know if that meant anything. I had no idea and soon put it out of my mind. Because I never followed up on that information, I did many extra months of wasted research. It motivated me later when I was looking back, to check everything. But, in this case, I didn't. So I plodded on, day in and day out with more setbacks than advances. I just kept going. I would hit gold soon, I was sure of it. Paper was strewn around my computer desk and censuses were coming out of my ears. I had to admit I was getting more than a bit frustrated. Doggedly, I went back to the newspapers and started to scroll through all the Scottish ones for 1863. It was about this time I had an email from a member of the Edinburgh list. The name, Mack, had come up in a newspaper he was scanning, and he sent me the link. I clicked on it, and there it was, an advert put in the paper by Sam looking for his family. At last! Shivers ran up my spine; I couldn't believe it. At last, my mate was there, and I could have cried. I jumped up and down which scared the shit out of the cat, and ran around the house throwing my arms in the air. I immediately rang Mum and gave her my news. She was over the moon at my progress. I couldn't wait for Tui to come home, so I rang her at the hospital. 'Bob, that's brilliant news, well done. I can't wait to check it out when I get home.' Next I rang Sam's parents. I could hear his mum breaking down in tears in the background as I told Wayne what I had found. It was the first positive connection to him. He still hadn't got his memory back, but he was alive and well, and staying at the Waterloo Hotel in Edinburgh.

This information had taken me over a month to find. Belonging to all the lists had eventually paid off. I came off the phone and sat and looked at the photo of the three of us, taken in Otahuhu in 1863. I looked at his face and I spoke to the picture. 'Got you, you big bugger, now all I have to do is find a way forward from here.' It was the big breakthrough I needed. I was still on a high when Tui came home, I grabbed her and we danced around the room. As I bent her backward and gave her a big wet kiss; the kids laughed at us, wondering what was going on. 'Well,' she said, grinning, 'I wish you would find that sort of interesting information every day if this is what I'd be coming home to.' 'Take a look, Tui, it's all there,' I happily responded. She sat down and went through it slowly. 'Oh, Bob,' she said, 'you never told me his hair was steel grey and that he was clean-shaven.' I looked at her. 'No!' I exclaimed. 'That's not possible.' I knelt down to look at the screen to read the advert again. In my excitement, I had neglected to read the description entirely, I just saw what I wanted to see. 'My God, Tui, he was grey, why the heck would he be grey?' 'Shock, Bob, plain and simple. With all those head wounds; the shock would have turned his hair grey or white. It doesn't happen all the time but in some cases it will. So it looks like in Sam's case he went grey, and I bet someone close to him suggested not to regrow his beard as it would make him look like an old man,' Tui explained. 'How the hell could I have missed that? Here I am set up as a so-called detective hunting for him, and I missed an important clue.' 'No, that's not true Bob, once the euphoria went, you would have sat down and reread the description right through. You are methodical.' 'Yeah, but I should have noticed that at the beginning,' Bob answered. 'Don't go beating yourself up, Bobby. It's a great find, and the first definite information you have found. Enjoy it.' I grinned sheepishly. 'Yeah, you're right as usual. Hey I have an idea, you know that friend of yours, the one who paints—what's his name?' 'Alan?' Tui answered.' 'Yeah, that's him. If I remember rightly, he's pretty talented when it comes to using Photoshop. Do you think he could change Sam's hair colour to grey on a photo? If I asked him, that is? I would like to see what he might have looked like back then. What say I put the photo on a USB stick, and maybe you could take it into work and give it to him?' My eyes pleaded with her. 'Okay, Bob, I'll take it into work tomorrow. Pop it on a stick, and I will ask him for you. Though there's no guarantee, as he works quite a bit of overtime.'

Tui's workmate, Alan, didn't hesitate and he finished the photo for me in just two days. I was elated as the altered photo looked marvellous. He had Sam not only clean-shaven with grey hair, but he had also dressed him in 1860s attire for me. Now he looked quite different, and I wouldn't have recognised him in the street if I had walked past him. He was still a good-looking bloke though, and looked quite distinguished with his grey hair. But the old-fashioned clothes made him look a far cry from the man I knew. I rang his parents and explained what I had done. They were fascinated with what I said and wanted to see the result, so I sent the photo over to them as an attachment. It seemed like it was only moments before a Skype call came straight back. 'I cannot believe that's our Sam, what a change.' 'You're right, there,' I explained. 'That is how he would have looked back then, or close to it. We have an opener now, so that's a big help. Now I need to find out if he left a paper trail in Edinburgh.' So over the weekend I plotted my next course of action.

CHAPTER SIXTEEN

Southland New Zealand

I wrote a list of the things I needed to do next: check the records of the Waterloo Hotel, and the army hospital in Edinburgh for any mention of his name as well as any other newspapers right up till Christmas 1863. Also there were the army discharges in Scotland to look at. That would keep me going for a while. The easiest would be the army records, I thought, but that turned out to be the hardest. The National Archives in the UK kept a tremendous amount of records, but sometimes finding what you wanted could be quite tiresome, and it was like that for me. There were so many links listed and to find the right one took me off on a tangent, frequently. Eventually I found the link to the medal page, and it was here that I found Sam's awards: the New Zealand Medal and Military Cross from the New Zealand war. Then that linked me to his army hospital records which told me that Sam was discharged on the 13th July 1863 with his last known address listed as the Waterloo Hotel in Edinburgh. The Chief Surgeon, Colonel Mcrea, signed it. I was elated; here at last were official records of Sam. I found another link to a gratuity of one hundred pounds that he was paid, though at the bottom of the page, I saw an additional fifty pounds pencilled in at the convenience of Scottish Command. It even told me the bank that he presented it to the Bank of Scotland. I sat looking at the computer screen;

these were superb records, and this was really interesting. So now, I knew he was in Edinburgh at least till July of 1863.

I wondered if there were any records of other guests at the Waterloo Hotel. Just as I was about to close the page, I saw a link to a website put up by a descendant of Colonel Mcrea's. I couldn't click on it fast enough. There wasn't much there for me as the records were a run-down on his life and marriage, and everything that would be of interest to the Colonel's family. But it told me that he was in charge of the military hospital from January 1863 until January 1865. It was the time frame I was most interested in. Also there were records of part of his diary written in 1863. On one page, it mentioned him giving away a Lady Gale at a wedding in a nearby church on the 20th of July. There was no mention of the groom. Not much help there, unfortunately, but this was more of a slow tramp rather than a race. At least it was progress, and I was slowly getting somewhere. A month or so ago I had nothing; now I had something concrete. Next, I had to find his movements from there. So I went back to look at the hotel. I searched on Google for the Waterloo Hotel in Edinburgh. Up came a swag of stuff but nothing to get very excited about. So I sent an email to the manager asking if they had any surviving archives from the past. I gave them my mate's name as Samuel Mack or McInness, who had stayed there in July of 1863. I didn't expect too much to come out of it but, in for a penny, in for a pound. In the meantime, I slogged on. Next, I thought I would check on all of the Edinburgh papers in July of that year. I expected that would take the rest of the week, but as it turned out, it gave me a further push and broke through a small brick wall. It was Friday afternoon, and I had stopped for a beer and a bite to eat. Usually, I went out onto the wee knoll to sit and look at the beach. But this day I sat back down at the computer glaring at the screen and munching on my sandwich. I was hoping that something would jump up and hit me between the eyes. It was then that I came across an ad from a menswear outfitter in Portobello. They mentioned their new design of more practical men's underwear called shorts. It went over my head for a minute. Then I thought, hey wait a minute, this is much too early for these underpants. It wasn't until the 1930s that boxers became the rage. But that was only a brand name, maybe the name, *shorts*, in this instance, was before the boxers. Let's face it, it's just a name, but it still seemed a bit early. I looked at the name of the company, Selkirks. A flag came up on my laptop screen from the app that my mate had made for me. All the names of Sam's family had been entered and would flag if they came up on my screen and one just did. Scratching my head, I thought, well this isn't relevant; this is just a firm's name, it doesn't mean anything. But I took another look at the ad and wondered how they came up with the name shorts. No one used shorts in this period. Hell, you could hardly show your ankle, and if you did, the girls would be fainting. It was food for thought.

The name of the shop was Selkirks, so I Google searched it. A few pages about the firm came up. I clicked on to their history link and discovered a blog about a Jewish bloke who started Selkirks back in 1850. The company had spread all over the UK and by the 1880s they had nearly one hundred outlets. They made men's clothing, women's undergarments, shoes, and started to sell clothes off the rack in 1873. That was unusual for this time, but this firm seemed way ahead of the pack. There was a small passage about a Mr Hyman, who started the business and then eventually his three sons took over when he passed away in 1869. Featured were designs drawn by Mr Selkirk. Apparently he completely changed the way men and woman used under garments. The firm was still going in 1980, but in 1982 it shut its doors after 132 years. The Hyman family then launched another business with lines this time in technology and medicine. An email contact at the bottom of the page caught my eye, and I sat back and pondered. This was weird, but my little flag was waving brightly. So I sent off an email to the address asking for any information on the Mr Selkirk, mentioned. Time to call it quits for the day; I went and picked up the kids.

A week later, I received an email from the Waterloo Hotel.. One of their staff who dealt with the archives was away but would be back in a few weeks. So they set aside my request to await his return, adding sorry for the delay. Well, at least they had an archive, so something might come up. There wasn't a reply from my Selkirk email, so it was back to the grind. Now it was time to take stock of what I had or didn't have. I'd no luck with my *Esk* inquiries; I'd been hoping to find diaries from ex-sailors. Nothing had come through from the hotel, but that may change down the line, and naught from the Selkirks shop. On the positive side, I'd collected information from the army hospital, about Sam's discharge, his money, and where he stayed, but nothing about Bella Wrightson. So I was a wee way ahead, but there was a long way to go.

At the end of the week, I reported back to Wayne and Mary by Skype. 'You're doing well Bob; this is more information than we thought possible after all this time,' Wayne told me. 'Yeah. But Wayne, we now need to know where he went to from there, and that is proving to be a problem. But if we get some results from the hotel it might be a way forward, so fingers crossed.' We finished our call, and I realised that this might be the right time to take the kids out for a picnic, on the weekend. It would clear my head and give me a fresh start for Monday morning. Before bed on Friday night I dropped a line to the Edinburgh list. I gave them all of my recent information including the blurb on the Selkirks shop. I queried if anyone knew someone who was, or is researching this Jewish family, or anyone who was researching the Waterloo Hotel, and if the name of Mr Selkirk had come up. Bugger, I had had enough; I switched off the light, and hit the pit. 'Hard day, Bob?' Tui asked as I climbed into bed. 'Yeah, it has been. It's funny, I never thought it would be this hard, but looking at the computer screen, day after day has tired me out. Look, I had been thinking of us all having a day's picnic, but let's go up to the crib for the weekend instead, and have a complete break.' We had a small holiday home up at Lake Hauroko that we didn't get to as often as I'd like. 'That's a superb idea Bob, we have nothing on this weekend, so let's do just that. We could get away just after breakfast; the kids do love it up there.' I fell off to sleep thinking about my much-needed break from the computer. A day or two off was necessary when researching or you could miss something important with inattention. I should have done this more often. Up at the lake, with the Fiordland National Park as your backdrop, you could blow the cobwebs out of your head.

It worked; I came home full of energy and raring to go, full of ideas of what I could do next. From then on, while I was doing this research, we decided to get up to the lake at every opportunity, though we would have to work around Tui's shift work. But every three weeks would still be good. Once I had dropped the kids off, I was into it again. I checked my emails, and I had three waiting two concerning the Waterloo Hotel and one about the Selkirks shop. I opened the last one first. It was from a woman who was a descendant of the Hyman family and asked if she could help. I questioned her if she knew about this Mr Selkirk and how was he connected to the family business, then flick off the email. Then I opened the other two. One was from a bloke who had photos of the hotel taken back in 1863. He asked me if I was interested in seeing the image. I answered yes and thanked him for his time. The second was from a lady who collected information about people who stayed at the Waterloo over the years. She had compiled a list and wondered if I'd like a copy. I just about dribbled on the computer; I was so excited. I sent an email back immediately, with a yes, please. My fingers were crossed that I'd receive something positive from that. I went back to trolling through the papers for July 1863; I had stopped looking through them when I had found the ad. But I was hopeful that there may be more information to glean there.

I was up to about the middle of the month when I came across a wedding notice on Monday the 20th 1863 of a Mr Selkirk to a Gale. The old flag in the app did a bounce on the screen again. Gale meant nothing to me and Selkirk didn't either for that matter, but it was Sam's grandmother's maiden name, and it did keep coming up. But who was this Gale? Where did she fit into the picture? There wasn't much to go on in the paper, just a few words to say it was held at two p.m. in the St Andrew's and St George's, a combined church of Scotland. It went on to mention the lovely Lady Gale married Mr Selkirk. The officiating minister was the Rev D Macintosh. A small congregation of thirty people attended and that included some army officers. The bride was given away by a Colonel Mcrea. I stopped and reread it again. I found I suddenly had trouble breathing and had to consciously remember to take a breath. There was more here than met the eye, that's for sure both army officers and the colonel from the hospital. So who was Lady Gale and who was this Mr Selkirk? I think I will have to follow-up on this one. I had taken all day to get to this point, and I needed to stop and think about what this meant. Were these good leads? The Selkirk name had come up again. Did it mean anything? I needed to give it a break. I'll leave it till tomorrow and see if the lady with the list comes back to me. I looked at my watch the kids bugger. I'd better get going. Saving all my stuff, I closed the computer and high-tailed it out of the house. Libby was going to swimming lessons, and if I were late she wouldn't be too happy she loved the water. As I drove over to Mum's, I felt I was near a discovery, though I didn't know how, but it felt near. Nearly three months had passed since I had started. I wanted to move forward, and I needed to as I was struggling a bit. Be it tomorrow or this week I could feel a breakthrough coming. Well you can hope. Then it came to me, I will check the church records for that wedding, first thing. It just might put some light on this Gale woman. Then I'll ask my researcher in Wales for the original certificate. She'll let me know the particulars immediately after she gets it. I sensed I was close; I knew I was close. It was just around the corner and near enough to touch. I looked at the photo I now had stuck to the sun visor. Sam dressed in clothes from the 1860s. You aren't going to lose me, mate. I'm not going to drop the ball, hang in there, my friend.

CHAPTER SEVENTEEN

1863 Shrewsbury England

We trotted through the countryside, leaving Shrewsbury behind us, and the day was perfect for our drive out to Shadymore. Recently shorn sheep gathered in small scattered mobs in the paddocks, and the smell of freshly cut hay was in the air. 'We are on our land now,' Bella eventually announced. To the left surrounding the high stands of corn and wheat, was good-looking farmland filled with cattle and sheep. In one area I saw chooks' and pigs' pens clustered together. On the right, the land was covered in forest with light undergrowth. This continued on up into the hills to disappear on the horizon. I gazed with interest at everything I saw. I could smell the country and now the forest, and it gave me a feeling of contentment. I noticed stands of oaks and poplar trees but I didn't know many of the other varieties. I recognised blackbirds, thrushes, sparrows and starlings, but a lot of the bird life felt foreign to me also. 'Are you familiar with the bird breeds in these parts, Bella?' 'Yes, of course,' she replied, 'and with all other types of fauna around here. But Amelia was exceptional in her knowledge of all the local wildlife, much better than me. For any questions she would be the one to talk to.' 'Do you have deer and wild pigs on this property, and are they a menace?' I queried. 'No, Sam, they are not, why would they be? I like to think everything is in accord with the natural order of things. Most wildlife kill for survival and are then, in turn, killed for food.' Bella responded. 'Do you have any *introduced* fauna on this property, Bella?' I asked.'From other countries, do you mean? No, I don't think so, Sam. Bella then called out, 'George, has any wildlife been brought in from overseas to our forest?' 'No, my lady, not intentionally, though we get a few birds over from the continent with the typical migration,' George answered. 'Do you have any problems with wild pigs, George?' I intervened. 'Only people poaching them, sir. The population has reduced quite a bit with that, and if it keeps up we will not have a boar left in a few years,' George replied. 'How about deer, then?' I urged, beginning to feel uncomfortable. 'We have a few different species on the estate, but they don't give us any problems though, but their numbers are dropping as well. To think the earl used to have to cull them in the past. Not now, though, what with the poachers taking what they want. We have had no luck catching the scoundrels either,' George informed Sam. His answers were all wrong and didn't make any sense; I felt confused. I couldn't understand why I had this distinct impression that pigs and deer were detrimental to the environment. Why on earth would I think that way? Something wasn't right. I jumped in with another question. 'What about stoats, ferrets, and weasels now they must be a menace around here, George? 'Well, if they get into the chicken runs, they are. But generally, not that you would notice, Mr Selkirk, and we do have a fur run once a year when we cull to keep their numbers down. But largely their numbers fluctuate with what's available for them to eat and then of course the weather plays a big part in it also. If we get a prolonged winter, their population is quite low the following summer,' said George. I sat back really worried. He hadn't said what I expected, and so I tried a different tack. 'Why do poachers steal from your property, Bella? Is it because of poverty, or greed, do you think?' 'I think it could be a bit of both, Sammy, and I guess it is something you can ask Father about.' I sat back quiet for a moment and gazed out mesmerised by the trees as they slipped by. I could feel them soothe me, and soon I found myself much calmer, and I realised being close to nature alleviated my stress. Then something caught my eye, an unnatural profile on the forest floor, or was it just a hunch. 'Hey, George, taihoa. Oh sorry, stop for a minute, please, mate. I just saw something that seemed out of place.' He hesitated then pulled up. I jumped out of the coach, 'I won't be a minute; I just want to check it out.' I then turned and walked into the bush, back towards where I'd caught a glimpse of something alien in such a pristine forest. Three metres off the road I came upon the tree I'd marked near the object. I searched around and found what I'd seen lying on the ground partially covered in leaves. I don't know how I could have seen it from so far off. Suddenly a big metallic type of voice in my head said, 'The force is strong with this one.' What on earth was that, where did that come from? I looked around to see if I could see anyone around that could have spoken. But I knew there wasn't anyone; it had come from inside my head. Once again I felt bewildered; maybe I am losing my marbles. I looked for a spot to sit down to think about that realisation, when suddenly I identified the object I'd found. My troubled thoughts flew out the window as what I'd seen was a bloody gin trap. This trap lay flat and open on the ground with cruel sharp teeth on both sides, waiting for any unsuspecting animal or even tramper for that matter. When one walks into the trap the mouth slams shut, with the teeth ripping into the leg, and sentencing the animal to die a slow, painful death. I found a stick, carefully pushed away the leaves and sprung the trap. I then tore it from its anchor. I hated them, they were brutal, and it pissed me off that whoever planted them had no feelings at all for how these poor animals suffer. I scouted around and picked up a trail the trappers had left as they returned back into the forest, their boot marks clear for all to see. There were two sets of them each with different sized boots. One had a distinctive pattern on the sole, and the other had a left heel that had worn down on the outside of the shoe. Going by the depth of their prints they weren't big blokes, about 1.6 to 1.7 metres that's about five foot three to five foot seven, and only about fifty-six kilograms which is eight and a half stone. I will know them if I see their signs again, and if all goes well, I'll catch those two buggers. There's nothing worse than having an animal caught in a gin trap. How the heck did I know all this stuff, I thought, because my mind didn't even have to think about it. I shrugged it off; I already had enough to worry about. I headed back to the coach with the trap I'd confiscated. George eyed the trap as I handed it up to him, 'Oh, the earl will not be happy when he sees that,' George spat. 'Yeah.' I glared. 'Him and me both. I tracked the blokes who laid this, for about fifty metres; what's that in yards, say sixty yards. I'll know them when I see their prints again.' 'Are you sure, Sammy? That's expecting a bit much don't you think?' Bella asked doubtfully. 'Yes, I'm quite sure, Bella; I sense that I am good at this. You know I felt right at home in there,' I said, indicating the forest. 'What I do find troubling though, is the bush or forest as you call it doesn't seem very much like what I'm used to. I kept imagining it would be denser with vines, but I did find it very comfortable moving about, and it felt quite natural to me. It's hard to put a tag on it.' 'That is wonderful, Sam. Well at least that trap will not do any damage,' Bella commented. 'Yeah, you're right, but I'm bloody wild about it because these gin traps are indiscriminate, they kill everything,' I said with passion. 'I'm positive I'll be able to sort this out for your Dad.' As we moved on at a slow pace I continued, 'I could clean out this type of rubbish for him. Mind you I'll have to get to know the property,' I added with a grin on my face. 'It'll be a good excuse for me to lose myself in there for a few days and see what I can find.' 'This is a part of you I don't recognise, Sam.' She smiled with admiration. 'Yeah, but I think it's the real me, Bella. Remember, according to that document we found, I was on a special mission. I could have been behind enemy lines for ages. I have this awareness that I know how to look after myself in the bush. Remember my gear, the colours that blend into a forest landscape, it will be handy here too.' 'Look, I do not want you hurt, Sammy, so no heroics as you have done your bit,' Bella gently scolded. 'Yes, don't worry you'll get no bravado from me, Bella, I promise. But if the wildlife is being depleted on your dad's property it needs to be sorted.' She looked up at me. 'My, I see a quite change in you, Sammy. It is as though someone has pulled a switch, and you are now both animated and focused. You know, I think I like it,' she said with satisfaction. I grinned with pleasure, then looked up and asked George, 'Are any other farmers in the area having poaching problems, George?' 'Yes sir, a few, it's not all the time, mind, we have runs of it,' George replied. 'Have you heard of any illegal selling of meat at the markets in town?' I enquired.'Well sir, I've not noticed, but I could ask around,' George responded. 'Yeah mate, do that but quietly, I don't want the sods to be aware as it's best to keep them in the dark till we know who they are,' Sam explained. 'Bella, what happens to poachers if and when they're apprehended?' She was grim when she replied, 'It used to be a hanging offence, either that or they would have been transported to Australia but that stopped about 1850. Now the sentence is more like up to seven years in prison. I don't like them hanging people, it's barbaric.' 'Well, maybe we will have to think seriously about coming to an arrangement of sorts with them. But if they are hardened criminals, well that will be on their heads, and altogether a different matter,' I said. 'I'm looking forward to getting the chance to do a tramp as I'm really impressed with this forest. Bella, what say we do it together like we did in Cape Town? It would be fun, and you could instruct me on all you know about the local flora and fauna. We could take my tent, the sleeping bag, and enough food for a few days. What do you say?' I asked hopefully. She grinned and announced, 'I knew my life with you was going to be unusual, but I did not know just how unusual that was to be. It would be fun, though my parents will be horrified, but yes, we should do that.' I sat back for the rest of the journey holding her hand. 'You know, I feel really content. It seems like it's been a while since I have felt like this,' I told Bella.

The manor came into view through the trees, and it had a large, circular drive of crushed gravel that passed by steps which led up to the main entrance, a double front door that was framed by two pillars. Oak trees shaded the drive on both sides as we approached. Bella squeezed my hand. 'Ok, my love this is it, don't be hurt if my father is abrupt, just be you.' Three figures stood at the top of the stairs waiting for our coach to pull up. I noticed there were no servants about, and I wondered what the old boy was up to. Perhaps he was waiting for a chance to get his claws into me.

As we came to a stop there was an almighty yell and an attractive young woman belted down the steps holding her dress up so she wouldn't trip over it. She reached the bottom of the stairs just as Bella stepped down from the coach. 'Bella, Bella,' she shrieked, and she grabbed her sister and hugged her not willing to let go. 'Oh Bella,' she cried, 'I missed you so much, so very much.' Both girls were in tears and laughing at the same time as they clung together. Bella eventually pulled away from her sister's embrace and introduced her to me. 'Ami, this is my husband, Sam.' Ami composed herself and wiped her eyes. 'I'm so sorry Bella,' she mumbled, 'I forgot my manners.' 'No, don't apologise, Amelia,' I whispered, 'you haven't seen your sister for years, and it's only natural that both of you are excited. Bella has been telling me all about you, and I can see that you are as beautiful as she is. I'm looking forward to getting to know you.' She looked a bit taken aback. 'Thank you,' she spoke softly with a cautious smile. 'Where are you from, Mr Selkirk? I don't recognise your accent,' Amelia questioned me. I smiled and said, 'I'm sorry, Amelia, I don't know, but as soon as I find out you will be the first to know after your sister.' She looked at Bella, confused. 'Sam had a head wound, Ami; he lost his memory, but other than that he is fine.' I stuck out my hand. 'G'day Ami, I'm Sam Selkirk, your new brother-in-law. I hope we will be friends.' She grinned. 'It is nice to meet you, Mr Selkirk, and I think I can see why my sister married you. Come along, I will introduce you to our parents.' Bella took my hand, and Amelia took hers and we climbed the steps as a threesome. I heard her whisper to Bella, 'What does G'day mean?' 'It is short for good day,' Bella answered.'Oh.' Amelia smiled. "That is bizarre.'

As we climbed the steps, the earl and countess stood back and waited by the door. Bella let go of my hand when she reached the top and stepped forward to put her arms around her mother, who immediately burst into tears then all three women started to cry. I didn't know where to put myself, so I held back, waiting. I was conscious of the earl standing quietly as he gave me the once-over. I made a decision and continued up to the top entrance, and immediately, I looked down on them all. I don't usually accentuate my height, but on this occasion I just wanted him to know that I was no pushover. Now he had to look up at me and I must have looked huge to him. Finally Bella pulled away from her mother, her eyes still wet with the pleasure of seeing her mum again after two years. She turned to her father. 'Daddy,' she said, and for the first time he smiled and hugged his daughter. I could see that he loved her; that he loved them all. I realised then that I'd have a hard job ahead of me, but I'll have to make it work to become part of her family. 'Mother, Father, I would like to introduce to you my husband, Samuel Selkirk. 'I could see that this was really distressing for them both. They had expected Bella to marry someone from the upper classes with a big village wedding and all of the paraphernalia that goes with it. But now there would be no grand wedding, not even a small one as it had already happened without their knowledge. A wedding they weren't even invited to. Instead they get this enormous, casual-looking bloke as a son-in-law. A man who took up so much space and towered over them all. A man who had silver-grey hair which gave the impression that I was much older than I looked. Well I could see this was going to be quite a challenge, but Bella was worth it. So I took the bit between my teeth and I stuck out my hand and said to the earl, 'G'day, sir, it's a pleasure to meet you at last, and you too ma'am.' I smiled at Bella's mum. The earl shook my hand limply as did my mother-in-law; they both didn't look too happy, with large frowns on their faces and pinched lips. The earl spat, 'Come, we have some tiffin set up in the dining room, we can talk there.' I looked down at poor, old George struggling with the bags and remembered I'd left my rifle down in the coach. 'Just a moment I'll just give George a hand, there's a bit too much for him to carry.' I quickly left and went down. 'Mate,' I said, 'Just stick the bags by the door, and I'll take them to wherever they put us.' He looked at me then dropped his head, smiled and whispered, 'Well, I never. This is a first, and it is most unusual, Sam, but there is usually an army of servants here to help. I'm picking the earl and the countess wants it to be a private affair. Looks like even the butler is stuck out the back, and he'll be put out by this as well, I should think.' I picked up the biggest bag, grabbed my rifle then stuck another bag under my arm. I left a couple of the smaller bags for George, and strode up the steps two at a time. When I reached the landing, the earl glared at me for not taking him up on his invitation immediately. 'Where would you like me to put these, sir?' I asked. 'Oh, just leave them there,' he said abruptly. 'I'll get the butler to arrange to put them in your suite later.' I could see it would take some time for him to come around. George came up behind me and placed his bags next to the others. 'Thank you George, we won't need the coach again, today,' he snapped. 'Thank you, my lord.' George turned and returned to his coach. I got the feeling he was only too happy to be right out of it. 'The dining room is through here,' the earl boomed at me, I grinned to myself, recognising this as his big voice that Bella had told me about. 'The ladies have gone through,' he continued.

I followed him down a splendid, thickly carpeted hallway. It was vast, and a large chandelier with gas lights hung from the ceiling. There were a multitude of family paintings adorning the walls, and the wooden cornices tucked under the ceiling were carved with animal scenes. I felt the hall looked cluttered though as there was an excessive amount of ornamental furniture pushed up against the walls. I noticed there was a staircase with a curved banister that led off the hall, that must lead up to the bedrooms. We walked on further and into the dining room which was huge. A long oak table with seating for twenty sat in the middle upon an enormous carpet square. I would say this room would accommodate at least sixty people on a special occasion. I guessed another table would be needed if they wanted to seat them all. I couldn't help but think that you could lose yourself in such a room. What a shame; such a massive table for such a small family. An enormous fireplace surrounded by a couch and armchairs stood to the side of the room, and additional large chairs were placed around the walls. I spotted gas lighting in there also. The girls were over by the large serving area, chatting away as we came in. I looked at Bella, and I could see she was happy to be with family. It made me feel a tiny, wee bit jealous and somehow left out. She saw my face and came straight over. 'Are you okay?' she whispered, 'you look as though you are in pain.' 'Oh sorry, Bella, I didn't mean for it to show. I just saw you with your family, and all of a sudden I felt lost. I'm okay now, and I'm happy that you are happy.' 'Sammy, I'm a fool, I should have realised that you might feel left out since I have family and you do not. Come on, the food is quite nice, so now what do you say? With tucker in your belly, and you will be a box of birds.' I had to laugh, which made everyone on the other side of the room look up. 'That was so funny coming from you, Bella; yes a bit of tucker would be nice.'

CHAPTER EIGHTEEN

Shadymore 1863

We all sat down, and soon I had my head down and got stuck into my meal, preferring to ignore any aggravation coming from the family. Quiet conversation fluttered around the room, but you could cut the atmosphere with a knife. When I cleared my plate, I realised that I couldn't stand it any longer. Something had to be done, and it looked like it was up to me to bring it out into the open.

I went over to the sideboard, deliberating on my best approach, and poured coffee for Bella and myself. I returned to the table and turned to my parents-in-law. They both sat with straight backs and haggard faces, I could see the stress of the situation wasn't doing them any favours. Amelia, realising something was up, leant back on her chair doing her best to hide behind Bella. I hadn't quite made up my mind how to handle it but I wanted to grab their attention, so I did what I normally do and I dived straight in. 'Well folks,' I started and looked at them directly. 'I've come to the conclusion that you both feel that I'm not the right bloke for your daughter.' I gazed at each of them in turn. 'But Bernard... Margaret... our wedding has already taken place, and that is an irrefutable fact.' Using their first names got them taking notice and both looked up at me with a jolt. I could see Bella trying not to smile, and Amelia's mouth had dropped open in shock. 'If you think I'm presumptuous to call you by your first names, well I'm sorry it offended you, but I'm not comfortable with titled names. Look, I don't want to call my parents-in-law by their title. I feel with me being a family member that that would mean I was subservient to you both, and it wouldn't be a good start for our relationship. 'You will have noticed that I speak quite different to you that I use different words. Now I don't know where these words originated from or who I am for that matter, but Bella found me headshot in New Zealand. She told me I had mates with me, but I can't remember them. I was a redhead back then, but now I'm grey, and she reckons that was caused by shock. So you must know that eventually when we have children, there will be a chance for you to have red-headed grandchildren.

'Now I don't know if I have a family of my own. I'm sure I must have a mum and dad somewhere, even siblings maybe, but I can't remember. Anyway you are all my family now, whether you agree with it or not. Both of you are now my surrogate parents, and I will do my level best for you to eventually think of me as a son. I know this is going to take time, and I won't expect it to happen overnight, but I sure hope I can make it happen for Bella and for all of your sakes. I'm uncertain with my loss of memory what skills I have that can help you, but whatever they are will be put to the benefit of the whole family. 'You know, Bella saved my life in New Zealand, along with a lot of other people as well. Your daughter deserves a medal for what she and the other nurses did. After enduring all that we went through we finally realised we were in love on our trip back from the southern hemisphere, and you can't beat love. It overcomes all obstacles. To tell you honestly, I had no idea that Bella was titled, but even if I had known, it wouldn't have stopped me loving her. Look, what I'm trying to say is, just give me an opportunity to prove to you I'm a good bloke. If I don't come up to your expectations, then I will willingly leave. But you must be aware that if I go, I will take Bella with me as

141

she is all I have.' When I stopped, a hush fell over the room, and everyone was waiting in anticipation of what Bernard was going to come out with. I waited for an explosion that never happened. He looked over at his daughter, and said, 'Do you know what it means to us to have you at this table again, Bella; all of us have missed you so.' Bella rose from the table and went around to her father, and lovingly told him, 'Yes I realise, and I'm so sorry to have left like that, Daddy, but I knew you would have tried to stop me, and I needed to do my own thing.' She hugged him, and continued, 'I thought about you all, every minute. You do know I would never have had the opportunity to see or do what I did if I had stayed at home. I even met an exciting man on my travels, and I do love him with all of my heart. You will to... I know it. Just give him some time to prove to you that he is genuine, that's all we ask.' She looked over at me with love in her eyes. 'You know Sam is a bit of an eccentric. He does not know how to ride or to even drive a gig or buggy. A lot of the things he sees, he believes they are old-fashioned, and he can come up with ideas that are not even invented yet. The most surprising thing is he can explain what they are for. So please be aware that although he's a bit different, he really is normal.'

Margaret, who had been quiet through all of the conversation, spoke up at last. 'I must admit, in my considered opinion, Bella seems to have chosen well enough, and we have had some young men here who I would not let go out with my worst enemy, let alone with either of my daughters. I feel you are a genuine person, Samuel, and I would like to try and get to know you better. Maybe you can accompany me to church tomorrow in Brittermore.' Inwardly I said shit, outwardly I said, 'It would be a pleasure, Margaret, and I will look forward to it.' 'My husband will not be able to go tomorrow as something has come up that is more important than God, but it would be nice to turn up with a

142

big man on my arm,' Margaret admitted. Bella was trying not to laugh. 'Oh mother we will all go, I'm sure the village would like to meet Sam.' I felt like a chunk of horseflesh, but I would have to go with the flow. 'We will not have to show you to your room, Bella. We have given you the blue suite, and you know where that is.' 'Oh, Mother that is splendid of you; that's a lovely bedroom.' We said our goodbyes for the moment. Bella took my hand and ushered me out of the door. As we went down the hall, she looked up at me with admiration. 'Well that didn't go too badly at all.' I grinned at her and answered, 'Yeah I survived two hours on trial, not bad eh?' 'You know, with us removed from the dining room it will give them all a chance to talk about us and draw some conclusions. Come along, my love.' She smiled. 'I'll show you to our suite, it is rather large.' She squeezed my arm. Our room was upstairs and down the far end of the house away from everyone. I was surprised when we opened the door as it wasn't just one room as I had expected but two enormous rooms.

The first room was a lounge and I immediately saw why it had come by its name. It had soft, blue-patterned wallpaper, along with blue carpeting, cushions, and curtains. It had a large fireplace surrounded by comfortable chairs, a table, and to finish it off, against the wall, a desk. The far room, a lovely bedroom, was decorated in blue, also. Here a big, four-poster bed covered with an attractive quilt dominated the room. I checked out behind the net curtains and saw French doors that led out on to a balcony overlooking the garden. The room had a large, walk-in wardrobe. Next to it was a door leading to a huge bathroom with a standalone bath, a counter-top with a basin and a huge jug for washing, and there was also a toilet. The colour blue was repeated in the patterned tiles. All of these rooms were as luxuriously furnished as was the rest of the manor. I don't know who had delivered our bags, but they were placed by the end of the bed along with my rifle. Bella jumped onto the bed. 'This is much more comfortable than I remember. We use to sneak in here as children, but the beds seemed so hard then. This bed is quite soft. Would you like to sit beside me, Mr Selkirk, and maybe we could even try it out if I'm not being too forward.' I bent over and pushed her down. 'I hope it doesn't squeak Mrs Selkirk,' I whispered as I kissed her.

We went down for drinks at six pm, and as we had hoped the house was returning to normal. I noticed the butler was out and about once again supervising, a footman and a maid in the dining room, who both dashed past us on an errand. One acknowledged us with a quick nod and the other a curtsey. We joined the family in the drawing room and chatted amicably with them for a while. Then Bella asked her father if there had been any mail for Sam. 'No,' was the reply. 'Well, his medals should arrive soon, so we will need to keep an eye out,' Bella said. 'Medals, what for?' he asked. 'Sam has been granted the New Zealand Medal and the Military Cross. It should have been a VC, but as the war had not officially started, they downgraded it to the Military Cross. So they will send them here,' Bella answered. 'A VC? What did you do Samuel?' he enquired. 'I don't know Bernard, that part of my memory has gone, but I'm sure Bella will know.' Her father turned to her while she enlightened her father. 'Sam, along with his Maori sergeant, saved a family from being slaughtered and their property from being burnt down when Auckland was attacked.' She put her hands up to her mouth. 'Oh Father we were told not to speak about the raid, so it's important that you don't mention a word about what I'm telling you. His Maori sergeant was killed in the barrage, and Sam was shot three times in the head with shotgun pellets when they fought off four of the Maori rebels.' The earl looked impressed and stated, 'That was a very brave thing you did, Sam.' Ah... things were looking up, he'd shortened my name, and we may be getting somewhere. Maybe he's even warming to me. 'Quite honestly I can't remember a thing, so the medals don't really mean anything to me. How the heck I came to be there, I have no idea. But we do have a feeling that I was on a special assignment of some sort behind enemy lines. Judging from what Bella picked up from my mates, we had been in the bush for months, but I'm not certain. Maybe that's why I felt at home in your forest.' 'Hmm,' he said. 'Well, if you do spend some time wandering around in the woods, it might jog your memory.' 'Yes,' I agreed, 'it would be enjoyable as well, but if it doesn't help my memory, that's the way the cookie crumbles I guess.' Bella laughed. 'What do you mean by that?' he asked with a frown. 'Oh sorry, I mean it's the way things will have to be. You know, what will be, will be,' I explained best I could. 'Ah yes. I do like that,' the earl slowly repeated my words, 'The way the cookie crumbles, very good. Have another Madeira, Sam?' 'Actually, I would love a beer,' I replied. He rang the bell, and the butler entered. 'Alfred can you get a tankard of beer for Mr Selkirk, please.' And just like that, he had come around. I think Bella was utterly amazed, but from my point of view it felt good. I really did want to have a family and with the earl accepting me like that, even if only partially, it made me feel quite elated. The beer turned up in a fancy tankard, and I had a couple of sips before I turned back to the earl and approached a subject that had been on my mind for a while now. 'I have something I would like to show you. You will be the only person, except Bella, who has seen it, but I would like your opinion. Would you accompany me for a look-see as it's up in our room?' He nodded, and I quickly finished off my beer and turned to Bella. 'Be back in a minute, love. I want your old man to look at my rifle.' Amelia nearly choked, and I saw Margaret give me a funny look, I don't think she had heard her husband being called an 'old man' before. The earl didn't hear well, I don't think he did.

Up in our room, I picked up my wrapped rifle to show him. 'This gun appears to be one of a kind; I don't think there's anything like it around, well I have seen none like it, either on board the ship or in South Africa. So I need your advice. If this is shown to the right people, maybe someone or some firm might be able to copy it.' I unrolled it from its canvas protection and handed it over. 'What do you think?' Bernard's eyes flew open, and his mouth was agape. 'What, what sort of gun is this?' he stammered. 'How is it fired, how do you load it?' Questions were flung around left, right and centre, and I did my best to answer them. Then I went through the routine, showing him how to load, attach the magazine, aim, and fire. 'My God, Sam, this is ingenious,' he stated eagerly, not being able to keep his eyes off the weapon. 'It is by far the best rifle that I've ever seen. This would put the UK on the map.' 'Well, this is a sporting gun. Anything for the army would have to be much more robust, but I'm sure a good gunsmith would be able to do that,' I stated. Bernard picked up a cartridge and rolled it in his hands 'The whole thing is extraordinary; these bullets are so unusual. You are right the gun is unique.' He picked up the scope and peered inside, and soon he turned it towards the window. 'Sam, I cannot believe it, this thing, what did you call it, a telescopic sight, is superb. Oh, yes, we will have to do something with this.' He was like a kid on Christmas day, so excited at this discovery.

'Yeah, well I was hoping you would have some contacts. If I could show this rifle to them, they might be able to reverse engineer this design and produce a sturdier weapon for the army. Of course, we would have to make a small profit on each rifle produced,' I asserted. 'We?' The earl stopped in his excitement and frowned. 'Yes, that's what I'm saying. This is for our family, and I'd like to add it to the family estate.' 'But, Sam, it is yours, you and Bella should take the profits,' he suggested. 'No, that's not what I intended, Bernard, I need to be able to contribute to the family coffers, and this is how I can do it. Well, it's a start anyway, is that okay with you?' 'Okay what's that word mean?' the earl questioned. 'Is it all right by you?' I told him. 'My boy, of course,

146

of course, it is an incredible gesture. I will have to think about who I can send you to someone who manufactures weapons. Ah, yes, I think I have the right person in mind. In the meantime we will keep it buttoned-up. 'You betcha. No one is going to see this baby,' I answered with relief that our talk had gone well. We left the room with Bernard shaking his head saying, 'I didn't understand any of that sentence, Sam.' We returned to the ladies in the drawing room.

Bella looked up apprehensively, but after taking a look at her father's face she relaxed. The earl was quite animated, and the women looked at each with amazement. 'I think...' He smiled looking quite smug. 'I have learnt some new words today. I will need to write down what they mean, so I can remember and grasp what Sam is talking about.' By now he was grinning from ear to ear, and the women were wondering what had taken place up in the blue room. We sat and talked a while and then Bernard announced. 'Come Monday, I'll make arrangements with George to give you lessons on how to ride and drive and then we will work out a time to show you around the estate. Later on I have a map I can give you that might help you find your own way around, though there are not that many paths on it.' 'That will be great. I'll look forward to having a look around. I could use the wildlife tracks as animals always head for water and shelter. But what I really would like is to learn all about the wildlife you have. Bella tells me, Amelia, that you are a whiz in that department. Oh, sorry, that means you are clued up, ah—you know your wildlife.' She smiled and replied, 'Only too happy to help with your education, Sam.'

'Oh, that's right, Bernard, I forgot to mention before.' I turned to him. 'I spotted a gin trap about two kilometres back, in your property. I asked George to stop and I went and investigated. I followed the spoor of the blokes who put it there, so I'll know them if I come across them again. George left the trap in the coach.' 'A gin trap!' spat Bernard. 'I despise them. I'll hang those men if I find them.' 'Oh, Bernard you know you will do no such a thing, but if we do catch them, I'm sure the constabulary will only be too happy to deal with them,' asserted Margaret. 'When I get a chance, Bernard, I'll take a look around and see what I can find,' I suggested, 'if that's okay with you?' 'Of course, of course, I'd appreciate that, thank you, Samuel,' muttered the earl, still distracted by the gin trap find on his property. The evening wore on and eventually I yawned. 'I hope you don't think I'm rude, but I think I'll head up to bed.' 'Yes, yes, sorry,' the earl mumbled, 'you have had a long day.' Margaret looked up and smiled, 'We will see you for breakfast and then we will head off to church for the ten a.m. service. So please be ready by nine am, Bella.' We all rose, and I shook the earl's hand and then continued on to Margaret. She held out her hand, but I stepped closer and hugged her. She was a bit taken aback but soon relaxed, so I kissed her on her cheek and murmured, 'It's nice to have a mum again.' 'Mum?' she queried in a low voice. 'It's short for mother.' As we left the room, and I closed the door behind us, I thought I saw her wipe a tear from her eye.

The morning drive to the church in the village of Brittermore was pleasant, and Amelia chatted to me about how the village came about. Apparently it was originally created mainly for the farmworkers. 'It was better to have somewhere for them to live near their work, than be scattered all around the district. There is a tavern, a church, and a few small shops, that is about all.' She turned to her mother. 'You know the houses really need to be updated,' she advised, 'some are in poor repair.' I set aside that bit of information, to be remembered at a later date. The small church, surrounded by trees sat next to its graveyard, it had a wooden steeple, and as we came through the village, the bell was peeling. What a lovely tranquil sound, I thought. A small cottage positioned next door was no doubt set aside for the vicar and his wife. Everyone waited outside the church until the countess, the girls, and I had gone inside. I couldn't get my head around how they treated titled people. It didn't stop them from giving me some funny stares though. The countess had her family seats set up in the front pew, and when we sat down everyone else took their places. Then the vicar came out to begin the service and he announced, 'I have to apologise. Our organ player, Mrs Dell, has taken to illness, so we will have to make do with just our voices today.' My head came up and so did my hand. Luckily the service hadn't started yet. 'Excuse me, I may be able to play if you want, just let me take a look at the organ first and I'll let you know,' I volunteered. Everyone looked up at me with odd expressions on their faces as I walked over to the organ. I sat down, pumped the bellows and I started playing 'Abide With Me.' After I had finished, the place was a hush, and the minister asked, 'Can you play the hymn numbers that are in the box next to you?' I took a few minutes to look them up. 'Yep,' I agreed, 'that's good as gold; you start, and I will follow.' I saw Margaret and Amelia gape at each other with incredulous looks on their faces, and Bella did her best to try not to smile. The congregation however seemed to enjoy it. The morning went well and everyone thought the music was uplifting. I played it a wee bit faster than they were used to, but it sounded okay to me. The padre was all over me at the end of the service, full of enthusiasm. So I volunteered, 'If you are ever stuck, just let me know, and I'll fill in for you.' I walked away knowing he would be going over my words wondering what I'd said. As we returned to the manor, Margaret turned to me, 'Samuel that was such uplifting music, can you play the piano as well?' 'Yes I can Margaret. If you like after lunch I'll bang out a few songs for you,' I offered. 'Bang out?' She pulled back looking doubtful, wondering how the piano would cope. 'Play,' I qualified. 'Oh,' she said, relieved that it wasn't what she envisioned. 'I think Bernard will love that,' she replied with a smile. With what happened at church then later with my music recital, by the time the weekend was over, I was the flavour of the month it felt like home. They had turned around in two days from strangers to surrogate parents. And for the second time since meeting Bella, I felt like I had a family. Bella shook her head and confided to me, 'This is so unbelievable, Sam, the way you connected with my parents in only a couple of days. It's so incredible I would have thought it would take months. I know they have seen in you, what I did on the very first day you opened your eyes. I'm utterly thrilled that we are all unified.' 'I'm happy too, Bella,' I replied with a smile. We stood on the balcony of our room and looked out over the farmland at the back of the manor. I could see the forest in the distance disappearing over the horizon. I felt I was home.

CHAPTER NINETEEN

Shadymore 1863

Over two months had passed since our first arrival at Shadymore; the time had flown as I settled down into my new way of life. First off, I was given a crash course on learning to drive a gig and coach, including hitching the horse up with the tracers, and soon I was quite capable of doing it myself without help. The day I did my first solo drive, the whole family were out watching me, admiring my progress. I felt a little foolish, but I didn't let it deter me and went on to have a go every day until it was second nature. George was my patient teacher, along with his eldest son, Tobias, as he gave me instruction when his dad was attending to something for the earl. Tobias knew his stuff, too. I felt quite sorry for him; the poor boy with a name like that, but his parents were proud to call him a biblical name. So when he was with me, I called him Toby. I was impressed with his ability when it came to the horses and the livestock, but he had a particular affinity with the local wildlife. Amelia always appreciated his help in her wee animal hospital.

Now, when it came to riding a horse, I was bloody hopeless. I liked the animals, and they seemed to like me, so that wasn't the problem. The horses would always nudge me or blow in my face hoping for attention. I, in turn, would rub their necks or scratch them behind their ears. But to actually ride on them, to physically get on their backs and ride just wasn't my thing.

I somehow couldn't get my head around it, so I put the reason for my difficulty down to my size. Of course it made me the talk of the manor, and everyone had a chuckle at my expense. I sometimes noticed the staff looking out from behind the curtains, or the footmen would find an excuse to be outside. They all used every ploy to get to watch me fall off again, and I was flung off a lot trying to control the beast. Even the earl merrily said it would not be worth my while to join the cavalry, as I was a hopeless case. In the end, I decided that enough was enough, so I went to the paddock where all the hacks were grazing, and in my biggest voice yelled, 'I surrender; you have won, and I'll never try to mount you again.' I wouldn't have been surprised if George, along with the groom, Richard, and most of the staff burst out laughing. So from that day onwards I always went by gig or coach.

Over time I made a point to chat with all of the staff, along with the gardeners, the groom, and his wife and family. I got on well with the coachman, George Cotton, and was fond of his two boys who spent most of their day grooming horses or cleaning out the stalls. His youngest also had the extra job of cleaning out the chicken coop. The groom, Richard, had three daughters, all under ten and a two-year-old son. They were a bit of a handful for his wife but since the cottages were well away from the main house, the kids could run wild. I asked them all about school one day, but they looked at me dumbly, and I was told there was not one this far out besides they were much too expensive. That can't be right, I thought, and pocketed that bit of information away for later.

I found it hard getting used to having servants, and deep down I really didn't like to be waited on by servile people as it all seemed degrading to me. Even though I had gone out of my way to get to know the staff, I found there was still a big barrier between us. It seemed to be acceptable for them to have an 'us versus them' mentality. It was acknowledged as the norm in houses of quality and everyone wouldn't have it any other way. I didn't want to upset the apple cart, so I only pressed gently and took the time to ask small personal questions. Eventually they came to like and except me for myself. We didn't get to be mates or anything like that, as I couldn't break through their barriers, but we became acquaintances. The butler was very standoffish in the beginning until I took him aside one day and spoke to him. 'Look, Alfred, I might not be your cup of tea, but we are all in this together. I'm not a fly-by-night, and I know you have the family at heart, so just relax around me, mate, and we will get on fine. Remember, I'm here for the long haul.' Seeing confusion on his face, I had to repeat it again translating each word. In the end after thinking it through, Alfred came around especially after he realised I was not just after their money and the prestige that came with my position. Very protective of the family was our Alfred. But having people running around after me regularly made me feel uncomfortable. Still, I got the impression that all of the staff felt privileged to work for the earl, so I guess that eased the burden a bit.

One day I went down to the kitchen to thank the cook for the excellent meal that she had prepared the night before but I soon realised that this was unacceptable, and she was most unhappy at my intrusion. I didn't know where to put myself as here I was in the kitchen with an out-of-sorts cook, and her two kitchen maids looking up at me all wide-eyed as if I'd come from another planet. Then I noticed the cook had been making something that looked comparable to a sandwich but not quite. With my mouth starting to water at the thought of a sandwich, I forgot my dilemma and asked her, 'Have you heard of a salad sandwich or a Dagwood sandwich?' 'No, Mr Selkirk, not that I recall,' she replied. 'Would you mind if I showed you what I mean?' I requested. She was starting to fume but I could see that she was doing her best to calm down. I added, 'It will only take me a minute to put it together.

They are superb for a quick lunch and are excellent to eat.' She reluctantly asked, 'What do you need?' So I made her one of my favourites the best sandwich ever. I included most of what I could find in her cool store. There was ham, tomato, cheese, coleslaw, beetroot, and lots of mayonnaise between two thick pieces of homemade bread, yum. I cut it into quarters, and passed a wedge over to her. 'There you go, Martha, try that.' By the looks on their faces I picked that I must have been the only one who called her by her first name. 'There's a portion for each of the girls as well. Charlotte, and Elizabeth, take a bite and tell me what you think.' They looked at the cook whose face reminded me of a chook's pinched bum, but they each took one. 'Well, what do you think?' I asked. Martha's face started to return to normal and she said, 'Well, I must admit, Mr Selkirk, that is an excellent morsel; yes, very nice indeed. You call it a salad sandwich, is that correct?' 'Yep, that's right,' I acknowledged. 'Okay girls, what do you think?' I asked. They frowned. 'Did you enjoy it?' 'Yes sir, it is splendid,' Charlotte finally spoke.'That's fantastic. You could add that to your vast selection of incredible dishes you prepare down here. I do believe, Martha, you must be the best cook in England.' Well, that got her in the right mood. 'Anyway, I just came down to say thanks for the delicious meal last night. So I'll leave you to it.' I returned upstairs. Once I left the room they all started to talk at once, and I heard the girls say in a loud whisper, 'What a lovely gentleman and oh, so big and handsome.' Martha and I got on like a house on fire after that. Whenever some new foodie idea popped into my head, I would go down to visit her and ask her opinion. I could tell in the end that she looked forward to my visits.

Amelia was a beautiful kid, and we became great mates as we hit it off so well. I was fascinated when she spoke about her animal hospital. She started it when she first cared for injured animals way back when she was ten years old. Since then she collected books on animal welfare for her hospital library and set about educating herself on the subject. Now she was really knowledgeable about the nursing and healing of the sick animals that came under her care. I felt it admirable for a person to accomplish this by themself, and without a degree under her belt. Because what she didn't know about the subject wasn't worth writing home about. So I asked her about her going to university, but she just laughed. 'Sam, you know women are not allowed to attend.' What! Surely that's not true; I couldn't believe that. I was sure women had degrees.

I worked hard to get my parents-in-law onside with me, most probably sacrificing some of my pride in the process, but I had to make an effort both for myself and especially for Bella. So it wasn't long before I had made real progress with our relationship, and I had Margaret now calling me Sammy, and Bernard calling me Sam. Once he spoke about what he would like to do with the estate and even broached the subject of its expansion, but that was something he was still unsure about. I sat and quietly listened and didn't push in with my ideas. It was early days yet for me to put my ten cents worth in, so I just nodded my head and agreed with him. Bella had settled back quickly into manor life, but after what we had done and where we had been, I felt everything was a bit too cosy. She needed something more to keep her occupied, something to challenge her. That's when I offered a suggestion, 'You know, the kids around here don't go to school because there isn't one and they can hardly read and write. What say you set up a small school in the village for them, and I bet you could fill it with twenty kids at least. I reckon all it would need would be you and one other teacher. Maybe you could also teach first aid to the older kids and at a pinch I could even teach them a bit of music.' She looked up surprised, her eyes bright with anticipation. 'Sammy, why didn't I think of that? I know the perfect teacher who could help. She lives in Shrewsbury and I'm sure she would be interested; I know a music teacher also. That is a fantastic idea; I'll need a pencil and paper. I could utilise Amelia for nature studies and there are a few other adults I know whom I could ask for help. Sam, this is an excellent plan!' I smiled to myself because all she needed was just a bit of a shove in the right direction and she was off.

Autumn was in full swing with winter not that far off, when I announced to Bella, 'I've been here two months now and I've hardly set foot in the forest. I need to get out into the bush before winter sets in.' I had no idea how cold it got here, though I had been informed that there would be snow on the ground with plenty of frosts and rain. I wanted to get out there and have another look around, as recently there had been a poaching incident that had gone wrong. One of the tenant farmer's pigs had gotten quite close to the bush line and had ended up getting caught in a gin trap. The farmer found the pig not long after it happened, but not quick enough, as it had to be put down. He'd lost a valuable sow and was not a happy bloke at all. Oh, he sold the meat, but part of his good breeding stock was gone. The only consolation was that the poachers never got the pig. I had gone out afterwards, scouting around till I was certain that it was the same familiar shoe pattern I'd discovered just before arriving at the manor. The sods were still around, and I decided I needed to spend time in the bush, gathering clues as to where their hideaway was. Bella hadn't been feeling one hundred percent for nearly a week, and now she kept rushing off to the toilet each morning. I was worried about her, but she said she was fine. 'It's just a cold, and it will be best for me to keep warm so as to get rid of it,' she told me. 'Look, there's nothing to worry about, Sammy; you go out and see what you can find. But be careful.' As she wasn't coming, we decided that I would take Tobias with me instead. I decided to go the following Monday, as Margaret had insisted I attend church on the Sunday. Then because I intended going, poor old Bernard felt obliged to go as well. I didn't have to play the organ this time, but I had a feeling the minister would have liked to see Mrs Dell under the weather again, so I could be the one to play.

It seemed like ages since I had climbed Table Mountain in Cape Town, so I had a real urge to get out there and be one with nature again. I sat quietly and worked out my plan of action for the trip. I came to the conclusion that it would best to circle the estate first, keeping close to the border; I was keen to see if I could pick up tracks going into the bush. Then we would head in towards the Welsh part of the estate where the gold mine is situated. Bernard had advised me that there was a small mining community living on site, and there's a track from Brittermore we could use. It was built for the wagons to bring the gold out, and the workers used it when going into town. Apparently there were three houses built close to the mine for the married miners, a bunk room and kitchen for the single men, and a cottage for the manager and his wife. I'd like to stop there and have a yarn with them, just to get their opinion on the matter and find out if they had seen anyone coming in who didn't belong. If there had been a road around the circumference of the estate, it would have only taken a day or so to walk around it. But moving through the forest, with no roads or tracks would be a hard slog. I would say a good four-or-five-day tramp, as we would have to clear a pathway as we went along. I'd picked that following the animal tracks would be the easiest option. I didn't intend going too deep into the interior, and would leave that for another time. I'd gathered there were a couple of lakes and rivers up in the valleys that I'd be keen to explore later. On this trip though, as well as keeping my eyes out for signs of the poachers, it would give me a chance to get a real feel of the place. Hopefully young Toby would clue me up on both the wildlife and bird life we'd see. Yes, I was looking forward to it. Amelia had me sit down with her and her books, and gave me a general idea of what animals were in the area, but I wanted to see them for myself. The earl had even shown me his old map of the area, and confided that even he didn't know what was in there. 'You will be a bit like an explorer on this trip Sam, but you will not be going too far in. I would, though, still be interested in a head count of what deer and boar you come across. I've been wondering why I haven't seen many deer come down to the meadow on the south of the property lately; they used to drink and graze there all the time. Now I am curious why they are not. With luck you might be able to pick up on something. 'Oh and just in case, I want you to take my Sharps rifle with you, and Tobias can use the shotgun. If there are poachers out there, we don't know how aggressive they will be, so it will be better to be more safe than sorry.' I wasn't looking for trouble, but of course if it arrived I wouldn't back down. Still, I thought it'll be best to keep any mention of guns under my belt; Bella would be most unhappy with me if she knew. But really, my main focus was to enjoy the freedom of the forest once again.

CHAPTER TWENTY

Shadymore 1863

Toby looked a bit like his old man; both with brown hair. He was only five foot six, but big, with broad shoulders and large hands which were calloused by the manual labour he did. He was a reliable and serious young bloke. I thought he should be out chasing girls, but he had no time for that and besides where the heck were they? On this trip, to help avoid being spotted by our poachers, he wore browns and greens to better blend into the forest, and his mother had sewn different patches onto his clothes to help with the look. He knew his way around a gun and it showed in his work habits, so I felt he was a good man to have along. He had organised food for the five days with my assistance and mentioned that we could snare a rabbit or two to supplement the food supply. I emptied the contents of my pack out on the floor and went through what I had. My camouflage clothes were still in good order so I would wear them. But the stove was useless as I had no gas, and all the dehydrated food was finished. I marvelled at the words that sprang to mind and my knowing their meaning, but it left me a bit perplexed. I went over my pack for one last check in case I had missed something, and when I opened the flap at the very top, out fell a small, waterproof parcel. I was surprised, as I hadn't noticed it back on the ship beforehand. 'What the hell was that?' I wondered. I sat on the bed, unwrapped it and saw that it was a brooch. The piece was silver bore the depiction of a plump bird standing in front of a fern leaf. The word 'kiwi' jumped into my head. 'Where did the brooch come from?' I thought. It seemed a bit out of place considering the pack had been in a war zone. The jewellery clip had a safety pin on the back so you could attach it to your jacket. I was scratching my head as Bella came into the room. 'What do you have there, Sam?' she asked. 'It's a brooch. Here take a look, the bird on it is a kiwi.' She admired the clip, enthusing, 'Oh, how pretty. The bird is rather unusual looking with its big feet and long beak, but I like that fern leaf. It reminds me of the ferns I saw back in New Zealand.' 'Of course it does. That's a kiwi on a silver fern; it's a New Zealand icon Bella.' Once again there was that understanding how did I know this stuff? Bella looked confused at what I'd said, but was keen to tell me about a kiwi she had once seen. 'When I was in Auckland, I saw one. It had been kept as a pet. Apparently it is a flightless bird and native to New Zealand. I was told its nostrils were right at the very tip of its long beak, so it could smell out insects while rooting around in the undergrowth.' 'Well, I wonder how the heck I've come by it; someone must have given it to me.' I picked up the waterproof paper it was wrapped in and noticed a slip of paper with writing on it that I'd missed when first opening the package. I tried to smooth out the wrinkles. It wasn't easy to read as the ink had faded, but I managed to decipher the words: *To my big big brother, with love, Mary.* I stood looking at the piece of paper, not believing what I had read. I had trouble breathing and suddenly everything went quiet, like the world had just stopped. 'What?!' I wondered to myself. I was stunned and unable to think. 'What did it mean?' Then all of the emotion of months of not knowing finally hit me. I burst into tears and sobbed. Bella did her best to calm me. But I was beside myself with grief, I was so upset. She just held me gently, stroking my back until after taking in big gulps of air I finally started to calm myself down. Her lap was wet with my tears, and

I was unwilling to speak, so sat whimpering. Slowly I quietened, and when I stopped, I raised my head. With my eyes still red from crying, I looked into Bella's eyes. I could see her compassion for me, but best of all, the love that was in her heart. 'Sammy, this is wonderful news; you have a sister, Mary.' 'Yes, I must have, Bella, but I have no idea who she is, as I can't remember her. Not even a flicker, I don't even know what she looks like. This is much worse than taking a shot to the head. I now know I have a family, but I don't know who or where they are. They're lost to me.'

I was depressed for days after that, so we didn't leave on the tramp immediately. Bernard eventually intervened and came up to talk to me. 'Look, Sam, this is hard for you I know, but you cannot live your life on a question mark, you have to live for now. Come on, you have a wife and a position to uphold. Look, it is tough I know, but I have an idea that might help. Whilst you are away, why don't I mount your brooch and its note for you in its own casing, to keep it safe and protected. Then when you come home, it will be on display for you to look at whenever you wish. I'm sure your sister gave you this present with her love, and would not want you to be miserable because of it. Now it is time for you to go out, and as you say, blow the cobwebs away.' I looked up at him and asked, 'Since when have you been so knowledgeable about my state of mind?' He grinned, pleased he got a reaction from me and answered, 'Ever since you arrived on my doorstep.' Then with even more support he stated, 'I cannot have my son-in-law wandering around in a pickle; you need to be out there in the forest clearing your mind.' I sat thinking on what he'd said. 'You are right Bernard, I'm acting like a baby.' 'Not so, Sam; this has come as a big shock to you. The best thing I would suggest would be to try and make your sister proud.' He got up and patted me on the shoulder. 'The cart will be here tomorrow morning at dawn and will take you and Tobias to the edge of the property.'

'Thanks, Bernard,' I said gratefully, standing up and shaking his hand, 'you are a really good dad.' He looked pleased at what I'd said. 'Sam, I never thought I would ever have the honour to once again have a son. So I'm thrilled to be able to say thank you, for being a wonderful son to me. And to think my lovely Bella made this possible.' Then he embraced me. That took me by surprise my god he hugged me so I hugged him back. 'We must not let the ladies see us,' he said, 'what would they think?' Before he left, he whispered, 'I believe Bella wants to talk to you as well, before you come down.' He left the room shutting the door quietly.

About ten minutes later, Bella arrived looking as healthy as the day I first clapped eyes on her. It looked like she'd recovered from her tummy bug. I smiled at her and stated, 'You know, Bella, your dad is an excellent bloke and I'm so pleased we are all family now.' She came over and put her arms around my waist. 'Sammy I'm really glad that you like my family as much as they do you. I'm just so surprised that it has happened so quickly. I thought it would take months, I truly did, but here we are all one, big, happy family. Do you know Father told Mother that he would do anything for you? It, how do you say, 'blew me away.' My father has never said anything like that to anyone outside the family. So I believe that we have knocked down the final barrier. Now how are feeling? Come and sit down beside me, Sam,' she invited, patting the bed beside her. 'Much better Bella, very much better.' I told her what happened and she smiled. 'What a good idea to have the brooch mounted. Even if you never find her, you will know you are being thought about, and she will always be with you wherever you are. Are you comfy Sammy?"Yes, I am Bella, but why? 'Good,' she said. 'How do you feel about children, Sammy?' 'Oh, kids are great Bella. I enjoy being with Richard and Mary's children why would you ask?' 'Well, Sammy darling guess what? You will have one of your own in about seven months' time.' I sat and stared at her, as it didn't click to start with. Then slowly the smile spread across her face and she beamed at me. 'You're pregnant,' I yelled. 'You're going to have a baby?' I jumped up and danced around the room, then grabbed her, pulled her close and kissed her hard. After recovering from the kiss, she said with a smirk on her face, 'So you're happy then, Mr Selkirk?"Bloody hell, Bella, I'm over the moon. That must have been morning sickness you had?' 'Yes, it was; it didn't last long thank goodness, just a week. Luckily mother picked up on it, but when I think back, I have missed two moons, and my nipples are very tender when you kiss them, Sammy. You will have to do so ever so gently now. Anyway, I do like it gentle as you know.' 'Oh Bella, I'm overwhelmed; I never once thought about having children.' 'Well', she smiled, 'the number of times you were trying to make them then really surprises me.' 'But it was exquisite making this baby, Mr Selkirk, and let's hope it continues like that in the future. Now don't you worry about me; you to go out and find those poachers. While you are away, I have plenty to do with organising the school, and we can talk about that when you come back. Now let's go down and give my parents the news. Mother knows of course, but father and Amelia will be as over the moon as you are.'

As we headed down, she stopped and looked up at me. 'I will have to be checked by our family doctor for confirmation. Mother and I will arrange that sometime this week. The only thing I'm concerned about is Mother. I know what she will be like; she will want to wrap me in cotton wool. You would think I was the first woman in the world to fall pregnant. Women are much stronger than you think, so I don't need that. 'I remember while staying at Auckland I was asked to pop over to Newmarket, to a plot of land that a few Maori women were tending. One of the women was due to have her baby, but by the time I got there, she was already in labour. I managed to deliver her child, though she didn't need my help. I cleaned the baby and once the placenta was expelled, she wrapped it in a flax cover, then took it over to a tree and buried it. She then went back to work with the baby strapped to her back. As I cleaned up, I looked over at this woman and thought, 'And to think; they believe women are the weaker sex.' After meeting her, it made me realise that keeping active is good for both the mother and child. So that, my love, is what I am going to do. Though do not worry; I promise you I will not have our baby in the potato field.'

We walked hand in hand down the stairs to the lounge, an enormous room that could also be employed as a formal ballroom. All they had to do was roll up the carpet, push all the furniture to the sides, and you could get over a hundred people in there. At the very end of the room was a long, low door close to the floor. When opened, they could roll out a stage big enough to hold a five-piece band. Brilliant idea, I thought. Bella's parents sat reading and Amelia had just been given a cup of tea by the housemaid. She asked if we would like a drink, but we declined and off she toddled. When she left, I poured a cup of tea for us both. I was doing my best once again, to avoid the staff waiting on me constantly. I handed Bella a cup, then I announced, 'I would like to thank you all for your concern over the past few days. It's been a real shock for me to find I have a sister. Though I don't remember her, she must be out there somewhere so I'll never forget that I have a loving family elsewhere. I can't do anything about my memory returning or not; maybe one day with luck it might. But in the meantime, I will put it to the back of my mind, as I have this family now to care for.' 'Now we have some news to announce that I'm sure you'll all be happy with, as both Bella and myself are.' I paused for effect, 'You are shortly going to be grandparents and an aunt.' Well, that was a bomb blast. Amelia flew out of her seat as if she had a bee in her bonnet. She rushed over to her sister and hugged her with a wide grin on her face. 'This is fantastic news, absolutely incredible.' Her mother beamed from ear to ear and clapped her hands. 'Bella,' she cried, 'I knew it, I just knew it oh how lovely.' Then her father rushed over to embrace her, saying, 'Bella, my dearest girl I don't know what to say. There could not be any better news. Congratulations to the two of you.' Margaret came over to me and put her arms around my waist. She looked up at me and acknowledged, 'Sam, this is fantastic news. You have brought nothing but happiness to our family and I thank you for it. We seemed to have been doing nothing but mope around, and now every day is different. I do not know how we have survived without you. I believe we were just standing still, letting the world go by around us. Then Bella turned up with this unorthodox man who speaks so differently, yet is so loving, intelligent and refreshing. I cannot thank you enough for wanting to stay with us.' Well, you could have blown me away with a feather. It's amazing when you think of it, how in the space of a few months we have become closer than some families do in a lifetime. I felt a bit embarrassed, and said, 'For the first time, I seriously think of you both as my parents, my mum and dad, and I know I will never be lonely again. Bernard was there for me when I was down, and I will be there for you both and Amelia when needed. Together we are strong.' We all stood together, and I pulled them into a circle and all of our arms draped over each other. It felt familiar somehow, like a footy game. Footy! What the hell does that mean? Once again, here was another word that randomly popped into my head. Will this ever stop? Anyway, that aside, I felt positive, so I affirmed to them, 'We are a team, and tomorrow I'm going out to do something for the team.'

CHAPTER TWENTY-ONE

Shadymore 1863

'No need to get up, take another hour as it's a bit early yet,' I said after saying goodbye. I kissed her on the lips, and Bella, looking a little smug immediately snuggled down under the bedclothes. It was dawn, and the air was crisp and clear as we climbed aboard the cart ready to be taken to our drop-off point. The earl came out to wish us well and finished with, 'Don't forget, Sam, no heroics. Bella would be upset with me if anything should happen to either of you.' 'We'll be careful Bernard, you have my word,' I responded, and waved as we set off down the drive. The sun was just coming up, and the day looked to be a good one. The morning's coolness felt good on my skin, and I could feel a hint of winter around the corner as the days were slowly drawing in. I felt alive once again and hadn't felt like that in a while. Finding my sister's brooch had set me back, but now I had a fresh start and was looking forward to getting out into the bush. Toby had also looked forward to this tramp, as he too enjoyed exploring the wilderness of the forest. He confided in me that he had hardly been away from the estate in all of his life, except for half a dozen times into Shrewsbury. Once again my mind registered how that was unusual, but if that was the case, what did I believe was usual in this circumstance.

We headed out east and passed the village of Pulverbatch, then swung south for about thirty minutes. I glanced at my map and announced, 'This will do fine here, George.' He pulled up, we all jumped down, and George addressed his son, 'Take care Tobias, remember I want you back in one piece, so do not do anything stupid, son.' 'Father, this is a good opportunity for me,' Toby pleaded. 'You know I love these woods, and if I can help Mr Selkirk out, then I'll be of service to him and be doing what I love.' 'Yes I know, son, you have wanted to get out into the woods for a while now. Just be careful, that is all.' George gave his son a hug. 'Look, I promise that I will keep a good eye on him, he'll be okay, George,' Sam assured him. We all shook hands and shouldered our packs as we started towards the forest. I turned and called, 'See you in five days.' We intended to circle just inside the perimeter of the forest looking for spoor. When we nearly reached Sledgemore village, we would walk into the mine, then come out to Brittermore, and eventually return by the road back to the manor. 'You okay, Toby, ready for our adventure?' I asked. 'Yes, Mr Selkirk I am ready and willing.' He grinned from ear to ear. 'Okay, but from now on while we are out here, I want you to call me be my given name, Sam. You know this place better than me and all about the wildlife, so you are the teacher here, but remember, it's Sam. Okay?' Toby gave me a nervous smile. 'If you insist, Mr ahhh... Sam.' 'Good, then let's get on and see what we can find.' In single file we headed on into the bush. Toby was quiet and observant, and there was a confidence about him while in the bush, not usual I would have thought in such a young bloke. We slipped quietly through the forest for about a kilometre then started to slowly head south.

Once again I had the impression that I was more used to a thicker jungle-like bush than this, but I still hadn't a clue why. I wondered if the bush was more impenetrable in New Zealand. This forest wasn't actually what you would call bush with vines or suchlike. There were some ferns around, but there weren't any huge tree ferns with long, drooping fronds as I'd expected. This

167

was starting to be commonplace for me expecting something that wasn't there. Anyway that wasn't going to take away my enjoyment today. I breathed in the earthy, pungent smell coming off the bush, and took pleasure in the quietness and the freedom of the tramp. I felt at home. Before we had headed out, we had gone over a few ground rules if we ever needed to keep quiet. We would use hand signals to communicate, and Toby had a good thrush call to use to make contact from a distance. So we settled on using one bird call to stop, and two to come forward slowly and be alert. His bird call felt familiar to me so when I practised it, it only took me about five minutes to get it right; I guess I had a good ear for sound. I was beginning to find out new things about myself. The first day we tramped south nearly to the edge of the boundary and then turned west. We talked when we could, and Toby explained to me about the names and characteristics of any creature that came into view. He took his teaching role seriously and flung out the names of birds that I didn't recognise: lapwings, nightjars, dippers, warblers, and jays, explaining their different peculiarities. We watched the squirrels scampering around in the trees and Toby told me they were stockpiling their food for the winter. When we came across a hunting fox, we sat and watched him until he disappeared. Then I surveyed the ground where it'd been foraging and picked up his spoor, along with the peculiarities of the species. I knew in the future if I came across a fox print again, I would identify it as fox and not a dog print which was similar. Next, we examined goat prints and I explained some of my tracking skills to him; he was a quick learner. We found no deer or pig spoor around though, something Toby said was remarkable as there was quite a big herd of red and roe deer in the woods and a sounder of swine. I don't think I had heard of the name a sounder of swine before, the words in my head were a mob of pigs Most of the trees seemed unfamiliar to me also, so we went over their names and aspects.

There were alders and ashes, beeches and birches, pines, oaks and maples, and other types too many for me to remember right off, but Toby knew them all. Then he progressed to the smaller bushes. Toby gave me a good grounding on our first day out, and I could see he thoroughly enjoyed being my tutor. He certainly knew this forest. When we passed a crab apple and a wild cherry tree still showing a little fruit, we gathered them for later. By four p.m. we decided to call it quits as it was time to set up camp, have a meal and an early night. The sun dropped below the horizon around five thirty p.m. but out here in the bush it got darker much quicker. We gathered wood and started a fire. I put the billy on and when it came to the boil, threw in some tea leaves. We had packed enough food for four full days, we could stretch it out to five, but we might need to hunt on that last day. We didn't mind as this was what it was all about, to go along with the fun of being out in the bush. We sat and yarned and got to know each other better. He spoke hesitantly at first as he had never conversed with anyone from the manor before, except Amelia, and that was only when helping her not just sitting and talking informally. So for him this was something unique. Toby slowly got the confidence to talk to me about his aspirations and ideas about how he would like to work in the forest and care for its wildlife. He spoke about how he really loved being in the forest and working with nature, and how he also enjoyed helping out Lady Amelia in her hospital, caring for the sick animals. He explained he had even picked up quite a bit of knowledge from her on animal welfare and their healing, but he felt disadvantaged as he couldn't read or write properly and had had no formal schooling. He grinned at me and while waving his hands around confided,.'It is silly, really, to have these thoughts there are no jobs like this for the likes of me, but it is a beautiful dream.' I looked at him and thought, bugger this kid would be a real asset to the estate. Maybe I should have a yarn with Bernard

169

and see what we could do about it. It would be such a waste to not use his potential to let it slip through the earl's fingers. Afterwards, I told him my story and then it was time to say goodnight and we turned in. As we closed our eyes we could hear the sound of bats flying over our heads and the distant hooting of an owl. It had been a really enjoyable day.

I woke to a buzzard squawking his lungs out high above the treetops. 'What the hell is he on about?' I yawned and rubbed the sleep out of my eyes. 'I think he has very likely picked up some dead prey and telling every other bird to keep out of his area,' replied Toby. 'We'll go and have a look after brekkie,' I suggested. It wasn't long before we had packed up and got away. By then the buzzard had gone quiet, but we had taken a bearing where we had last seen him glide down, and after fifteen minutes we came out onto a small meadow. The buzzard had his head down feeding on a boar that looked quite large from this distance. We crept in as close as we could without frightening the bird, and I touched Toby on the arm and whispered. 'The pig's in a trap; will the buzzard attack us if we get too close?' 'No, if we make a bit of noise, he will just get out of the way.' So we jumped up and starting yelling at the buzzard. He lifted his head, grabbed another piece of juicy flesh, flapped his broad wings and cleared out of our way. He didn't go far though, just up into the largest nearby tree to sit and watch us while he chomped into the meat he took with him. We closed in on the boar. It startled me as I'd anticipated it to be a big solid pig with a large chest and shoulders and long hair covering its body. But this one was quite different than the picture I had in my head, as it was much smaller with an entirely different shape altogether. Yes I'd say a completely different breed, and one I'm not familiar with. This boar was a female by the looks of it, and it looked like it had been dead for about twelve hours. 'Shit,' cursed Toby. 'Sorry Sam, it is not right to swear, but this is terrible the boar tried to chew her own leg off, poor thing, what a way to die. These traps are a curse. Don't people know the damage they do?' I scouted around the area and came across three sets of footprints. Two of them were very much like the ones I had seen before all those weeks ago, but it looked as though they had changed their boots. The other fella was similar in height and weight. 'This sign, mate, is close to the one I saw before. Can you get anything out of these prints?' He looked down at the spoor then up at me, crestfallen. 'I'm sorry,' he screwed up his face, 'not really, Sam.' So we crouched down and I pointed out the evidence I could glean from the footprints with a stick. You could tell by the depth and length of the print, the weight and shoe size of the person who left it, also how they walked and their height. I continued with other clues I could pick out in their distinctive marks. Then we scouted around and found a small piece of material caught on a low tree branch, it looked like a piece of tartan. After an hour of instruction, I asked, 'Well, do you think you got any of that?' 'Yes, a small fragment but I think I will need you around more often to get it right.' He grinned. 'Yeah, mate, I suppose it would take time. In my case I haven't got the foggiest idea how long it took for me to pick it up. I just have all this information tucked away upstairs in the old noggin with no idea where it came from. Anyway, we will know these blokes if we run into them again. How far is the nearest village, do you know Toby?' 'I think it is Wentnor, about five miles as the crow flies,' he replied. 'Ok, I'm not saying they are from there, but they have to be from one of the neighbouring villages otherwise the meat will go off. Looking at their footprints, I'd say they left this trap about this time yesterday, so they could be back within the next twelve hours or so, probably earlier, to pick up the carcass. No doubt they would be aware that the rapiers and wildlife would feast on the meat if they left it too long. We'll have a scout around further out and see if we can pick up which direction they went. I'm pleased we brought that rope, mate. If we capture these buggers we will have something to tie them up with. We need our guns loaded with safety catches on, because we don't know who we are dealing with.'

I took the lead examining the ground going in a westerly direction. The spoor was easy to follow as the hunters were not trying to cover their tracks. Every twenty minutes or so we found another trap which we sprung and left behind, we will pick them up on the way back. We crossed over a small creek when I nodded to Toby. 'Notice anything different?' He scanned the ground and scratched his head, 'No I can't, Sam,' he answered. I crouched down and pointed. 'Look here, next to the creek, there's an unmistakable mark that's been left by the butt of a gun. So now we know they're armed, whether the weapon is for hunting or not, they have a gun, so we need to be even more careful.' Searching further, Toby said, 'I think this track has veered away from the village and it appears to be heading towards the gold mine.' 'Yeah, you're right, I think we now have a good idea where they're from, so what say we head back to the pig and wait till they return? You okay with that mate?' 'Yes of course, Sam.' So we turned and chatted as we headed back, and that's when Toby spoke of his concerns. 'I can understand people poaching if they are starving and homeless. I can accept that. But if this proves it's for greed and profit, then that's a terrible thing. It really worries me that these men might be some of the earl's own miners. The idea of anyone stealing from their own employer, especially the earl, it just does not sit right with me. It's the trust issue and what he expects from his workers. If this is true and he finds out, he will be mad fit to bust.' 'Tell me about the gold mine, Toby,' I broke in. 'Is it underground?' 'No Sam, it is an open cast and not big at all. They have never had a problem with the people there in the past, so I'm not sure what is going on.' I told him what I'd been thinking about. 'If it had been underground, they may have stored the meat down there, out of sight and out of mind so to speak. Anyway, we will know soon. When we get back we'll set up a hide and see what happens, and if they're not here by dark, I reckon we could each do two hours on watch and two off. Are you happy with that?' 'That is fine by me, Sam.'

Within a few hours we had settled into our hidey hole and had an excellent view of the pig. It was getting a lot of interest from a fox, a family of stoats and a few crows that were diving in and hopping around the carcass. But when a falcon swooped down, every animal scattered. I found this enthralling, and I felt really happy. It came to mind that this is what I love, being outside with nature. Toby schooled me some more on all the birds and animals as they came and went. 'Sam,' Toby whispered, 'look to your left and see that movement, that is a badger.' He came out of the woods for a second, and I could see his black-and-white snout and part of his grey body as he sat up sniffing the wind. He must have had a whiff of us as he scooted back into the bush. We didn't light a fire, as that would've been a tell-tale sign, and would've made them aware of our presence. So we sat on the ground and ate the food that the cook had made for us: bread, cheese, fruit and a big piece of cake. 'I'll have to give her a kiss for this cake, mate.' I grinned. 'It's wonderful.'

CHAPTER TWENTY-TWO

Shadymore

It was pleasant sitting in the bush listening to the sounds of the animals bickering over their meal when everything went quiet. The fox had crouched down in fear and then was up and away disappearing into the bush, and the birds on the ground had vanished. I tapped Toby on the shoulder aware something was up as I started to scan the surrounding forest. It wasn't long before it was obvious what had disturbed them. I could hear people moving through the forest without a care in the world sounding like a herd of elephants. Three men broke out of the bush onto the meadow, and I could immediately see it was who I'd been tracking. They were as I had picked, all short, and about the right weight. Each had big, bushy beards, and wore waistcoats with sacks over their shoulders. I noticed an old bloke who wore a tartan shirt and carried a heavy, old Bess rifle. 'Sam I recognise them. They are from the mine, alright,' Toby said in a hushed tone. I was aware that they all packed knives and looked as though they could use them, so I would have to keep my eye on them. I whispered to Toby, 'I want you to remain hidden as you are my insurance, but if you have to shoot, fire above their heads. The more noise the better. They're not leaving here of their own free will, I want those blokes.' He gave me the thumbs up as I disappeared into the bush. I was going to outflank them and come up from behind.

As they reached the kill I could hear them swearing at each other. 'The bloody birds and pissing fox have been at the meat, now we won't get as much for it,' one of them groused. 'Oh stop your bellyaching, just cut it up. We have done pretty well up until now, and this is just bad luck. We should have come back quicker, that's all,' the middle bloke insisted. By this time, I had sneaked up behind them. I slipped my rifle off my shoulder, quietly released the safety catch to off and stood up. 'What's going on here?' I murmured. Well, they just about pissed their pants. You should have seen the shocked look on their faces as they swung around to face me. The old boy came around with his rifle ready to fire, but I stepped inside his outstretched arms just as he was trying to bring the gun to bear. I put a lot of force into the jab of my rifle barrel into his guts and winded him badly. He dropped to his knees and gasped for breath. The youngest looking bloke, a scrawny little fella, came at me with his knife. I smacked him by swinging my rifle into the side of his head. He crashed to the ground, but that didn't stop him as he tried to slash at my leg. I bent down and managed to grab his wrist as he attempted a second slash. I yanked it up towards me, gave it a twist in the opposite direction and I heard the wrist bone snap. He squealed like a stuck pig and fell to the ground clutching his hand to his stomach. Two down. By now I was in a compromising position as I was coming up from breaking the bloke's wrist, when the third joker came running at me. As he was short he had to reach up, but he still managed to pummel my head with his fist. Although I was nearly at my full height, I didn't have time to move out of his way and he got me right on my cheekbone shit, he had a punch on him I was going to have a bloody, big, swollen eye after this lot. I shook my head to clear it in time to see him come in again. I went left and he followed me. I then came back on my right leg and threw a right-handed uppercut connecting on the point of his chin, and he went down for the count. By this time, the old boy had managed to sit up and was trying to train his gun on me, and that's when Toby let fly with the shotgun. It scared the shit out of me and by the look of terror on the face of the old bloke him as well. His dive for the dirt was comical. They were all lying on the ground when Toby came out of our hide, reloading the shotgun. As he got close, he growled, 'Anyone who so much as blinks will have a bellyful of shot.' He looked at the old boy. 'Ah hello, Mr Davis, how are you today? And this must William and John, no doubt.' 'Tobias, what the hell do you think you are doing?' snapped the old man. 'Well,' he smirked and replied, 'I'm stopping you from stealing, for a start. Tell me why are you poaching. You work at the mine, and I thought the earl paid you good wages.' The old bloke just clamped his mouth shut. 'Cat got your tongue?' Toby grinned. 'Get the rope, Toby, we will tie them up and take them over to the mine. Does the manager know what you're up to,' I demanded from Davis, 'or is this a more private affair that you're involved in?' He just scowled at me and still didn't answer. The middle bloke, John, was supporting his wrist and whimpering. William was still out cold. 'I want some answers from you, Davis, and if you don't tell me, I'm going to kneecap you. Do you know what that means? You won't ever walk again on that leg, and if you still won't talk, I'll kneecap every one of you I don't give a shit. You were found stealing, and I'm sure the sheriff in Shrewsbury will have a nice dirty cell for you to spend your days in. You can sit on your bunk all day long and stare at the door, because you won't be able to walk anywhere.' William moved his head and started to come round, then tried to sit up. We waited until he was upright, before Toby gave me the rope and I tied his arms behind him. Then I bound their dad, the old bloke. I didn't bother tying John as he looked a bit pale nursing his wrist. 'Let me take a look at it,' I said begrudgingly. One bone had broken through the skin, so I hunted around for two pieces of wood. 'This is going to hurt.' I grabbed his damaged hand then held the arm with my other hand and pulled. He screamed as the bone slipped back into place with a click. I put the wooden splints against his wrist and wrapped his scarf around it, making it tight, then used Williams scarf to make a sling for him. He had tears in his eyes after I had finished. 'Give him a drink, Toby, he's in shock. That whisky in my pack should do it.' He came back and handed it to me. I cracked open the bottle. 'Now take a big swig of that.' He took a swallow and coughed his guts up, but he kept down the second swig.

'Right, my friends, let's get down to business,' I started. 'Are you really that overworked and underpaid that you have to steal? Who will go first to tell us why you're stealing from the earl?' 'John muttered, 'He has more than us. Anyway, we are just taking what is not missed.' 'Doesn't he pay you a good wage working at the mine?' A thought hit me and I frowned. 'Have you blokes been stealing the gold as well, because if you have you could be put away for a very long time.' They both looked at their father. 'Oh, you stupid bastards,' I cursed. 'Tell me, do you live in one of his cottages?' Toby answered for them, 'Yes they do, Sam, and I think they are paid fifty pounds a year. I only receive ten, and I would love to collect their wages.' 'Do you really want to work in the mine, though, Toby?' I asked, surprised that he had an interest. 'Well,' he grinned while answering, 'maybe... they will need to hire more men after these three go for a long holiday.' 'What about your wife, mister?' I addressed Davis. 'She died three years ago,' Davis replied. 'Got any daughters?' 'Yes, one. She is fifteen and does the cooking for us. Not much good for anything else,' the old bloke spat, and I slapped him on the cheek. 'You are a prick. Do any of you own a boot with a pattern on it like a big zed?' I enquired. 'Yes I do, why? They are at home,' John answered. I grabbed William's feet and lifted them to see his heel was just starting to wear on the left boot. 'Your other boots have worn down, William,' I scoffed. 'How do you know that?' he frowned. 'You've been putting out gin traps all around the estate, I retorted. The last one killed a farmer's pig, and I saw the mark of your boot right next to the trap. I've also seen them all around the estate near set traps, over the last couple of months. Now tell me; I'm a bit curious. You can't have got them all, so where are the rest of the deer and pigs?' They just glared at me, saying nothing. I pointed my rifle and fired. The bullet went right between the old blokes legs. He jumped in the air; not a bad effort with his hands tied behind his back. 'Okay, mate, tell me the truth or the next one goes through your knee.' I deliberately loaded the gun, and I could see his lip start to quiver. Toby turned to me. 'Sam, don't muck around with him. Shoot William instead; he is the mean blighter, and he treats everyone with disdain, and is a bully to boot. Oh, let me do it, he won't be missed.' I looked at Toby in a new light as he turned the double-barrelled shotgun towards William. This kid was good. Well, the change in William's face was magical. 'No no, I'll tell you.' His father turned and snarled at him, 'Shut your trap, you little coward.' That didn't stop William, as all he could think of at this point in his life was self-preservation. 'We have run a fence line for three miles so the deer and boars cannot go down to the meadows. That keeps the animals nearer our way, and we can kill them away from prying eyes.' His father tried to headbutt his son then screamed at him, 'You little shit, I'll kill you.' William rolled out of his way. 'Where is this fencing, William?' roared Toby. 'About two miles inland from Sledgemoor. Some deer and boars escaped through, that is why we set our traps to catch the ones that got away,' William explained. 'How many in the gang? Are all the rest of you mining workers?' I snapped. 'There is no one else,' William replied, 'we keep it in the family.' 'Does your sister know?' i enquired. 'Yes she does, but she is so scared of Da

178

she would not say a word' 'Okay, I think I've heard enough. Right fellows, let's get you back to the mine.' We stood them up and tied them together with the rope around their waist. 'Toby, you walk behind them with me, and any mucking about; if they try anything at all, I want you to shoot both barrels at their legs. The way this shotgun spreads you will get them all with one shot. I will be by your side. They all know the way back to the mine so they can lead let's go.'

The roped group headed towards the gold mine and were mainly quiet. That is, except the old man who was fuming and continually disturbed our peace. 'What's all this to do with you anyway,' he growled at me. 'It has nothing to do with you; you're not even from around here.' 'Well you see, mate, you're wrong there. I'm part of the earl's household as he's my father-in-law, and when you steal from him, you steal from the family, and that makes me angry.' That shut him up for a bit, then he grumbled, 'You are not English.' 'I'm as English as you are,' I answered, 'I just talk differently. So why don't you belt up for a while.' When we got closer to the mine, a thought nagged at me so I asked, 'What about your daughter? Who will take care of her?' 'Who cares,' he snapped, 'she can earn more on her back anyway.' I whacked him with just a light tap of the barrel of my rifle I thought, but it made him fall and brought everyone to a halt. 'What a thoroughly miserable bastard you are,' I barked. 'Your daughter will be better off without you. No wonder your boys turned out bad.'

We arrived at the camp in the late afternoon when the miners were just finishing for the day. They saw our group and all stopped to stare, but we continued on to the manager's cottage. I saw a curtain flick aside when we arrived, then seconds later the manager came bounding out like a man possessed. 'What the bloody hell is going on here?' he demanded, looking at me. 'Why are my men tied up, and who the bloody hell are you?' he blustered. His eyes moved to Toby. 'Tobias, answer me, what is this all about?' Seeing him calm a little I stepped in. 'G'day, Mr Williams.' Toby had given me his name. 'I'm Sam Selkirk and these men of yours have been caught poaching the earl's wildlife.' 'What!' he spluttered, then scowled at his employees and addressed the old bloke, 'Is this right, Alun?' Davis kept his head down not answering. 'John, is this right?' Then William piped up, 'Yes sir, and I'm sorry.' The manager turned back to me looking crestfallen. 'What is your first name, Mr Williams?' I asked. 'Owen,' he replied. 'Have you a place we can put these blokes under lock and key for the night? Tomorrow I'll have to take them into Shrewsbury,' I said. 'Yes, we can put them into the food store for the evening,' Owen responded. 'Okay, Owen, they won't run off,' I stated. 'I intend to watch them all night. Just let me get this sorted out first, mate, and then we need to have a talk. There could be more going on here than meets the eye.' Owen disappeared inside and brought out the key to the food store, and we followed him to the wee hut. He opened up, entered, and cleared space for the three prisoners to sit. 'I'm disappointed with you, Alun, and to think I recommended you to the earl. You have not only got your family into hot water, but you have also given me a bad name as well.' I checked their bonds. 'It's not going to be comfortable for you blokes but that's your own fault; we'll see you in the morning. Remember Toby and I will be camped outside this door tonight so any funny business, any yelling or fighting, I'll come in and thump you,' I hissed, as Owen slammed the door. Owen observed, 'You will want some food, Mr... what did you say your name was?' 'Selkirk is the name, mate just call me Sam.' 'I'll have to tell the other men, Sam. I cannot keep this a secret as they have all seen Alun's family locked up. My god, this will slow down production, though I'm sure we will get some good men from the village or from Shrewsbury to take thier place. I just don't understand it,' he said, shaking his head. 'He pays us well, what the hell were those buggers thinking of?' 'It's greed, Owen, just greed, mate. I hear the old man has a daughter. Would she be home, do you think?' I asked. 'Yes, the poor little thing. I never liked the way her family treated her, but what are we going to do with her?' Owen questioned. Toby jumped in. 'We might have room at home, Mr Williams she can stay with us.' 'But will your parents accept that, Tobias?' 'Yes, I'm pretty sure they will. We cannot leave her to her own devices or she would be another one for the poor house, and I would not want my worst enemy put in there.' 'That's a good idea, but it will be up to her of course,' Owen stated. Turning to me, Owen asked, 'Did you want to say something, Sam?' 'Yes mate, we need to search the cottage these blokes lived in. I suspect you might find gold hidden there.' 'What,' Owen gasped, 'you are not telling me that they have been stealing the gold as well? You know we have a pretty good system in place to prevent that sort of thing.' 'Well, it's only a suspicion at the moment, but if it's as I expect and we find some in the cottage, your system may not be working that well,' Sam said.

We walked over to the Davis house and Owen informed me, 'The wee girl's name is Eliza, Sam.' I knocked on the door and it was opened by a just a slip of a girl. She was petite with blonde hair and had sorrowful, blue eyes. Her feet were bare, and her clothes were old and worn, but she had a lovely, wee figure. We explained what had happened and her eyes started to brim with tears. 'I don't know why the men in my family are such rogues,' she cried. 'All they have done is make my life miserable.' 'Eliza, I think they might have been flogging, er... I mean, stealing gold as well. Have you any idea about it?' She looked up at the three of us. 'It's not your fault girl,' Owen uttered. 'You are not responsible for the things your menfolk do.' 'You had better take a look under Da's bed, and you will find a loose board there. He didn't think I knew, but I have watched him, and it has been going on for over a year now, well, ever since we came up to the mine.' I could see Owen was really livid, and his face went a funny shade of purple. We pulled the bed out, and I removed the loose board, then stuck my hand in and felt around. There were four leather bags of gold which we bundled up then returned to the main room. 'Thank you Eliza, you did the right thing. Look, don't you worry now, you'll be alright. We will sort this out and be back tomorrow to talk.' We returned with the gold to the manager's house and he brought out his weights. Mumbling under his breath, he gingerly placed each bag on the scale. 'Two pounds each. My god!' he roared. 'There's eight pounds in weight. That is worth over 500 pounds sterling. The earl is going to have my guts for garters.' 'Don't worry, Owen, it's over now, and it'll be returned to its rightful owner. Look, mate, I'll make sure that he gets the facts right; you did your best, but the system will always fail if someone really wants to be dishonest. Can we get in touch with the earl now?' Sam retorted. 'Yes. I can send a cable to the manor,' Owen answered, unsure of where this was heading. 'Right, then I'll write it out and you can send it over for me,' Sam replied. 'Sam, look, I'm sorry, but I have never seen you before; just who are you?' Owen asked, exasperated. 'Oh, I'm sorry, Owen, I forgot to mention, I'm the earl's son-in-law. I married his daughter, Bella, a few months ago. ' 'Oh my giddy aunt, you must think I'm a real fool, sir?' 'Not at all, mate, we will just have to tighten up the process around here, and I'm sure you can do that. The earl would not have employed you if he thought you were a fool.' A cable was sent with all the information I'd gleaned, and thirty minutes later we got an answer.

Keep men locked up. Stop. Constabulary will be there in the morning. Stop. Write out your statement so they can take it with them. Stop. Tobias can do his verbally and you can sign it. Stop. Good work will be up to see you and Owen tomorrow. Stop. I want all the men there so no work tomorrow. Stop. On full pay. Stop. It was signed Shadymore.

Owen's wife left her cooking and announced, 'I have prepared dinner for you all. If you are going to spend the evening out guarding the hut, you will need to be fortified.' Owen stood up and introduced his wife, 'Sam, this is my wife, Olwen.' 'Lovely to meet you and, oh, I can smell something delicious coming from the kitchen,' I said. We sat all down at the table, 'You didn't need to do this, Olwen. We have food we could have used.' 'It is fine, sir, and my pleasure. You will want something hot. There wasn't much extra work involved, believe me; please eat your fill.'

Toby and I spent the evening under the stars taking turns to sleep. I was pleased that within a few days we had broken the poaching gang and recovered a fair amount of gold. A job, I thought well done, and a lot of the credit had to go to this young bloke next to me. I could not think of Tobias as a kid. He was a man; he thought like one, and he acted like one. Soon he tapped me on the shoulder. He was awake and it was my turn to have a snooze. It came to me as I drifted off to sleep; I needed to tell the earl that Toby is a real asset.

CHAPTER TWENTY-THREE

1863 Shadymore

The next morning the Davis gang, in need of the toilet, were beside themselves trying to attract our attention and woke us with all of their hollering from inside the hut. We escorted them off to the long drop and by the time this exercise was finished, Mrs Williams had delivered their breakfast. 'This will tide you over until you are in Shrewsbury,' she said gruffly, and handed them all bread and honey along with a cup of water. Before leaving she couldn't resist giving Alun a piece of her mind on how he had let his sons and daughter down, then walked away in a huff, growling, 'You will get your just desserts, Alun Davis.' Later in the manager's office I wrote out my statement and passed it to Owen. He went over it with Henry, a miner, who had literacy skills, and they both signed along the dotted line. Then I transcribed Toby's statement as he slowly dictated it to me. I read it back to him; he signed it with his mark and then the witnesses added their signatures.

With the paperwork out of the way, we went back outside to keep an eye on the Davis mob when we heard the snorting of horses coming up the track. The police, a sergeant, and two constables had arrived. They were quite big men I felt, larger than others I had seen around. They wore black uniforms with badges on their chests that read Shropshire Constabulary. The rest of the uniform included flat caps, brown belts, and nightsticks in their side belt. The sergeant took control immediately and with his nightstick out, shouted, 'All right you prisoners, into the wagon now.' He looked like he was only too happy to crown someone if they gave him the runaround. The wagon was a black, closed-in affair with an open cage door at the rear with steps leading up to it. Inside were seats on both sides and ankle bracelets attached to the floor. The constable made sure they were seated separately so there was no hanky-panky. 'I will be sitting right here watching you lot. There will be no talking on the journey, and if you so much as move without asking, you will get my baton around your ears. Do you all understand?' They nodded their heads.

Earlier, I had visited young Eliza at her cabin and explained what was happening with her family and mentioned that she couldn't remain here alone. I told her if she came along with us we may be able to find work for her. She agreed but was still upset at the sudden change in her circumstances. Now she sat not far from the wagon, crying. Toby went over to her and I heard him say tenderly, 'Everything will be alright, Eliza. These things have a way of turning out for the best; just have faith. My parents have plenty of room at home, and I'm sure they will be happy for you to come and stay with us. That is if you agree with it of course, and I'm sure the earl will give the go-ahead to finding you work on the estate. That is where I work, you know,' he said proudly, 'so you will know someone there.' He placed his arm around her shoulder, and I noticed she didn't try to pull away. I turned away with a grin on my face.

Once the prisoners were in the wagon, Mrs Williams came out with some tea and cake for the officers. 'Well thank you, Mrs Williams.' The sergeant smiled and said, 'This is most appreciated.' They sat and sipped their tea as I handed over our statements. 'Thank you, sir,' the sergeant acknowledged. 'It was brave of you to go up against a man with a gun, and I am so pleased we have

185

the offenders at last. We have spent a great deal of time doing our best to find them, but we never had a clue. Of course it is such a large area, and we only have a small staff. Their case will be held at the courthouse next week, by the way, but we will send you a cable to let you know the exact day. I will expect you there along with young Tobias Cotton.' He turned to Toby, who had come over with Eliza. 'You did well, lad. We are always looking for good men. If you decide to give up your job with the earl, pop in and see me,' he winked. Toby looked well pleased with the suggestion but said, 'Thank you, Sergeant, but I really like working for the earl. I'll give it some thought, though. Thanks for the offer.' The sergeant nodded then announced, 'Well it's time for us to leave; it will take us a few hours to get back to the station.' We all shook hands then the driver flicked the reins and off they plodded. The name, Black Maria, jumped into my head, whatever that meant, as we watched them heading down the road to disappear around the first bend. I walked over to the manager's cottage and sent another cable to the manor. I explained about Eliza and told them that Toby had made a suggestion for her to stay with the family. Then I asked if they would get the countess's permission for her stay. And as I knew George would be on his way up here with the earl, I said it would be appreciated if someone would give advance warning to George's wife about it all. I didn't want her to turn up and be told there was *no room at the inn*. She was disturbed enough as it was. Owen called out about an hour or so later to say I had received a reply. The cable confirmed that she would be welcome to stay with the Cotton family and that there was work available in the garden for her as well as various other bits and pieces. I told Toby the news. 'Oh, that's wonderful, Sam. I'll go round and let her know.' Eliza had returned to her cottage to pack her things and with the help of Olwen, had put together all of her brothers' and father's personal effects. 'Eliza,' Toby yelled, 'I have good news. You can stay with us, and there is work for you as well.' For the first time, she smiled, and Toby noticed how good-looking she was and couldn't help but return her smile.

Back at the manager's cottage I asked Owen what would happen to the Davis's things. 'Well, Sam, they won't need them where they are going, so I'll take them into the village and we will auction them off after the trial. I'm picking they'll be away for quite a while and the money collected will go to Eliza.' He stopped, scratched his head then continued, 'Do you realise this was a hanging offence ten years ago? But now Alun could go away for twenty years and the boys could get fifteen each I think, since gold was stolen. What stupid, greedy people they are. I'm pleased that young Eliza will be taken care of, though. You know, I think young Toby might fancy her, the way he follows her around like a lost puppy.' 'You noticed it as well?' I said with a grin. 'I reckon his old man might have to build a brick wall around her,' I joked. 'Old man Sam?' He queried. 'Sorry Owen,' his father. 'Oh right' he frowned 'yes, you are right, Sam. I think that a brick wall might be a good idea too.' Owen laughed. I was silent for a moment and said, 'At least the poor girl will see what it's like to live with decent people. I have a lot of time for George Cotton.' I looked up and speak of the devil, I saw George coming up the track in the gig at a fast pace with the earl beside him, waving his arms when he saw me. Everyone went quiet as the gig slid to a halt in a cloud of dust. The earl jumped down and grabbed my arms. 'Sam, my boy, are you and Toby alright? My god, look at your face. You really have a lovely black eye. What's Bella going to say?' 'I'm good as gold, sir,' I told him. I didn't want to use his first name amongst his workers. Good God, am I starting to follow the expected rules of etiquette? I had no idea, but I certainly didn't want to embarrass him. 'We are okay, one of the blokes got a lucky shot in, but other than what you see, we are fit and healthy.' George had alighted and went over to his son. Toby grinned at him, 'It was quite an exciting day, Father, but we got them. You know they had been stealing gold and poaching for over a year.' The earl turned towards Toby with a look of shock on his face. 'A year did you say, Tobias a whole year?' 'Yes, my lord.' 'Owen!' he bellowed, looking around for his manager. 'I'd like to see all the men in the kitchen right now, please.' He turned back towards me. 'Come, Sam, explain what actually happened.' I relayed our story, including Toby's part in it, and about Eliza informing us where the gold was hidden. He was thoughtful for a few minutes. 'Right. Don't you worry, I will deal with this. I want you both to find that fence line and take it down for me. I will see you and Tobias when you get back to the manor. Then I will consider an appropriate reward for both of these young people. So you toddle off with Tobias, and I'll see you in a few days.' He shook my hand, 'I'm thankful for what you have done for me, Sam. I really am.' He left and I went in search for some tools to help us dismantle the fence. When I returned I saw Toby talking to his father, and heard him tell his dad what had been arranged for Eliza, and that the countess, and his mother knew about it. Toby then called Eliza over and introduced her to his dad. 'Father, this is Eliza, and I'm sure she will be a big help to Mother.' Eliza curtsied. George looked at his son, then at the girl, and I could see that he had noticed that there was something between those two kids. He was uncertain at how to handle it, but looking at the wee lass, gave her a radiant smile anyway. 'I'm sure my wife, Sarah, would really appreciate your help, young lady,' George said to Eliza. Looking at my watch I realised it was time we got a move on, so I called out to Toby, 'We have another job to do, so we'd better get going.' Toby turned to his dad and asked if Eliza could go back to the manor with them. 'That's fine son if it has been arranged by the countess we will take her back. I'll talk to the earl.' Toby then picked up his backpack and murmured softly to Eliza, 'You will be alright now.

Father and the earl will look after you since Mr Selkirk and I need to get back to work. I'll see you when we get back.' We both waved as we headed back into the forest.

It was a bit of a slog, but eventually we found what we were looking for. The illegal fence was three miles long and it completely blocked the migration pathways of the deer, pig, and goats to the meadows below and water further on. That meant three miles of wire to cut and it wasn't just one strand, but three. As we worked along the line removing each section we found a couple of decomposing deer tangled in the barrier. Toby was furious and his eyes blazed, 'They deserve to hang for this alone the bastards!' he spat. And then remembered who he was with. 'I'm sorry, Sam, I realise it is no excuse to swear, and I apologise, but it makes me so mad.' 'I hate any sort of trapping myself, so I'm inclined to agree with you. That is unless there is a need to cull, and then it must be done in a humane way. As far as I'm concerned to trap and just leave these animals to starve to death is criminal.' It took us over two days to cut and coil the wire, and as there was too much for us to carry out, we stockpiled it safely to be picked up later. When the job was done we erected a hide, then hidden from view we waited to observe any deer movement. It wasn't until the next day that we saw the first sign of them. Mostly, we heard them rather than saw them, but they moved on down towards the meadows to feed in an intermittent stream for the rest of the day. We managed to count about twenty-three altogether, but there was only one stag amongst them. 'This is a worry as there are not many Scottish red deer there and only a handful of roe deer,' Toby informed me. 'I hope there are more up near the lake. That is about five miles east of us and they sometimes wander down this way.' I had kept my eye on the passing boar and had only picked up about half a dozen, and I was sure there was only one male in that lot also. That will need sorting quite quickly, otherwise they will soon disappear from this area altogether. We had

189

seen foxes, badgers, polecats, rabbits, and bird life in abundance in all the small grassy areas of the forest. But we didn't spot any snakes as it was getting a little bit too cold for them. I shivered when I saw the spoor of weasels and stoats though, I couldn't help but feel in the back of my mind, that they needed to be eradicated, but Toby said their numbers were quite normal and didn't need any attention.

The next morning we headed home with a reasonable amount of information to pass on to the earl. He had some work cut out ahead of him, and I'd say he would have to do an extensive breeding program, otherwise he could lose all the deer and pig population that he had left in this forest. Thankfully, we found the goat population was in a healthy state with over fifty head, and we saw a few rogue sheep. The exercise was a good starting point, but he would have ended up with nothing if Toby and I had not caught the Davis mob as they had just about wiped out most of his game. I'm picking the earl could surely lose a few more to the cold weather coming up as we had a winter to get through yet. 'A job well done I'd say, Toby. It was a pleasure to work with you, mate. When we pass the pub, I think a beer is in order, my shout.' He grinned and with pride said, 'I think I will enjoy that, Sam.' 'Yeah, so will I mate,' I said with anticipation. As the late afternoon sun was setting low in the sky we headed directly to the Sledgemore Tavern. I ordered a tankard each and we sat with the dying sun on our faces savouring the last warmth of the day, along with the fine taste of our ale. We arrived back at the manor after the sun had slipped below the horizon to a well-earned meal and a soft bed. I had missed Bella and had been looking forward to cuddling into her on a chilly night and to breathe in the smell of her hair. It concerned me that I had a lot of explaining to do about my face as my eye and cheek were still quite bruised. But I kept feeling that it was not as bad as it could've been, coming off a rugby field. What the hell was that all about, I thought as I drifted off to sleep.

CHAPTER TWENTY-FOUR

1863 Shrewsbury

I didn't see much of the family for the first couple of days. We spent most of the time just catching up in our room. We ate, bathed, and slept when we could. Well... sometimes we slept, but I had missed her and she me. You know, she could be quite a hussy when she wanted to be and quite honestly that suited me just fine. When we discussed her school project she bubbled over with enthusiasm and said she was eager to move on to the next stage. She had put in a lot of organising in the five days we were away and had already received a reply to a letter she wrote asking for assistance. It was from a friend who was only too willing to move out here and start up a school in the district. By return mail, Bella had proposed the wages of seventy-five pounds a year, and her friend was very happy with that. She planned that she would pay the salary out of her father's allowance. She then mentioned that she had already set aside one hundred pounds for school equipment, but what was really needed now was a school house that would suit everyone. According to her she had been waiting for her father to come back from the mine so she could talk it over with him, but he had stayed on in Brittermore village for the past few days hoping to solve the estate's security issues. Apparently he only just arrived back the same day as I did, bringing with him the young girl, Eliza. 'Sammy we really need a suitable school building, maybe one with a small bell tower,' Bella suggested. I thought it over for a minute. 'Well, Bella, if you want a new building, it will need to fit in with the rest of the village as the whole town is built in Georgian architecture, and it's what makes it so attractive.' She looked up startled by the idea. 'Yes of course; you are right, it would be a shame to upset the architecture.' Then her eyes lit up with enthusiasm as another idea came to her. 'What do you say we get an architect in to design one for us? If you like, we could even ask Angus McDonald he is qualified. Would he come down here and do our designs, I wonder? What do you believe? We have his parents' address somewhere. Should we ask him? He can even stay here as we have lots of room, and I'm sure Mother and Father would not mind if I ask them.' I grinned from ear to ear because her enthusiasm was infectious. 'That's an excellent idea, Bella, and it will be brilliant to catch up with him again.' Bella immediately bounced up and rushed out of the room hoping to get it organised before I could change my mind. I was starting to realise that when she had a bee in her bonnet she didn't muck around. So a cable was sent out and all we had to do was wait for an answer.

Bella had recently spoken with Amelia about her giving lessons in the school, and she had been only too keen to set aside some time for an animal health and well-being program. 'Amelia has been busy writing out some lessons on her subject already. I need to see that musician I know as well. He is a young man about my age, but he has been thinking of emigrating, so I'm not sure if he will be available. Anyway I will talk to him when I get into Shrewsbury next.' 'Well, I answered, 'I have to go to court in town next week with Toby, so maybe you could come as it will give you the chance to catch up with him. Whilst we are there it would be a golden opportunity for us to visit Selkirks and to take in my new designs for women's lingerie. I'm also looking forward to seeing how much Selkirks's first quarter brought in. Oh and we must open a joint account at the bank that we both can access whilst we are there.' I suddenly realised what I had said and chuckled. 'Thinking about it, it might be better if you show the underwear designs to his wife or maybe a female salesperson. I can just imagine how embarrassed everyone would be if I turn up and say, Hi folks I have these wonderful women's creations to show you, then display the unmentionables for all to see. Can you envision the heat emanating from everyone's faces? It would burn the shop down.' Bella giggled. 'You might be right there, so yes I had better be the one to do that.' 'Also,' I continued with even more eagerness, 'I have been thinking of introducing off the peg buying.' 'What on earth is that, Sam?' Bella asked. 'Well, when we go in to buy a jacket, most of the time it has to be made especially for you. But if they had some already made up and ready for sale in different sizes, using common chest measurements, it might only need a small adjustment to fit the customer perfectly. We could start off with, say, a fitting similar to your dad. Say the measurement around his chest is about thirty-eight inches, then for smaller men we could make a thirty-four-inch size, and then for bigger men, say, up to forty-two. Jackets would be made to fit those sizes, and any customer can come in off the street and buy right off the rack and even wear it that night as any necessary alterations could be done on the spot. The same goes with the trousers using waist and leg length measurements. The cuffs could be taken up whilst you wait. What do you think, Bella?' 'You know that is quite an idea, Sam. It's something that never occurred to me before, but it sounds like it could work. You are quite clever coming up with all these unusual concepts.' Delighted with her admiration, I carried on, 'We could even do it with women's clothing. What do you think about that?' 'What a thought! That sounds wonderful buying a dress off the peg now that would be something. I would be very happy to purchase that way. But sadly somehow I don't believe any of the privileged ladies would be interested, especially if it's the same style as what the common woman would be wearing. If it is not unique and the latest fashion from France, it would not be good enough. But luckily there are more lower and middle class people around than aristocracy. I think if the dress were well-made, I would buy a selection for everyday wear at least. But I must say, I'm a bit fussy when it comes to dressing for more formal occasions.' That surprised me and I said, 'Oh I didn't have that impression, Bella, but anyway if we can service the middle classes, then I think we could make a killing.' 'What was that you said, Sam?' she questioned, not comprehending my meaning. 'Oh sorry, Bella, I mean corner the market.' 'Ah yes, I understand that but "a killing," where did that come from?' she queried. 'I don't know, Bella, it just popped out like most things.' As we had a lot to accomplish in Shrewsbury next week, we talked over a plan to stay a few nights at Nursery Cottage and to return home after we had completed our tasks.

I finally met up with Bernard the next morning, sitting alone at the breakfast table. He told me it had taken him some time to work out a revised program for the mine security, but he thought he had a plan that would work. 'Bernard, have you thought of using a changing room?' I enquired. 'When the employees come to work, they undress in one room, walk through into another, and change into supplied overalls or coveralls, leaving their own clothes locked up in the shed. At the end of the day, they reverse the procedure. That way, they have no way of walking out with any gold. The overalls are removed that night, brushed down to clear away any gold clinging to the fabric, and then washed. A fresh pair would be available for the staff the next day.' A stunned look crossed his face as he replied, 'Sam, that is such a simple concept why didn't I think of it? What a brilliant suggestion. Where do you get these solutions from? I must cable Owen about your scheme first thing after breakfast. It just requires a couple of connecting changing rooms and clean coveralls for each day's work. So the costs won't be considerable either. As a bonus, it will be an opportunity to give some women in the village work, doing the laundry. That is marvellous my boy; just the ticket. 'Now then, after I've sent Owen's cable, I would like to see young Tobias in my office, and after that I want a word with Eliza. I need to ask Tobias if he would be interested in becoming a forest warden for me. Do you think he would be interested Sam? Maybe you could help school him up in your area of expertise.' Suddenly feeling excited for Toby, I replied, 'I can tell you now, Bernard, he will jump at the offer. It is right up his alley; you won't be disappointed with choosing him. The kid is a loyal young bloke and won't let you down. But I'm afraid he can't read or write, so he needs to have lessons.' 'Right, I will think on that one. But those words you said what were they 'kid' and 'bloke' and 'up the alley?' Hmm... let me get this right. A kid is a boy or a young man, a bloke is a male... but you have got me with that last one.' I laughed and said, 'Sorry, I forgot myself again. You are getting good at this though, Bernard. By "right up his alley," I mean it's a job he was born to do.' My meaning took him by surprise, 'Is it? Now that is really interesting,' he said, stopping a moment to give it some thought. 'Okay Sam. You know, I think you are right.' He smiled and said, 'You know, I am actually picking up your language after all these months.' 'And I yours,' I grinned. 'Yes, I am aware of that. I heard you call me 'sir' the other day at the mine; it surprised me a little,' Bernard conceded with a smile. 'Well, I am learning.' I changed the subject. 'There's another thing I've wanted to talk to you about whilst I have the chance. As we have to go into town next week for the court case, I've been wondering if you have an account with the Shrewsbury bank?' 'Yes I do, why?' 'Well, my quarterly cheque from Selkirks will be through and it needs to be transferred into the estate account.' 'Now are you sure you want that Sam? After all it is your money, and I wouldn't be offended if you changed your mind.' 'We have been over this before, Bernard; it's family money. Now I doubt it would amount to much to start with, but I need to feel I'm contributing.' 'Well, you are already doing that Sam, there is no doubt there, you and Tobias have saved the estate nearly five hundred pounds worth of gold after catching those criminals. If that is not contributing, I don't know what is.' 'Yeah, well, that's different. Now my next project I want to discuss is concerning the rifle.' 'Yes, well as it happens, I know the director of munitions quite well, and he has just returned to London after a trip over to the Continent. What say I arrange an appointment for you in London with him, maybe for the beginning of November? You can pop down with Bella and stay at the summer house whilst you are there; I'll sort that out for you. I will ask him to have a couple of his best gunsmiths available for you to consult with as well. I would suggest you take the train down, stay a week or two, and remember whilst you are there to have a good look around to see if anything is familiar.' 'Are you sure, Bernard? There is a lot of work to get done, and we do need to go over the wildlife situation.' 'Yes I am sure, Sam, besides it would be good for you and Bella to have time alone together. I'll give you the names of a couple of people whom you may want to meet up with whilst you are there. Mind you, I don't know how they will react to you. As you may have noticed, there are a lot of snobbish, titled people around quite unlike us I may add but saying that, there are some genuine ones out there who have a few brains in their head and are worth looking up. I will give you a few of their names, those who can be arranged quite easily that is, so you can introduce yourself. Now I am sure there will be no doubt that Bella will like the idea of doing a bit of shopping, so I will let you tell her the good news. Now, what is your best suggestion for Tobias's reading and writing lessons?' 'Oh I think Bella and her teacher would be the best option for that, Bernard; I'll have a yarn with her.' 'Oh yes a "talk" my, I'm impressed at how I am deciphering your language.' 'Yes, you are coming along quite nicely,' I noted, smiling warmly. 'Now, talking about Toby's tuition reminded me to tell you I believe it's important to reach for the highest potential of the people working for you, and if they all can at least have a fundamental education, it will turn out much better for the estate in the long run.' 'Do you think so, Sam? That seems a lot to ask; how would that work?' 'Yes I do, Bernard. Even learning to count makes a person think they are worthy. Take the housemaids. if they had literacy skills, they would be able to include other jobs in their day, like writing out the menus and recipes for the cook. This would free them up to concentrate better on their own job. You have good people working for you, Bernard, and they're worth the effort to educate. They are like a big family, and most of them generally like working for you. You know, young Toby was offered a job with the constabulary the other day, and he turned it down as he wanted to continue working for you. That's a feather in your cap, as I have overheard some terrible stories about some of the other big houses. So, Bernard, you are a good bloke and appreciated.' 'Now you are embarrassing me, Sam. Did you say he didn't take the job with the police?' 'No he didn't; he wants to be here and with what you are going to offer him he will be your man forever.' 'I have always tried to be aware and look out for the people that work for me Sam, and even now I am mindful of the need to put some thought into the hours a lot of them work.' Pleased with his answer, I told him another of my ideas. 'Well, you could always try a roster, Bernard. Split the day from five a.m. to two p.m, and from there, two p.m. till midnight, and see how that works for you. It would mean employing more people though, but you would always have a refreshed team each day. This would allow the ones who need to learn to read and write, to have time off to do that.' 'Where do you get all these ideas from, Sam; it is such a simple solution! We must go through the strengths and weaknesses of your suggestion later on today. In the meantime, let's get the young fellow up here and we can have a yarn.' He grinned, proud of himself. 'Well if you can say it, so can I. Bring him into the office, Sam, if you wouldn't mind. Thank you.'

Tobias was really nervous, as he very rarely had been up to the big house, let alone had a personal interview with the earl himself. I tried to reassure him, but it didn't help, so when we got to the office you could see the sweat on his forehead. Not wanting to muck about, considering the state he was in, I opened the door and announced that Tobias was here. The earl stood up and came round the table with a smile on his face and the welcoming words, 'Come in Tobias and take a seat over by the window. Would you like some tea?' 'No, my lord, thank you, though,' Tobias said timidly. 'Right, Tobias; I don't want to beat around the bush. I have a job offer for you. Would you like to become the official forest warden for the estate? It would mean leaving home and living close to the woods. I would expect you to keep an eye open for poachers. I don't want to ever again see what happened with the Davis people. 'Now before you give me your answer, let me go through a few particulars. First of all as part of your employment you would need to be able to read and write and to know your numbers, as I want good accounts of the population of the animals we have. I thought we would build you a cottage near the forest line, so you could keep a good eye on things. Sam has informed me that we will have to do a breeding program for both the red deer and the boar; this will be part of your job. I think a rise of salary to fifty pounds a year would be a good start, and when your education increases and you can read and write, I will increase it to sixty pounds. Now would you like a drink, and have time to sit and think about it?' Tobias just sat there like a dummy, with his mouth open and a silly grin on his face. He suddenly jolted out of his shock and shut his mouth tight. Then he started to babble, 'My Lord, of course I will take the job. I have never thought of anything else but the estate forest.' Then his mind shifted into overdrive. 'Once we get the deer population up, you could have a small cull. I'm sure we could get some gentlemen to pay for a hunting experience. The income alone for just one hunt would pay for my wages for a year, your Lordship.' 'Ah, Tobias, you have thought this through already.' 'Well, my lord, Sam... ah... Mr Selkirk and I were talking about it whilst we were up there in the forest. He suggested there was so much potential there, that both the upper and middle classes would pay just to come out here for the experience, even if it was to just walk around. The possibilities are endless.' 'Good, young Tobias; that's definitely an idea for the future. So since you are now my forest warden, your increased wages will commence from today, and starting from next week your education will begin. Mr Selkirk will liaise with Lady Isabella to arrange that.' Tobias rose and shook the earl's hand, saying, 'I'm your man, sir; I will not let you down,' He turned and walked to the door with a big grin spread over his face. 'Oh, Tobias will you send young Eliza in, please?' A very nervous young lady entered the office, curtsied, and then stood in front of the earl, wringing her hands. 'Eliza,' the earl announced, 'I want to thank you for your honesty, and for showing Mr Selkirk where to find the gold. It must have given you conflicting emotions as it was your men folk that were stealing. Now in recognition for your support to the estate and to me and of course if you are agreeable I would like to offer you work as undercook in the kitchen. That would mean fifteen pounds a year to start with. And as a bonus for your help in capturing the villains, I would like to offer you twenty pounds reward which will be put into a bank account in Shrewsbury under your name.' Her eyes were like saucers, but she soon found her tongue. 'Twenty pounds that's a fortune, my lord.'

'Well, young lady, you deserve it.' 'Yes, I would love to work with Mrs Williams; I have been helping her out over the last few days. She has so much knowledge, and I could learn a lot from her,' Eliza said with conviction. 'Can you read and write Eliza?' the earl asked. 'Only a little my lord.' 'Right, this will also be part of your duties, to learn, we will liaise with lady Isabella. Good then, it's settled. I'll see Mr Harrison the butler, and he will arrange everything.' 'Thank you, my lord, I won't let you down.' He rang a bell and the butler arrived. 'Alfred, would you take Miss Davis down to the kitchen? She is now the undercook. Mrs Williams knows all about it as I have spoken to her. Would you also ask Mrs Young to arrange accommodation for Miss Davis as well?' 'Yes, my lord.' They both left and the door closed quietly behind them.

The earl looked delighted and turned towards me, remarking, 'Well, Sam a good morning's work, don't you think? Now let's discuss the matter Tobias spoke about; do you think this would work?' 'Too right, Bernard. How many of your friends have never had the opportunity to shoot, because they just don't have the acreage that you have. Of course, it has to be in a controlled environment and only when we need to cull because of an overpopulation of deer or boar. Anyway, I'm picking they will pay the earth. You might, out of interest, put some feelers out.' 'Feelers, Sam that is a new one what does it mean?' 'A tentative enquiry, to find out if anyone is interested. I bet that anyone living in London or any of the larger cities would give their eye teeth for a chance to shoot your wildlife.' 'Eye teeth?' 'Ah... they'll be really keen.' 'Oh, I get that now,' he said with a grin. 'Well let's do that then.' 'Also, Bernard, I've another proposal tramping, hiking. That could be a lucrative wee business for a lot of city people as well. We could build a few accommodation houses for them to stay in whilst in the forest. I'm sure Tobias's expertise would come to the fore there, and I can help out as well. A lodge on the lake would be a great experience for a city dweller. Summertime or late spring would be ideal, so there is a bit of time to think things through.' 'Well my boy, you have given me a lot to think about this morning. Keep those ideas rolling; they are a goldmine,' Bernard said eagerly. Suddenly he was thoughtful. 'You know, Sam, I never really thought that much about the forest before.' He glanced out the window looking out over the estate, and then turned back. 'But now I can see it through your eyes. You are right; the potential might be quite lucrative for us all, and it really could be a nice little revenue-maker for the estate. We could employ more people and create wealth for us as well as the whole community.' 'Actually, Bernard, you just said not to stop the ideas, so I've another suggestion for you to add to your list to think on. I think your nursery should be closer to the estate. You will save time and money in the long run. Do you really need the cottage in town? What with trains now, how often have you personally used it? If it becomes necessary and you need to stay overnight, you can stay at the Shrewsbury Arms.' 'Well it hadn't crossed my mind; it just always has been that way. But you may have a point there, Sam. I'll give earnest thought to it.' He looked tired as he turned to the clock on the mantelpiece. 'Looks like it is time for luncheon, my boy,' he advised. We both turned and headed out the door to gather with the family in the dining room, ready for our dinner.

CHAPTER TWENTY-FIVE

1863 Shrewsbury

Our week had flown by before we knew it, and it wasn't long before we headed into Shrewsbury for the court case. Bella and I sat in the back of the coach going through the plans for the day while Tobias drove. The courthouse was an imposing, modern Victorian building with marble columns. As we walked up the stairs to the main courtroom, Bella left us to call in to Selkirks to discuss the designs we had agreed on with the proprietor's wife. She had plenty of time as I had the impression that we would be in court for quite a while. As we entered the courtroom, I had somehow expected to see a quiet hum of lawyers circulating and a crowd of witnesses patiently waiting to be called. Instead I saw utter chaos and the noise was inconceivable. People were up standing and arguing with each other across the room, each doing their best to be heard above the din and showing no respect whatsoever to the court. Soon the judge walked into the bedlam, stepped up onto his platform and sat down in his high-backed chair. But the crowd ignored him and continued. A look of distaste crossed his face and he slammed his gavel on the plate with a big, dull thud. Sadly, that wasn't enough so he too had to resort to shouting at the top of his voice. 'Everyone be quiet!' Slowly, the courtroom drifted into silence. When all was quiet, he boomed, 'Bring up the prisoners.' Alun and his boys had to be dragged up the stairs from the holding cells below the courtroom. Finally they came before the judge, and looked exhausted. I noticed John with his arm in a sling was still pale-looking. William kept his head low, but I could see he had a bruise surrounding his mouth where I had hit him, and their old man was doing his usual mouthing away at anyone who cared to listen to him. The judge glared at Alun and commanded, 'Shut up or I will go harder on you, you grubby, little man.' Looking down on the three blokes he continued, 'You are all accused of gold robbery and poaching. How do you plead?' 'Not guilty,' Alun blurted out. 'What? What's that? Not guilty, you dirty, stinky, little man. That's absolute rubbish,' the judge shouted back at him. He turned back to the court. 'Mr Selkirk, where are you?' I raised my hand. 'Ah Mr Selkirk, my good man. Tell the jurors your evidence.' So I relayed to the court what had happened, then Toby followed suit. 'Splendid, thank you, gentlemen,' he replied after we had had our say. 'Defence council have you anything to say?' 'All I ask is leniency for the sons Your Honour' he pleaded. The Judge then turned to the jurors, 'You have heard the evidence guilty or not guilty.' The twelve men huddled together for about a minute then one popped out of the pack, and stated, 'Guilty, Your Honour.' 'So be it.' He scowled at the accused, 'The three of you have been found guilty on all charges by your peers. Though indeed, you should all be hung; luckily I'm feeling lenient today. Alun Davis, you are hereby sentenced to thirty years hard labour. You will be sent to HM Prison in Skye and be banished from this Shire for life. If you ever come back, you will be hung. Remove him from the court, officer.' Alun swore and cursed as they dragged him down the stairs. The judge's icy glare swung around to fix on both William and John. 'You two are incarcerated for twenty years hard labour and also banned from this Shire for life. William Davis, you will go to HM Prison in Bradford, Yorkshire, and John Davis to HM Prison on the Isle of Wight. Take them down, officer.' He banged his gavel down, 'Next case,' he bawled. I was dumbfounded as I had expected more, and it was all over in fifteen minutes. 'Thank you, Mr Selkirk, Mr Cotton' the judge called as Toby and I left the court to catch up with Bella. I walked away quite bewildered as this didn't seem right to me; they didn't even get a chance to defend themselves. But Toby assured me that his father had told him that this was the way it usually went.

Bella made real progress at Selkirks. The saleslady in charge had written down all of the particulars Bella had told her about my ideas for 'off-the-rack clothing' and said she would send it, and my designs, on to Aharon Hyman in Scotland. Before she left, Bella was given an envelope addressed to me from Aharon himself. When she passed it to me I opened it immediately. With a letter it included a cheque for 150 pounds. I was overwhelmed and proudly showed it to Bella. 'That's wonderful, Sammy. Your designs have certainly taken off, and she smiled with delight. 'I guess our next port of call will be the bank. 'The first day I had spoken to Bernard after returning from removing the fencing, he had taken me aside and told me he would increase Bella's allowance to include me, and he had bumped it up to fifteen hundred pounds a year. I tried to argue with him, but he was adamant, 'Look Sam, don't you realise you are a significant member of our family now, and it is only right that you should be included. The money is there for both of you and it's even more crucial now, considering our first grandchild is on the way. This was an important decision for both Margaret and I, and we sincerely believe that it's right. Besides all that, you have just saved us hundreds of pounds. Then there is the percentage coming in from Selkirks and we haven't even seen the outcome of your rifle, yet. I think that, quite frankly, will be worth thousands, so you deserve it.' As we walked up the steps and into the bank, we heard a door open behind the tellers and watched the manager lose no time speeding across the bank towards us.

'Lady Isabella,' he gasped, 'what a pleasure to see you again, and you, sir you must be Mr Selkirk.' That took be back a bit because how the heck did he know my name? I was buggered if I could figure that one out. He urged us into his office and waited until we sat down, before he seated himself behind his desk. Then asked how he could help. Bella answered, 'I want my account name changed to reflect my married name and then changed over to a joint account. Also we have this cheque to put into the estate account.' It was normal, I had recently found out, that men had complete control over their wives' accounts and with the gentry it was even more so, but I didn't want that. I had expected to see his surprise at her suggestion, but he was a professional and didn't bat an eyelid. Joint accounts had been around since 1860. It amazed me what money can do as he made it such a simple procedure, our joint account was soon set up, the money from Selkirks deposited into the estate account and we were out of there in ten minutes.

'Right. Lunch?' I remarked rubbing my hands together. We walked up to the Shrewsbury Arms looking forward to a good old-fashioned pub meal. Toby said he would go somewhere else, but I insisted he should lunch with us. It was a good meal, and Tobias talked a lot about his lessons and his teacher, Gwen, who was a bright, young woman of thirty. At the moment she used the church as the schoolroom and most of the children had already enrolled. She had also begun lessons for the adults as well, of which Toby was a student. Apparently she had a way about her that brought out the best in her pupils. I mentioned to Toby that my friend, Angus McDonald, would be here next week to start the designs for the building of the new school house, and that I was looking forward to catching up with him. I added that we had decided to ask Angus to design Toby's own small house up near the bush line and close to the main forest pathway. We spoke then about what was ahead of us as the days were starting to close in towards November, and Toby had a few ideas for us to consider. We had planned to head down to London at the beginning of November for our appointment with Lord Percival Winter, who was a director of the Enfield munitions factory, and a good friend of Bernard's. I was quite looking forward to meeting him to confirm if my rifle had a good chance of becoming viable.

Conscious of the approaching winter, I took every opportunity I had to go out with Toby to check out the wildlife. I still had this pull for the bush and it was something that was always with me. We now had a much better idea about what was happening in the forest and found that there were more deer than we had originally thought plus a few more wild boar. That brightened our day. I also took the chance to tramp up to the lake to check it out and to scout around for a suitable place to build an accommodation lodge. I had in mind to build something suitable for tramping groups, or as I was told to call them, rambling ventures, but there were other options I wanted to go over with Angus when he arrived. It looked like we had enough work for him to stay until spring.

'After lunch I think I'll try and catch up with John,' Bella stated. 'He is the musician I told you about, but the trouble is I'm not sure where he will be. His father is a woolsorter and works for himself along with his partner in the centre of town, so he will know. His woolsorting sheds are that big brick affair in the square. Let's pop down there together after we finish our lunch. We may be able to find him and entice him into becoming our music teacher at the school, even if it's only for one day a week.' We caught up with John's father, Isaac, just as he was heading off for a late lunch. 'He's at home, Lady Isabella,' Isaac declared. 'I'm heading back that way now, and you are both very welcome to join us; it will be no trouble whatsoever.' We all piled into our coach, and Tobias drove us to Isaac's house in New Street. As the three of us walked into the house, we saw a slightly built man in the kitchen just finishing his meal. Isaac ushered us into the reading room and called out, 'John, Lady Isabella and her husband are here to see you when you have finished.' He turned to us and spoke, 'Please sit down, and my son will be with you soon. While I have a moment with you, Lady Isabella, would you be good enough to ask the earl to call on me the next time he is in the town? I would like to discuss the quality of some of his merino wool clippings and to ask him if he is willing to sell Nursery Cottage. I noticed over the last few years, he is not using it as much as he used to and wondered if he is likely to sell. I'm willing to give him a fair price for it as I would like something bigger, and that house would suit me nicely.' 'Of course, Mr Clough, I will pass that on to him. You know that is most fortuitous because not that long ago, Sam spoke to him about letting it go as it would be more convenient to move the nursery out closer to the estate. That would free up the house, and it might even turn out for the best for everyone. But of course, it is my father's decision.' She smiled, curbing her enthusiasm. Isaac rose when John entered the room. 'Well, I must have my luncheon.' He shook my hand, 'It has been a pleasure to meet you, Mr Selkirk. Lady Isabella, it has been such a delight to catch up with you again. If you will excuse me.' He left the room.

Bella acknowledged the young man and said, 'John, this is my husband, Samuel Selkirk, and he is a musician just like you.' As John looked up at me, and I had to smile. We might both be musicians, but that's where the similarity ended, because in looks we couldn't have been more opposite. He only stood about five foot two and had a small stature to match. His eyes were blue, he had high cheekbones, and light brown hair, but when he shook my hand, he had a firm grip for such a slightly built bloke. 'You play then, Mr Selkirk?' John asked. 'Yes, I do, John: piano, harmonica, mandolin, and guitar.' 'Excellent! Music is truly an international language,' he smiled, then added, 'how can I help?' Bella went into her explanation about her school and how she wanted to have a music teacher for it, even if it was once a week. 'I'm not sure, my lady,' John replied. 'You see I am now betrothed to Elinor Smith, and we are to be married in the spring. The church has recently approached me and asked if we would like to join their group of Anglicans going out to New Zealand. They have even offered us ninety acres in the north of the country for nine pounds and a house section in Auckland, free of charge, so all I have to find for us to emigrate is another ten pounds. The offer is so attractive, and it's all we can think about. My primary occupation is engineering and they are needed out there. So I might have to decline your offer, and I'm truly sorry to let you down.' 'Not at all, John. It is a wonderful opportunity, and we are thrilled for you, but what are your parents' opinions about you both heading so far away?' Bella enquired. 'Oh, my parents, and my sister, Margaret, are not happy not happy at all. It does not help that we are such a small family. We have had much the same response from Elinor's family. But I have this wanderlust within me; it has been with me all my life, and it is time to do something about it. I heard that you been out there yourselves, what's it like?' John asked her. Bella looked at him. 'Well, it is a raw, young country and you would be stepping back in time as you will have to live in fairly basic conditions. But John, you do know there is a war going on out there at the moment and quite honestly it could go on for quite some time. However, if you are prepared for that, I'm sure you and your wife will do very well as the country needs young people for it to grow. One bit of advice though: if at all possible, learn the native language as it will go a long way to making your life there, easier.' He turned to me, 'Do you have any guidance for me, Mr Selkirk?' John queried. 'John, mate, I'm sorry. I lost my memory out there. I have only a vague recollection of bush. So if you are going to farm you are going to have to do a lot of clearing before you can bring a farm online, but I do wish you the very best.'

We turned to leave and he added, 'I'll try and do a couple of lessons for you before we go, if I can. 'As the coach pulled away from the house, Bella sat forward, and uttered, 'You know, Sammy, New Zealand always seems to come up at every turn, and I was taken aback when you mentioned the bush. Has something triggered for you?' 'Oh no, no, not really, Bella. I just have this vague feeling that there's bush everywhere.' 'Well I'll admit there is a lot of it over there and it's like a jungle with the vines. Luckily there is nothing in the forest that will eat you,' she teased. But I was distracted and suddenly felt sad, so I spoke almost to myself, 'Yes, I seem to be drawn to New Zealand so I must have spent a lot of time there. I wonder if that's where I was born.' 'Well, Sam,' Bella said, doing her best to lift the mood, 'if you had been, wouldn't someone over there be looking desperately for you and there has not been one enquiry at all.' 'Yes it's strange. Maybe all of my family have gone, even my sister, Mary. I'm sure she would have tried to find me. Oh well, Bella, let's change the subject as we seem to always be going around in circles, and let's face it, your folks and Amy are my family now.'

We continued on to Nursery Cottage and spent the rest of our time there enjoying having the place to ourselves. Toby slept in the servants quarters and used his time looking over the tree nursery. The next day after a late breakfast when we were about to head back to the estate, we received a cable explaining Angus would arrive today from Glasgow on the evening train. 'Great news.' I grinned. 'We will wait, and take him home with us, it will save us a second trip.' Just before eight that evening, the train clanked into the Shrewsbury station with sparks and smoke rising out of the funnel and steam spilling all over the platform. The carriages slowly slipped by until a final clunk as she pulled to a stop. We desperately looked up and down the platform hoping to spot him but it wasn't easy in the crowd, then we heard him call, 'Och mon, over here.' The

Scotsman waltzed down the platform in his tartans with a bag over his shoulder, supported by his partially amputated arm which was all he had left after the skirmish in Auckland. In his good hand he carried a big carpetbag. He dropped his bags, grabbed Bella and swung her around, kissing her on both sides of her cheeks. Then it was my turn. He seized me and gave me a generous hug. 'It's so good to see you both, it really is.' His cheeks were flushed red and he spoke fifty to the dozen. We collected his gear and he walked beside us feverishly waving his arms about. I don't remember ever having seen him quite like that before as he was always such a quiet bloke, but it looked as though he had come out of his shell entirely. Back in the coach I told him that Bella was pregnant. 'Oh my goodness, Bella, you should have said. I would not have swung you around like that.' 'Don't you worry, Angus. I was perfectly all right, and besides it gave the populace something to talk about.'

The next morning we left the cottage early. As we all climbed aboard the coach I took the chance to introduce him properly to Tobias. Then I went on to explain that he was the ranger for the estate, and once he had done the designs for the school, we would like him to design a house for Tobias. 'We wanted it to blend in with the surrounding forest,' I explained. 'That sounds incredible.' Angus grinned from ear to ear. 'Anything else I can do while I'm here as I've no other work planned at the moment. I'm awaiting a reply from a firm in Glasgow, so right now I'm all yours.' 'Well,' I replied, 'we would like a design of an accommodation lodge up on the lakeshore. Maybe even a few accommodation houses around the forest nestled into the bush where walkers can overnight in comfort. I have a few more ideas for you as well, but I'll let you settle in first. I'll let Bella do the honours of introducing you to the family. You could be here for a while, mate.' I laughed. Once we arrived at the manor the introductions were soon out of the way, and then everyone felt more comfortable. Angus quickly relaxed and talked eagerly to Margaret until Amy walked in. She had been out the back fixing some bird's wing so she didn't join us immediately. 'I need a bigger place Father, I'm too cramped in my little room outside.' She wiped her hands on a piece of towelling, looked up, and then stopped dead when she saw we had a visitor. 'Oh,' she whispered, 'you must be Angus.' I looked at my mate. He was entranced as he looked at her, and I could see he was tongue-tied and unable to speak. I leant over towards him and whispered, 'Shut your mouth, mate, you are drooling.' That jolted him out of it, and he swallowed and stood up. 'Er, um, Lady Amelia.' She came over and looked up at him with her big blue eyes and smiled broadly. 'Any friend of Sam's is a friend of mine.' He tried to smile back but he was still in shock. 'Umm, it's a pleasure to meet you,' he stammered. Bernard broke up the embarrassment with, 'We will have Tiffin in the drawing room. Now come along it is warmer in there.' So we all turned and followed the earl.

Amy and Angus hit it off right from the first moment, to the point when you saw one, you would see the other. They went everywhere together. I was surprised my in-laws just accepted it like that it was most unusual. I wondered if Bella marrying me had made a difference to the way they thought now. Angus was not from a titled family, but he was educated and his family were well-to-do. He was a workaholic though, and in no time at all had produced drawings for the school house. Then we had an expedition up into the forest to look at the site I had in mind for Toby's place. Angus was keen to get an impression of how I wanted it to look, and both Bella and Amy accompanied us. Toby and a couple of other men joined us to survey the area and to prepare for the trail clearing. They were particular and were keen to make things look just right in Victorian eyes. A few weeks later Angus had finished the preliminary drawings for Tobias's three-roomed house along with the lake lodge, plus small comfortable huts we could use for the forest rambles. He had even designed an accommodation block for single men, adjacent to the pub in the village for the tenant farmer's labourers something we had discussed at length. Lastly, we turned our attention to upgrading the village's cottages. Everything was coming along smoothly and there was talk of marriage in the air as Tobias was courting young Eliza. Apparently everyone seemed to think it was the perfect age to marry, so it was funny that I felt that they looked too young. But I had noticed that the majority of people didn't seem to live to a very old age, maybe that is why they wed early. Still... I wasn't comfortable with it.

CHAPTER TWENTY-SIX

1863 Shrewsbury

It was the beginning of November when Bernard mentioned that his friend, Lord Winter, had arrived home from Europe and would like to have a look at my rifle. If I was able to get down to London, I could stay at the earl's London residence in Ladbroke Square, and then the lord could make arrangements to visit. Bernard had gone on to say that Lord Winter was concerned that I didn't walk around London or travel by train to Enfield with such a rifle. The impression he had derived from Bernard had told him it was revolutionary. So it was arranged for Bella and I to take the train down to London and spend a week or two there with the hope that Lord Winter would be impressed with the weapon.

As it was becoming quiet on the estate at this time of the year, we both agreed it was a good opportunity to have some alone time together again before Christmas. Besides we could do a bit of Christmas shopping for the family while we were there. Bella was nearly four months pregnant now and everything was advancing along as it should, but to me she seemed to be a bit bigger than I would have thought. However she was as healthy as a horse and the pregnancy was not holding her back. Now that November was here it was beginning to get quite cold, and frost covered the ground most mornings. We even had a couple of light snowfalls up on the hills near the lake. We had planned to start the building of the school house about the middle of the month and Bernard wanted to have Tobias's house up and liveable about a couple of weeks after that before the winter really set in. Angus liked to keep an eye on the builders when they were working in case there were any problems, so it looked as though he was going to be around for a while yet. The site for the lodge on the lake had been cleared but any building work wouldn't start until spring.

Bella and I were looking forward to the trip to London. Bernard had arranged for the London housekeeper to prepare, then run the summer house for us, and we were to take sixteen-year-old Eliza, along as the cook. Apparently she was coming along nicely with her new cooking skills under the cook, Martha's watchful eye. We also heard she was progressing well with her literacy lessons and was now reading anything she could get her hands on. But one of the cleverest things we discovered about Eliza was that she had a natural talent as an artist. It seemed that her talent was unlimited, and she could draw and paint anything and everything. It was hard to believe how much she had transformed from the little girl we found up at the gold mine, and I doubted she would be a cook for long. I felt she was going to be quite an asset to the estate in the future. Now that Tobias was courting her, she was a happy, young woman, and also very excited to be going to London. Shrewsbury was the furthest she had ever been in her life. The day of travel had finally arrived, and Eliza packed all the food to be taken with us for our first week in London. She sat up front with Tobias so they could say their goodbyes, both bundled up from the cold as he drove to the station. We sat inside which was a little warmer and waved madly to passers-by as we rode into Shrewsbury. On the train to London, Eliza sat in our compartment which raised a few eyebrows, but it didn't concern us. Besides it was a chance for her to do some initial drawings for her painting. She had pushed us both, to do our portrait, something she had wanted to do for a while now, and we had finally agreed. It was a long, uneventful trip, and five hours later we arrived at Waterloo Station in London tired. We hired a buggy, loaded it with all our gear and set off for Ladbroke Square. The house, a flash, three-storied terrace building was warm and cosy as we entered, and the housekeeper, Mrs Forest, ushered us into the drawing room. Eliza then went straight to the kitchen to sort out her provisions. We settled in, had a small cold meal and then had an early night. A cable was sent to Lord Winter the next day letting him know we had arrived, and his reply came back immediately. He would be down to see us tomorrow at eleven a.m., and he planned to bring two of his best gunsmiths. We had a whole day to fill in so we spent the time wandering around Kensington Gardens. Both of us found it pleasant after being confined on the train the day before. Sadly, I had hoped since the gardens were well known, that a fleeting memory might strike me as I walked around. But no, I still felt the familiar feeling of being out of time and nothing sat right with me. I didn't want to burden Bella with my thoughts as I had come to realise that this was going to be an ongoing thing with me. I will always be looking for that something that would trigger my memory. Up until now, no memories had surfaced. I sometimes felt like a duck out of water.

Mrs Forest answered the door at eleven a.m. the next day, and a rather burly bloke with a large, round body stood there it was Lord Winter. He had an open face that was flushed, a large nose, bushy eyebrows, and long sideburns. He shook my hand with a smile on his face when he introduced himself, and I noticed his hands were big. He then greeted Bella and asked after her parents. He stepped aside for the blokes behind him. 'Mr Selkirk, this is Mr Jonathan Clark, our senior gunsmith and his assistant, Mr Henry James.' We shook hands and I asked them all to follow me through to the study where I had my rifle sitting on the middle of the table. I closed the door and turned to Lord Winter. 'Well, my lord, there she is. Take a look and see what you think.' The gunsmiths pushed past Lord Winter to get to the rifle first. Jonathan Clark looked at me and asked, 'Can I pick it up?' 'Of course, fellas, I answered, 'fill your boots.' That got a few stares but fill their boots they did. Bella and I sat down on the couch while the three of them were whispering, and I heard lots of 'good God... how' and 'before its time.' Then they turned to me. 'How do you come to have this rifle, sir?' Henry James asked. 'I have no idea, fellas, but I'm inclined to believe that I owned it before my memory loss as you can see my initials are engraved on the stock along with some numbers 2013.' Clark couldn't resist saying, 'But it's made in Japan, and I have never seen the Japanese make anything like this, it is well beyond them.' Can you produce a rifle like this?' I asked earnestly. 'Oh yes, sir. After seeing this I'm sure we can. It will take some time maybe about a year but by then I think we should be able to come up with a serviceable rifle for the armed services.' He looked through the scope and was astonished. 'This is unbelievable and utterly fantastic. Can we take it with us, sir? 'Of course' I replied. We will need to strip it down to find out more about it and how we will approach the design work. I'd say it looks a little light and maybe more suitable for hunting, so we would have to make ours more robust. But the rifle is a breakthrough and remarkably years ahead of what we have now. It will revolutionise the way guns are made, I'm convinced of that.' Lord Winter smiled broadly and stepped forward. 'I have a contract here for you to sign, Mr Selkirk. I know it is a little early to push this on you, but we need to move forward quickly as our fighting men would benefit tremendously from it. I think you will be happy with what I have proposed. The short of it is we will pay you one thousand pounds now for the rights to copy and two shillings for every one we sell. Now I know you might think at the moment it is not much, but at the last count, we produced eight hundred thousand of our latest Enfield.' Looking at his gunsmiths he added, 'This prototype could fabricate millions. If you sign this, you will be a very wealthy man in your own right.' I stood and reached for the rifle. I then demonstrated how to fill the magazine and how quick it was load and fire. Their mouths dropped open, and they looked absolutely astounded. 'Why did we not think on these lines,' Mr Clark cried, 'it's so simple now that we have seen it.' Each of them took repeated turns to break it down and reassemble it again. I had to admit they were over the moon.

Bella and I left the room explaining that we would organise some lunch for everyone, but in fact that was already sorted before they had arrived. It was just an excuse to leave the room for a private yarn. I don't think they even missed us as they were so engrossed with the rifle. 'What are your thoughts, Bella?' I asked. 'Sammy, I think one thousand is too low. Ask for fifteen hundred and two percent of all sales including the two shillings per rifle. They are going to make a lot of money out of this. When you think of all the men in the armed services all around the empire, he is right; it could be three or four million in sales and that is a colossal amount. I think it is only fair, don't you, my love? Remember we have to think of our child's future now.' I had to smile. 'Dark waters run deep, Bella. You are a hard taskmaster. Okay, kiddo, let's ask for what you suggested and see what sort of reaction we get from them.' Mrs Forest popped her head around the corner. 'Lady Isabella, lunch will be served when you are ready in the dining room.' 'Thank you, Mrs Forest. Give us about ten more minutes.' We returned to Lord Winter and his employees who looked up and smiled. 'Well, Mr Selkirk, we are very excited about this rifle so have you come to a decision?' Lord Winter questioned. 'Yep, we have, sir,' I replied. Fifteen hundred up front and two shillings per rifle, but we would also like two percent of the overall sales as well.' His smile vanished immediately. 'That is asking a bit much, old fellow,' he blustered. 'Not really,' I replied, 'we could be producing millions of rifles and two percent is not that much to ask. Or...' I looked down at Bella, 'you can drop the two shillings, and pay us ten percent of all sales,' Sam demanded. 'Ten percent? No, no, that is quite out of the question. No, we will leave it at two shillings and two percent plus fifteen hundred up front, with the dividend paid into your bank quarterly.' I turned to Bella. 'Is that to your satisfaction, my love?' I asked. 'Sammy, I think,' she said with a grin, 'in your language that will be good as gold.' I turned to Lord Winter. 'You have a deal, sir.' 'Marvellous, Mr Selkirk, I was sure we could do business together.' He was back to his smiling self once again. He brought out the agreement and included the additional changes to the contract. Bella and I then read it through and signed along the dotted line. I noticed that he had left the actual totals blank, and I realised we could have hung out for more. But we were both happy with the outcome. 'A good deal; I'm so pleased, thank you,' he gushed. 'Now I have good news for you. We have been discussing that the way this rifle comes apart, we might be able to produce it even faster than we had first envisaged. So that means my good sir, madam, you will start getting your rewards sooner rather than later.' We gave him our bank details, and he said that we would be informed every step of the way. Our money for the rights would be deposited in the estate bank account within the next few days. We all shook hands and Bella announced, 'Come, gentlemen, we have luncheon ready for you all.' With that we turned and a bunch of happy blokes followed us out into the dining room.

CHAPTER TWENTY-SEVEN

Southland, New Zealand 2019

I had just dropped the little bloke off at Mum's after taking my daughter to school. Arriving home I made myself a cup of coffee and went outside to my wee knoll to put my thoughts in order. I felt a bit down, saddened that I had somehow let myself down, and I had been so optimistic when I had begun the week. In the distance I could see Stewart Island with a black smudge on the horizon behind it. I smiled, as I knew that was an indication of a good, southerly blow on its way. Well that was something to lift my mood. I love the sound of the rain on the windowpanes and the roof. Throw in the howl of the wind screaming around the house, what more could I need to blow the cobwebs away. You can't beat a rip-roaring squall in the deep south of New Zealand; it makes you realise that your troubles are nothing compared to their power.

I had just sat down at the computer when she hit. I immediately had this cosy feeling and my troubles melted away; I felt content once again. A tiny inkling of good things to come, came to me. Was this the day I'd been waiting for? I opened the first of the emails that arrived overnight. It was from a descendant of Aharon Hyman, a Mrs Akers who was knowledgeable about her family line. Apparently this Aharon Hyman had owned the first Selkirks shop in Portobello, Scotland. Before I had even started to read the email I felt a quiver run through me. Was this another indication that here was the break that I was waiting for? With anticipation I settled down to read her mail. It appeared that Mr Selkirk had met the original owner of Selkirks back in 1863. They entered into business together and eventually they asked Samuel to be a director of the company. He later told Aharon his story of memory loss, and how when he had first heard the name Selkirk spoken by the cab driver, he had felt such familiarity with the name, he decided straight away to take it on as his own. She added it was providential as their customers presumed that he was the owner and it took away the hassle that the Jewish owners had previously experienced, so it was a win-win situation, she reckoned. It wasn't untruthful, just convenient. She then explained that the family was privileged to be associated with the man. I was in shock. I stopped for a minute and just stared at her words; here was the precise information I wanted and I couldn't believe it. Within a few minutes of reading this email, I had knocked a bloody great wall down. I now knew that Sam had changed his last name to Selkirk. His grandmother's parents name was Selkirk and that feeling of association with the name must have touched his memory, so no wonder he felt comfortable with it. I was over the moon with this information. I got up and went over to his photo on the mantelpiece. 'Got you, you bugger. It has taken a while, but now I can find where you ended up and what sort of life you had.' Knowing that he ultimately had a directorship in the firm, he must have finished up reasonably well off, well that's a relief. Mrs Akers went on to mention a book she had found, written as a diary with numerous other bits and pieces. The writing was so small and difficult to read that she had to go over some of the content a few times, literally with a magnifying glass, to understand what was written. The connection between the two families had taken her a while to figure out, but in the end she had managed to make some sense of it all.

Sam and Aharon had, in the early days, just shaken hands to agree on a small commission on the sales of men's underwear that Sam had designed. But going over the figures, she discovered that they were extremely popular, and the shop did very well, thank you very much. Of course so did Sam, as his commission increased, but it didn't stop there. He continued to come up with other clothing ideas, one of which included a woman's bra that was way ahead of its time. His wife, Lady Isabella, had presented that to the women of the company, herself. Taihoa, hang on a minute, what the hell was that, back up there his wife, a lady?! The word screamed in my head a lady? I read that again, yes that's what she'd said, that's astounding. I had gone from him securing a directorship, to a marriage that I had not even found out about, all in one email. Now I find his wife was a member of the aristocracy. I had worked for months to gather this sort of information myself, and here it was delivered in one single email unbelievable. Well, of course there was a lot here to confirm, but my god he had married, he had been happy and shit a brick; he married a lady, to boot. How on earth did that happen? Mrs Akers went on to explain that all these designs originated from the Shrewsbury outlet, the one the oldest son, Aaron had managed. Who, incidentally, she said was her third great-grandfather. I was now on information overload and I loved it. It would take me a while to get the details straight, but man, I now had some knowledge to share with Sam's mum and dad in Dunedin, they would be thrilled to bits. I reminded myself not to run before I could walk as there was a long way to go yet, but I couldn't help but smile from ear to ear. Then the thought came to me Shrewsbury, why there? I had had him in Scotland, that's a long way from Shrewsbury, especially back then. Why travel on such a journey, as I figured it would take a good eight hours by train back in the 1860s? I came alive, another mystery; it looked like a lot more fact-finding was in the pipeline, and I rubbed my hands together in anticipation. Leave off! I was going off the beaten track again. I chastised myself *Drop it for now!* and just read what Mrs Akers has to say, then it would be time to mull over her message. It was understandable though; I was pretty excited after all these months to find something about him at last, so I shouldn't be too hard on myself. I went back to reading the email. She continued, it was no mean feat for Sam to be welcomed with open arms by a Jewish family, but he must have made a big impression on them. As a whole, she said, they kept to themselves or within the family. So for Sam and his wife to enter their lives like that was huge. She added that the whole family were invited to Sam's wedding in a Christian Church. Now that must have been a hoot, she said; I bet it would have turned a few heads in those days.

In 1869, Aharon died, leaving the eldest son Aaron to take over and the shops then expanded rapidly right throughout the UK. They had made a decision early on to not go upmarket, selling to more affluent consumers, but to keep it affordable attracting both middle-class and working-class buyers. Anyway they kept true to their word, and the shops never looked back. The Selkirks and the Hymans were close all their lives, and even today parts of the families are still in contact. I'm sad to say I have never had the privilege of meeting any of the Selkirks, myself. Of Sir Samuel and Lady Selkirk, all I know is they were both ahead of their time. I gather before Lady Isabella's marriage, she was a Gale from Shadymore. I hope this email has given you some insight into Samuel's life and his connection with our family. I'm sure there are photos around in the attic somewhere. When I get a chance, I will scan the images and send them to you. I hope this information has helped in your search. I went back and reread the email again *Sir Samuel what!* That had flown over my head when I had first read it. Sam was knighted? His title kept rolling around in my head. What the devil did he do to be knighted; my god this was mind-blowing. It looked like I had much work ahead of me. That excited me, and I looked forward to the prospect of discovering more. Then I addressed the last piece of information Mrs Akers gave me: Gale, now that rang a bell. Let me think... Lady Gale... oh heck, there was a Lady Gale staying at the Waterloo Hotel in Scotland at the same time Sam was there. Was that her, I wondered, could that be Sam's wife? Isabella... hmm... well that could be shortened to Bella. I got up and walked past his photo, heading over to the coffeepot. I grinned at his image. 'Hello, Sir Samuel.' Somehow I couldn't imagine Sam as a knight of the realm, but according to Mrs Akers he was one. My hand had a slight shake as I poured my coffee was it excitement? Probably. All of my tension over the last few months, searching in every nook and cranny, had been swept away in one day. Still, I was in seventh heaven having Sam's surname, finally, and knowing about his wife, Bella. I really felt like celebrating, but I knew more investigating was needed before that. So taking my cup, I sat down at the computer once again.

Right. First thing's first. I flicked off an email to my friend in Wales who bought certificates in the UK for me. I asked for the marriage certificate for a Samuel Selkirk to a Lady Gale in Scotland in July 1863, most likely from mid-month onwards. I didn't have to wait long as an email came back to say she would do it in the morning. So as daytime in Wales was night-time here meant I might even have it tonight, that is if she could find it. Great, that should fill in some significant gaps. Then I returned to the email and read it repeatedly until I had it in my head word for word. Having those names was a breakthrough and a lot of the little things started to fit. I considered Lady Gale, now she was intriguing. She was a lady before Sam married her but in that case he would have remained Mr Selkirk. So he must have done something worthwhile to be knighted. Now, if Bella was this Gale woman, and Mrs Akers *did* mention Shrewsbury was where those designs had originated from, then Bella's family must come from around that area. Was I getting off the beaten track here? I didn't have the documented proof that she came from there, but my mind was saying I had enough to go on. If I had a quick look and was wrong, well, I wouldn't have wasted too much time. I googled the name, Gale in Shrewsbury, and bingo, I got hits all over the place. It looked as though the family had been there for a few hundred years. The Gale estate was about twenty kilometres from Shrewsbury in the Shire of Shropshire. It stated the size of the property and that it was one of the first private parks and forests to open up to visitors in the UK. The park specialised in conservation and breeding endangered wildlife. The information went on to say the park has been kept in its virgin state, since way back in the era of King George III. All credit must go to the earls of Shadymore, who have kept the tradition up for over one hundred and fifty years. Included in the park were sleeping cabins for those on rambles. That must mean huts for tramping. There was a fifty-bedroom lodge by the lake with hot pools and a treetop cableway was the mod of travel to reach the lodge. To protect the surrounding forest from vehicles, there were no public roads in or out of the lodge except an unsealed service track on the Welsh side of the property for emergency purposes only. Apparently when it was built, it was fifty years ahead of its time.

The bells in my head were ringing so loud it is a wonder my neighbours the closest was about five hundred meters away didn't hear them. This sounded so much like Sam's influence, it shouted out at me, I just know it was him. He had to be involved with this estate. After all, Sam had a degree in conservation, so it must've been him, and if it was, what a credit to him and his ancestors for their effort. The piece included info up to the Earl of 1863 Bernard and his wife, Margaret, and also on his father and grandfather but nothing of the later ones well not in this particular search anyway.

Maybe they wanted privacy, in which case I might have to come from another angle. But I didn't want to spend too much time just yet on this part of the search. I had earmarked it as important for later when I definitely had their marriage certificate. I hoped that would come tonight. Funny, as I was reading all this stuff I was getting all these goose bumps at the back of my neck, it was as though Sam was looking over my shoulder. I felt his presence all around me, and determined that I must be on the right track.

CHAPTER TWENTY-EIGHT

Southland, New Zealand 2019

I struggled out of my chair. Boy, was I was stiff, and I needed to stretch my muscles. I walked into the kitchen and put on the kettle. I think I drink too much coffee these days. I glanced up at the clock, and it was nearly lunch time. How did that happen as it didn't seem that long since I had taken the kids to school. I looked over at my mate's photo once again and asked him out loud, 'Is this you, Sam? Have I really found you because, mate it has all the hallmarks of your expertise.' I went goosy all over again. Back at the computer I checked my latest mail. The first was from a lady, who sent me a compiled guest list, on a PDF file, of those who had checked in at the Waterloo Hotel in Scotland back in July and August 1863. As it was nicely laid out in alphabetical order, I quickly searched through it and suddenly, her name jumped out at me. I did a double take because I couldn't believe it; Lady Isabella Gale in room thirty-three, and right next door in thirty-four was Samuel Mack. This was too much of a coincidence for it not to be them. Everything I had read earlier seemed to be confirmed and my heart soared. There was a reference below it to a wedding breakfast with a note that a Colonel Mcrea had given the bride away. Then, as an afterthought, Samuel Selkirk was added, with "Mack" in brackets. As I read those words, tears poured down my cheeks, this was total confirmation without the actual document I was waiting for. My next thought was how on earth did he meet her? But only for a moment I couldn't concentrate as my emotions kept getting in the way. After all, four years had had gone by since he had been removed from my life, and that of his parents, and I missed him terribly. I sat glued to the screen staring at the information, but not really seeing a thing, because I was blubbering like a bloody, little kid. Get a grip on yourself mate, don't be such a wussy, I chastised myself. How long I sat there heaven knows, but ever so slowly I got my act together. Then I checked the time again. Shit, the kids, time to pick them up. Forgetting my mental state, I was out the door as if I had a fire cracker up my bum, and I ran to the car.

Later that night when Tui arrived home from work, I got her to look over all of the information that I had received that day. My mind was still in a bit of a fuddle and I wanted her wise council. She read everything without making a sound and jotted notes down on a notepad, then finally stopped, looked up at me and smiled. 'I can see it has been an emotive day for you Bobby, but I think you might have cracked the first part of the puzzle.' 'After going over all the facts that have been sent to you, this is how I see it. Sam arrived in Scotland on the *Esk* with Bella, his nurse, which I believe is Lady Isabella Gale. I'll tell you my thoughts on why she changed her name, in a minute. "Isabella" comes up so many times that it's too often to be coincidental, so I'm reasonably sure that Bella is an abbreviation of her name. Now, what I find interesting is for her to change her name, come out to New Zealand, and work in Dunedin where there was rampant cholera, then later move north and get caught up in the Auckland incident. I'm picking she must have been a particularly strong woman. If this is her, I'm guessing she changed her name to conceal her identity so she could perform her nursing duties freely and without hindrance. Now if she had gone by her real name, she would have had problems at every turn. So going by the facts

227

I'd say she was a remarkable woman well ahead of her time. Yes, I'd like to add, my kind of woman.' Tui grinned broadly. 'Anyway that's my opinion, and I'm sticking to it.' She shook her head and continued, 'It looks like Sam must have had an enormous effect on her. There he was, a man without any memories, so he had no past to speak of, and yet she still saw in him a man that she could love. As you know, back then, the landed gentry didn't marry for love or not that often, so this woman must have had a fair amount of backbone to go up against the norm so she would have attracted attention.' I smiled at that, and I remembered back to the day I had first come across Bella. 'You know, Tui, you're right. I met her twice, and thinking back now she left quite an impression on me. She sure as hell had the sailor boys hopping when they came to collect Sam to take him down to the hospital ship. The second time was when we went on board the next day. Sam had been in and out of consciousness since he'd arrived, and she had sat up with him most of the night. I felt then that she was caring and had a big heart. There were no airs nor graces about her; she just worked to get the job done and was a strong-willed lady, to boot. So yeah, I have to agree with you on that one.' Having Tui beside me and quietly going over the details helped me get over the emotive journey I'd been on since receiving this material. As I started to think logically once again, I joined in with my thoughts. 'The Waterloo wouldn't have been cheap so they must have had money. Though when you think about it, Sam did have his army gratuity, and if Bella was a lady, she no doubt would have had money tucked away somewhere. But I know Sam's strong views against being a kept man, so I bet even though he'd lost his memory, one of the first things he would have done would have been to seriously think about how to get his hands on some cash.' I put a question I'd been thinking over, to her. 'So how would he have met the Selkirks in the first place to get his fortune started, do you think? I can guarantee they wouldn't have

228

been in the family's circle of friends, being Jewish and all.' 'Maybe,' she surmised. 'Sam bought himself some new clothes. That could have been when they met up, in the Selkirks shop.' 'Yes that works. I bet when he saw the shop front with the name Selkirks above the door it would have triggered something inside him, as it was a name well known in his family. Anyway, I know he didn't like the name, Mack, that's for sure, he only used it because I gave it to him. We all went by different names back then so we could remain incognito. But he hated his, so that was probably the reason he dumped Mack and chose Selkirk as his new name.'

I had taken over the conversation and Tui was content to let me have the floor. It looks like all I had needed was a shoulder to blub on and now feeling better, I was on a roll. I sometimes worried about what the after effect of going through the time warp, returning badly wounded and losing my friends, had on me. Had I completely recovered from it yet? Getting as emotional as I had today hadn't happened to me for a long time, but the latest events had brought it all back. Anyway I was over it for now. I'm so thankful that Tui is supportive, as I couldn't do without her. 'Okay, where were we?' Tui jolted me out of my reverie. 'So he changed his name to Selkirk.' I answered, bringing my attention back to our task at hand. 'Then he went to the newspaper and inserted that ad in the daily paper under his old name Mack as he presumed it was his family's name. He announced he was home and was anyone out there missing a bloody, big Scotsman with a funny accent. I have a strong feeling that that didn't get him anywhere. Then they decided to get married, I wonder if his name change was a problem. Looking over the research we've collected, I'm guessing not. I'll know later when that certificate comes through for me.' 'Then there was a wedding reception at the hotel,' Tui added eagerly, 'and the colonel from the army medical hospital gave the bride away. We don't know who else attended, but we can assume there might have been some of his mates from the ship at the ceremony. Also if Bella had a bridesmaid, it could have been one of her on-board nursing friends.' It was my turn to interrupt. 'But if the colonel gave her away, that means her parents didn't attend?' 'Well, she might not have even invited them,' Tui said as the idea popped into her mind. 'Remember, she was marrying a man below her station in her parent's eyes. Now, if she were married before she took Sam home, they would have just had to accept him. Sam's figure of speech would have been quite different to what was spoken back then, and the gentry were inclined to look down their noses at anyone different from themselves. So to go against conformity then would have been like walking on coals. If this was the scenario, it was pretty brave of her, still, it looks like she was a determined, young woman. I'm guessing his words would have had a few of them scratching their heads in wonder, don't you think? Anyway I'm sure that the Gales would have eventually realised what a great bloke Sam was. So how are we doing now, Bob?' 'Great, I'm really pleased with all the information we've collected today. You know I think we've got the beginnings of his life in the UK stitched up. I will be able to confirm all the details as correct later tonight I hope. I think it's neat to think that he was happy though. You know the way Sam was with his solid beliefs on conservation, and then to plant him into the middle and late nineteenth century when those ideas were more or less non-existent, I can imagine he must have fought tooth and nail to protect the forest from logging. I'll research the estate a bit more once I get that email. Also I don't want to delay getting in touch with his mum and dad so I'll ring them tomorrow, I promised I would keep them up to speed and this is the first positive finding of Sam's life. I know they will be tickled pink, it won't bring him back, but it will be some sort of closure for them. 'Then a thought struck me. 'Out of curiosity, I wonder how he got his knighthood.

Now that would be interesting to know. Anyway, his parents will be proud, what parent wouldn't be. Hey I wonder if being married into a titled family had any influence on his being awarded the order. No! Knowing Sam I doubt he would have accepted the title if he hadn't received it on his own merit. He might have lost his memory but I doubt very much he would have lost his integrity.'

Finishing our analysis for the moment, Tui and I took our cuppa out into the conservatory and watched the last of the storm slip north up the east coast. I felt contented and at peace with myself. For me, finding Sam was a healing process that I didn't think I needed. It's been a long time since I came back from the past of 1863 full of bullet holes. I was completely buggered then, that was until Tui nursed me well again. She was my strength she still is, and I'm so grateful she found me. I just hadn't realised that although my body had mended physically, I had a ways to go, yet. As Tui prepared for bed, I tidied my desk and checked the mail, nothing as yet, it will still be early over there, so I'll check it in the morning. It excited me discovering all I could about Sam's day-to-day life in another time period. With this unveiling I knew I would recover as well. I was getting there, but many questions still rolled around in my head. Did they have children? What happened to his rifle, and how did he survive the overall environment of the nineteenth century? There was still a fair amount of sleuthing to get on with, but I now had something concrete, and I was over the moon. What was most surprising to me was I knew in my heart I was spot on. It was this awareness of Sam around me that made me so sure. At last I climbed into bed, and turned to Tui, kissed her and said, 'The confirmation hasn't arrived yet, I'll check in the morning. You know honey, if it weren't for you I would still be that shaking jelly you found when you first knocked on my door. Don't ever leave me; I couldn't do without you.' 'Oh, Bobby, don't be silly, you pull yourself down too much, and you were unwell back then. Now you are on the mend and much stronger than you think. All the way through your investigation, you have been methodical and persistent in your search. You have done this all on your own. Just know that I'm always here to support you if you need it.' We snuggled up against each other. As I drifted off to sleep my last thought of the day was that I can't wait to get up to find the marriage certificate from my friend in Wales, and -------- ------------ blackness I was out like a light.

CHAPTER TWENTY-NINE

London November 1863

We spent the week shopping and sightseeing in what was often referred to as dirty old London. The smell of dung was the worst we had come across so far. It permeated the air along with soot and smoke, and at times we had to watch where we stepped to avoid the muck strewn about. Nothing seemed familiar or commonplace to me; in fact, I felt like a tourist. But what I really found disconcerting was that I couldn't break the thought that everything around me seemed so old-fashioned somehow. I told myself I was being foolish as I was the only one who felt that way, but this awareness of being out of time kept reoccurring. These feelings confused me. Oh, I was comfortable within myself, but I didn't want Bella to think I was reverting to being weird again, so I kept a lot of these impressions to myself. To take my mind off these thoughts, I suggested we go and gawk at Buckingham Palace. Bella smiled at the word I'd used and told me she had been there only once before herself. However her parents had visited a few times at the invitation of the Queen, and they had even attended the Queen's wedding back in 1840. Now, that date 1840 rang a bell. It felt significant to me somehow, but why, I didn't know. I felt something significant had happened then, but the more I thought about it, the less apparent it became. In the end, as nothing came to mind, I shrugged my shoulders and surmised that it may have been a special year for someone I loved. I put the thought aside.

I had recently heard that they had just opened the first underground train line in London, which travelled across town from Paddington. I mentioned to Bella that I had hoped to give the tube a go. 'What was that you called it the tube? Where on earth did that come from? Oh, never mind. When you come to think about it, it is the perfect name,' she said with a laugh upon reconsidering. So my plan for the day was for us to go exploring and include the new line in the itinerary. First, we would go to Paddington and take the underground to the zoo. Now that was a place I was extremely keen to see; then we would continue on to Kings Cross. From there we would change to Victoria Station and maybe if Bella was feeling up to it, cast our eye over the Queen's palace. That should fill up the day nicely, and we'd work out our meals as we went along. After deliberation, we decided to ask if Eliza wanted to come with us. Fear showed on her face immediately. 'I won't fit in, My Lady,' she said, nervously pulling at her clothes. 'Nonsense Eliza, of course you will. It's not as though we are going to meet royalty; we are just sightseeing, and it will be educational for you.' So it was all arranged.

As it was November, it was starting to be a little chilly at ten a.m. in the morning, so the girls made sure that they were well wrapped up with suitable scarves and gloves. It was a splendid day, and the cab arrived on time to take us to the station which was about a twenty-five-minute trip. Once at the Zoo, the first thing I noticed and took umbrage with was the bizarre way they caged the animals. I found it quite disconcerting that they were not displayed in a more natural environment. But soon my interest piqued when I realised the zoo had an extensive collection of exotic animals, some of which as far as I could remember I had never seen before. It wasn't long before I lost all perception of time. Finally, Bella had to step in and tell me that she needed to eat. The words 'time flies when you are having fun,' jumped into my mind. Frowning,

I puzzled over where that idea had come from. All throughout the day, young Eliza looked on amazed at what she saw with her eyes as big as saucers. As soon as she jolted out of her trance, she took up her sketch pad and furiously drew as fast as her hand could go to record much of what she saw. Eventually, we found a dining room near the station where we relaxed and ate our lunch, while Eliza, between mouthfuls of food, babbled on about all she'd seen. Once lunch was over, we continued our trip on the underground to Kings Cross. We were pleased we had brought Eliza along with us, as we found her pleasant company. She had opened up to us as if we were best friends, and had chattered to us both continuously about her impressions of the day. Elisa had recently polished up her accent, trying desperately to rid herself of her Welsh way of speaking, and now spoke like an upper-class young lady. So anyone passing by would have hardly noticed any difference between the two young women. Still, to my way of thinking, I had liked the way she had spoken before. It made me angry the way people placed others in little boxes because of the way they spoke. It was one of my pet dislikes. At least in my case, they couldn't pigeonhole me as they couldn't get a handle on my way of speaking. Of course, this was concerning to a lot of people, but I delighted in making the buggers second-guess.

Nearing the end of the day, we planned to catch the train from Kings Cross to Victoria Station and hoped to have time for a quick look at the palace, before returning home in a cab. But when we arrived at Kings Cross, the platform was unexpectedly crowded, and people were just milling around without purpose. When we climbed aboard our train, we were informed that the crowd was waiting to see Queen Victoria, as she was out and about today. We were told she was on her way home to the palace in her own special train that was following ours. The young women whispered to each other, and then Bella turned to me, 'Sam we would love to see her ourselves. Do you think you could find a good place for us to observe her at the next station, that is if the wait is not too long? I haven't seen her since I was a child, and Eliza has never even seen the Queen.' I rolled my eyes. 'Ok,' I agreed. 'I'll find us all a good vantage point, but I have a hunch that we won't be the only ones.' When we arrived at Victoria station, stepping down onto the platform we headed out to the front of the terminal. The road was even more crowded than at Kings Cross, and at the bottom of the steps stood a black carriage hitched up to two white horses. Waiting beside it was a groomsman and a couple of aids ready to assist the Queen when she arrived. The roadway was swarming with cops on crowd control, preventing the unruly from getting too close to the carriage. As Bella and Eliza were both short, I had to search for a favourable place for them to see the royal entourage. I would have no trouble finding a spot myself, as I was tall enough to look over most heads. Soon I found an excellent viewing platform for them on the base of the left-hand column. There was just enough room for them both to fit and no one could block their view from there. I lifted them up; it got a few frowns, but the girls were happy. I settled into a place nearby and watched the crowd and the police with interest.

Soon I heard clapping, and a roar went up as the Queen arrived with her young daughter Beatrice. They stood at the top of the stairs and acknowledged the crowd. They were accompanied by the royal entourage which included a couple of ladies-in-waiting and her companion John Brown. Bella whispered his name to me when she saw them. The Queen was a short, sturdy wee thing all dressed in black as if she were going to a funeral, and her daughter was cute like all seven-year-olds. All eyes were on the Queen as the royal group moved slowly down the steps towards the carriage. Everyone including the police bowed in reverence as she passed, and no one even bothered to observe the crowd milling around.

But that alerted me; I felt the cops should have had their backs to the royal group with their eyes vigilantly searching the crowd for any troublemakers. This was bloody slack protection for any dignitary, but especially for their Queen. I noticed she had just arrived at the carriage door when I spotted something out of place in the throng. Three blokes walked as though each had a broom up their bums. They appeared nervous and tense and were all dressed the same in long coats. But I seemed to be the only one who took a blind bit of notice of them. As they drew closer and closer to the carriage, out of the corner of my eye I saw one of them undo his coat; then it dawned on me that the bugger had a gun. A split-second later, the second bloke had pulled out a revolver, and then the third moved to the other side of the carriage.

Beatrice had just settled inside the carriage, and the Queen was in the process of entering with her head in and bum out when these blokes made their move. I didn't think first fool that I am but I pushed forward through the crowd and shouted, 'Vicky get down, there are people with guns.' I yelled loud enough to get her attention, but the mob heard, noticed the gunman, and started to shriek as they scattered. The next time I had to roar even louder above the din, 'Brownie there is a bloke with a gun to your right.' I broke from the crowd and ran at the first bloke just as he jumped onto the running board of the carriage, aiming his shotgun inside the coach. I hit him on the side of his face, and his head slammed back against the door frame of the coach. This put his aim off as he lost his balance, and the shotgun ended pointing up towards the roof as both barrels exploded, blasting a fist-sized hole in the coach body. The horses got a hell of a fright, and the coachman worked hard to control them as I saw the second man move to fill the gap where the first one had been. I grabbed him from behind, pulled him from the running board, then smacked him as hard as I could with my right fist. He yelped as he rolled on the ground, but came up with the gun in his hand as he pointed it at me and pulled the trigger. I thought, shit this is it, and time slowed down, but the revolver didn't fire. A piece of his coat-pocket lining had gotten caught on the firing pin and jammed everything. Not giving him a second chance, I rushed in and gave the sod a bloody good whack to his nose, a knee to his groin, and then smacked him once again in the side of the head for good measure. He collapsed to the ground moaning. By this time, the bloke with the shotgun had picked himself up and tried to come at me from behind. He rushed me, holding the gun reversed, attempting to crown me with the butt. But I managed to duck, and kicked out, hitting his knee and putting him off balance. As he staggered back, I closed in on him and hit him twice. He went down and this time stayed there. By now the cops moved in. It might have been twenty seconds maybe less since the ruckus had begun. But at last, they arrived in numbers and dragged the third bloke away, bleeding from his head, towards the Black Maria. Then the other blokes were manhandled into the carriage after them.

Finally, the inspector turned towards me. Before a word could be uttered, a commanding voice from the royal carriage demanded, 'You sir, I would like to speak with you.' I walked over to her carriage. 'Are you both alright, Ma'am?' I asked. 'Yes, perfectly,' she answered. 'I want to thank you, sir. If it had not been for you and your warning, I would not have had the chance to throw myself as protection over my daughter. If I had not done so, we could have both been with our Lord by now.' 'I'm pleased to be of help, Ma'am, I had to get your attention and thought if I yelled loud enough you would hear me.' 'Well I have not been called Vicky for a very, very long time, and you certainly did alert me. My thanks to you Mr...?' 'Selkirk, Ma'am.'

Bella had managed with Eliza's help to get down from her perch and had arrived at my side. She curtsied to the Queen and turned to me. 'Are you okay, Sammy?' she said with worry in her voice. 'I'm okay, Bella.' The Queen looked at us both. 'Lady Isabella Gale, I believe?' 'Yes, Your Majesty,' replied Bella, curtsying once again. 'But not Gale now; my married name is Selkirk. This is my husband, Samuel.' 'Good,' she nodded. 'Are you residing at your summer house at the moment?' 'Yes, we are, Your Majesty.' The Queen nodded once again and stated, 'Tomorrow at ten a.m, my coach will pick you both up and bring you to the palace.' With that, she turned and called, 'Mr Brown, are you well?' We heard a muffled answer, and she called out to the driver to drive on. The horses were still skittish from the recent excitement, but the coach moved out of the station and headed towards the palace with the cops running along beside.

We stood a bit speechless for a minute. Now that the Queen had gone, Eliza joined us and asked if I was alright. Then the inspector of police approached us once again. 'Sir,' he said, 'I want to personally thank you for your effort on behalf of our sovereign. I'm at a loss as to how we managed to miss those villains. On your very own, you stopped the assassination of our Queen, and our nation is in your debt.' I leant forward. 'Would a bit of advice be taken in good spirit and not as a negative?' 'Yes, of course,' he replied looking confused. 'When you are guarding dignitaries, make sure your men are looking at the crowd, not the dignitary. This is why those three blokes got so close to the Queen. As the crowd shuffled forward, your men didn't notice the trouble brewing. I'm sorry they were just not vigilant enough.' 'Thank you, sir; I'll have to look into that definitely.' 'It's just a thought,' I replied, 'something for you to work on. Now Inspector, if you don't need me anymore I think I will take my wife home and have a beer.' He grinned. 'I think sir you have earned it.' I gave him Bella's card with the address of the London house, and Shadymore printed on it. He thanked me and gave a small bow to the girls. I took Bella's and Elisa's arms and went looking for a cab.

Once we were home, Bella broke down in tears in the privacy of our bedroom. 'Sammy I was terrified when I saw you being shot at; I thought I was going to lose you forever. What would I do without you?' I held her close and comforted her. 'Bella love, please don't worry. Yeah I know I was lucky that the bloke's gun got caught in his pocket, but you must know by now that I'm a lucky bloke. I have you in my life, after all; that proves how lucky I can be.' She didn't seem altogether convinced. Funny though, it didn't bother me that I could have died back there, it just left me on a high. Maybe I had been in situations like that before, and I was used to it. Of course, I didn't like anyone pointing a gun at me, that's for sure; I found it quite unnerving. But I guess instinct took over. I defended myself as though it was the most natural thing to do. I didn't need to think about it. I continued to cuddle Bella for some time until she calmed. I then thought of Eliza and wondered if what had happened had upset her also. 'I had better check up on Eliza as today's event might have distressed her.' But Bella wasn't going to let me out of her sight just yet, so we both went hunting for her. But Eliza had handled it well. She told us she had been afraid for my safety at first, but when the man had his gun on me and she saw the way I handled myself, she felt certain everything would turn out well.

When we arrived home, Eliza had gotten straight in and made an excellent dinner for us both. It's the way she had learnt to deal with stress in her family. 'I just buried myself in my cooking to get my mind off all the nasty things happening,' she explained. 'Anyway, because of that, I'm pleased to announce dinner will be at seven p.m.; does that suit you, My Lady?' We sat down to a delicious roast meal and talked about the day that was nearly at an end and deliberated over the day to come. 'Fancy actually speaking to the Queen today and being asked to attend the palace tomorrow. What an opportunity, Sam; not many of us get to have that privilege. Amelia is going to be so envious,' Bella gushed. 'I suppose the Queen will just want to say thanks,' I muttered. 'I guess it's not every day that someone tries to shoot you. It will be neat though to get a look at the inside of the palace; I'll look forward to that.' It had been quite an eventful day, so we headed off to bed early. Besides, we had to be ready for the royal coach at ten a.m., and you don't want to keep the Queen waiting. So it was early to bed and early to rise for us both.

We were ready to go when the coachman arrived on time at our door. As we headed out and stepped up into the coach, Eliza and Mrs Forest rushed out to wish us luck. It was only about a thirty-minute drive, and as we turned onto Constitution Hill, Bella said she was feeling nervous. Then I started to feel a bit apprehensive as well. But as soon as we entered through the main gates of the palace and saw the sentries present arms, it lifted me, and I felt my self-confidence return. When the coach arrived at the main entrance, the coachman climbed down and assisted Bella out, while I descended. I looked up at the palace and saw an orderly officer come down the stairs to greet us. He introduced himself as Captain Millar and informed us he was our escort to the ballroom. The palace was exquisite, and I was in awe of the surroundings. I didn't think I had ever seen anything quite like it in all my life, memory or no memory. Large paintings of kings and queens mounted in golden frames covered the walls of the hallway, and in pride of place was a massive portrait of Victoria with her husband Prince Albert, surrounded by their children. Lush carpets hid any sound we made as we were escorted further into the royal residence. Looking around, I was gobsmacked, and even more so when we arrived at the ballroom, as the room was packed full of people. The Prime Minister was there with the leader of the opposition along with other civil servants, and also military personnel from The Queen's Guard were in attendance. I also noted a full orchestra.

'What on earth!' I said quietly to Bella feeling a bit bewildered. Our escort entered and led us right up to a small dais. Bella stood on my left and looked nervous as hell, though I wasn't much better. Then the double doors swung open and in walked the Queen herself attended by two Scottish orderly officers. The band started to play the National Anthem, God Save The Queen, and everyone stood at attention. When that was over, The Lord Chamberlain announced my name and began to describe my brave exploits of the previous day, when I saved the life of our Queen Victoria and Princess Beatrice. I was then asked to step forward and kneel on the investiture stool, and it was then that it hit me Bloody hell, she's going to knight me I couldn't believe it. I felt confused, my mind was in turmoil, and I could hardly remember kneeling on the stool. Then she placed this rather big sword on either side of my shoulders. All I could think about was, for god's sake don't slip. Then she announced, 'Arise Sir Samuel Selkirk.'

Tears welled up and filled my eyes. She looked up at me and declared, 'Sir Samuel, I cannot thank you enough for what you achieved yesterday. You put your life at risk for your Queen, and this, sir, is a just reward. In the days gone by, kings would have lavished land on you. Those days are in the past, but I can do this to acknowledge my thanks. I invite you and Lady Isabella to luncheon with my family and me, and then we can all talk informally.' She turned, and the band started to play as she went out through the rear door. The Prime Minister came over and shook my hand, as did the opposition leader. 'Well done old chap, well done.' We chatted for a while longer, and then I noticed Bella was missing. Where the heck is she? My eyes desperately darted around the room until an orderly approached me. 'The Lady Isabella has gone through to the Queen's apartments, and I'm to take you through now sir if you will?' With relief, I said goodbye to the government officials and followed the orderly. We passed the courtyard, the music room and the royal closet, until with a discreet knock on the door I was shown into the Queen's private lounge. Bella was sitting by the fire with a small glass of sherry, chatting away to the Queen as if it was an everyday occurrence. By the look of her, she was over her nerves and right at home. After all, with her father being an earl, she had mixed with the gentry all her life. The butler offered me a Madeira. I would have rather had a beer, but beggars can't be choosers. The Queen turned to me, saying, 'Your wife, Sir Samuel, has been telling me much about you.' 'I hope what she's told you is favourable, Your Majesty; I'm sorry I have no knowledge about my past to enlighten you more.' She smiled, 'So I understand. However, I found what she told me to be very encouraging, very much so. I think I will have to keep an eye on you, sir. You have the potential to be of great benefit to my kingdom; I do wish you luck in the future. Please sit down; we will go in for an early luncheon in an hour's time.'

The whole day passed in a blur. At lunch, we were introduced to a few of the Queen's children, including Princess Beatrice. I asked her if she was okay after yesterday's incident. That brought a frown. 'You weren't hurt, I hope?' I asked again. 'Oh no, mother threw herself on top of me, and all I heard was the shotgun blast, and part of the coach roof fell over us. We were not injured thanks to you, sir.' That surprised me, as I didn't expect her to be so well spoken as she was only seven. We chatted often throughout the afternoon with the eldest son, Prince Edward, and we got on very well. The Princes Leopold and Arthur were quiet, but I found Princess Louise an unusually intelligent and entirely practical child. The Queen was called away for an hour during the afternoon. There was a noticeable collective sigh of relief when she left the room, then all the children began to open up to us and became quite animated. Overall we had a splendid day with them, but I found it an absolute eye-opener on the dynamics of the royal family. We saw the Queen as a sad and bitter woman who spoke harshly to the children at times. But the kids were charming and went up in our estimation, especially Louise and Edward. At the end of the day when the Queen dismissed us as queens do, we trudged the long journey back to the main entrance, descended the steps to the waiting carriage and continued home with a sigh of relief.

CHAPTER THIRTY

London November 1863

Mrs Forest and Eliza were eagerly waiting to hear about our experiences at the palace, so Bella got in first and made her announcement, 'Sammy is now to be addressed as Sir Samuel Selkirk.' Both women stood with their mouths open in shock, and then Bella filled them in on what happened at the palace. That was a great ending to our day of days, but the day's repercussions didn't stop there. The papers soon got a whiff of what happened, and the next morning we had reporters around to get the story. I invited about half a dozen into the dining room for a yarn, and some tea and cake. They all went away happy as sandboys, armed with my life story up to date. Next, we sent off a cable to Bernard and Margaret and told them our news. A cable returned almost immediately full of gushy stuff, so I gathered they were pleased. Then a policeman called around to reassure us that I would not be needed in court following yesterday's incident, as all the men had confessed to the crime against the Queen. I asked what would happen to them, and the inspector speculated that the Queen would probably step in and be lenient. Apparently, it had happened in the past, and they had sent the perpetrator out of the country. We found out later that this is indeed what happened. As Australia was not a convict settlement anymore, they had to officially ask their government if they would take one of the wrongdoers. They had agreed, then another was sent to Canada, and the last was shipped out to India. All were never to be heard from again.

What a week! When we left London, we were on a high as it indeed had been an exciting holiday. We not only had luncheon with the Queen, but we also had made an excellent deal on the rifle as well. Then to top it all off, I was knighted for my troubles. Earlier that day at the palace, I had made an offer to the Queen to visit us at Shadymore by the lake when the lodge was built. I could see she was pleased with the invitation but demanded that we give her plenty of notice as her time was restricted. She smiled at my next request and gave us her permission to call it The Victoria Lodge. We arrived home to a fanfare. All the locals had either read the papers or had heard the news, and the roads were lined with villagers and some of the staff waving and clapping as we drove up to the manor house. Bernard and Margaret were beside themselves with excitement as was Amelia, and Angus stood quietly and smiled a lot. On arriving, we sat for hours on end repeatedly telling our story. Finally, I had enough and announced that tomorrow I was going bush for a couple of days. Early the next morning I buggered off, keen to experience the quietness of the forest once again with Toby. This was a much-needed break, and it cleared my head. Winter was just around the and each day was a reminder that the next few months were going to be bleak. I didn't expect many of my estate improvements to be made then, so I was hoping to check up on what had been done and take a look at some of the pathways Toby was putting in.

Having a knighthood changed things for me. It didn't matter now how I spoke or acted; I was automatically accepted into the higher echelon of society as I had saved the Queen's life and no door was closed to me. Bernard was amazed at the deal we had negotiated over the rifle, and when our first payment of fifteen-hundred pounds arrived in the manor house bank account, we celebrated. We included all of the staff for the occasion and organised a substantial meal with music added. Local musicians John Clough and his Orchestra were employed to play. I sang a few numbers myself during their break. No one had heard these songs before, but everyone enjoyed them and clapped along. This was an excellent buildup to the highlight of the year, Christmas Day when we planned to have a good old-fashion party for the entire estate.

By Christmas, Bella was five months pregnant and exceptionally large. It worried me until the doctor from Shrewsbury visited one wet and windy day and announced that she was having twins. Well, that was one for the books. No one had had twins in their ancestry as far as the family was concerned, and it was no good asking me, as my history was a blank. One day I whispered to her, 'If you get any bigger, I'll have to roll you around the room.' That took her aback for a second or two but she smiled when she realised I was joking. Her mother's wails at my remark went on for much longer though. Bella glowed with happiness. Childbearing came easy for her, and she took everything in her stride just as well, because she was determined not to let pregnancy hold her back. She gave First Aid lessons to the students and still used her nursing skills wherever they were needed. She even managed to continue with her school program throughout her confinement.

On Boxing Day 1863, Toby married Eliza. She was now sixteen, and Toby, seventeen. The couple looked so young, like babies to me. The wee church was full as everyone turned up, so that gave us another excuse to have a party. As Toby's house on the edge of the forest had been completed, they spent their honeymoon there. As a wedding gift, I promised that when the first fine weather of spring came, I would shout them both to go anywhere they wished for two weeks on a proper honeymoon. We had lost a good cook, but Eliza said that if we ever needed her, she would come back. Of course, that never happened as she was busy looking after

Toby and using her spare time to paint. She did, in fact, never look back. The paintings she completed of Bella, myself and all the family are hung in the manor house. As she was becoming renowned for her portraits, she asked Bella's advice on how much to charge as her work was sought after. After a lot of thought, it was emphatically decided for her to charge 20 pounds a portrait, but after she painted Victoria herself, it went up to over one hundred pounds. We were thrilled for her as we had watched her go from a child of a thief to a royal portrait artist, but the thing I liked most about her was that she never changed, except for the way she spoke. She was as committed as her husband was to the estate and included in her paintings the wildlife she dearly loved. She was a delight to watch, and many times I saw her sitting in a hide, studying the birds and forest creatures. She also spent time with Amelia in her animal hospital, getting up close to the animals so she could draw in all their details.

From the first day of spring the estate improved week by week. First, we got our teeth into building the lodge near the lake, Angus had done some fantastic drawings for its log cabin design which blended into the surrounding forest. Smaller tramping huts were constructed of a similar design, as the tracks were pushed throughout the estate. We built hides near the breeding grounds of various animals, treetop lookouts for birdwatching and others for night time viewing of the bats nearer the fruit trees. I had also marked positions of future hides on the tracks where the foxes, deer and pigs roamed. In all of this time, Toby's classroom education was coming along nicely. Both he and Eliza filled their shelves with books on wildlife and painting, and also veterinary science and poetry. Within a year, they were utterly literate. Their teacher deserved the thanks for that, as she had spared no effort in heading them in the right direction. Toby's first report on the state of the forest was clearly written and a joy to read. His summary included all the numbers and percentages of game he hoped to attain and covered all he envisioned in the new year. Bernard was impressed and accordingly increased his pay, not to sixty pounds as promised, but to eighty. I had to laugh, as there was a method to his madness. Margaret had seen how talented Eliza was and didn't want them to head for brighter shores. She had even arranged an outlet for Elisa's paintings. They were sent to a London gallery owner, a friend of Margaret's, and from there they were quickly snapped up. Soon she couldn't keep up with the orders. But Eliza explained to all who would listen, if there were not enough paintings to keep up with demand, then they would sell at a higher rate. Who would have thought it? She was no dumb cluck. As I'd promised, I asked Toby and Eliza where they wanted to go on a belated honeymoon. They both said Scotland, as they wished to see the Red Eagle in its natural habitat and Eliza wanted to paint it. So that's what I arranged a trip to Edinburgh to stay a fortnight at the Waterloo. I also gave them an introductory letter for Rory, with cash for the use of his cab while they were there.

In the summer of 1864 Bella finally went into labour. She had been huge and in the last couple of weeks had found it difficult getting around. Our lives were going to change from now on altogether, and we were both excited and apprehensive at the same time about it all. It proved that Bella's instinct was right, for her to keep busy walking and working throughout her whole pregnancy. It gave her a problem-free labour and the twins popped out within a few hours, much to my relief. We were blessed with both a boy and a girl. The little fella had the hair colour of his mum, and my wee daughter had the red locks of her dad. I shed a tear when I was introduced to them. My mind was now entirely focused on the future of my children. I couldn't let whatever was in my past interfere with their future. I shut that part of my brain off. Maybe one day I'd think about my past naturally, but from now on the family would take precedence. We named the young fella Bernard Samuel Selkirk, and his sister Mary Isabella Margaret Selkirk. I swallowed hard when Bella suggested giving our daughter my sister's name. It was the happiest day of my life. I thought that if my parents were here today, they would be proud, as proud as Margaret and Bernard were. I had never seen them so happy before, and so adoring of their grandchildren. I walked outside and sat on the steps overlooking the driveway to just gaze out at the forest of Shadymore. This was my place and my family's now, and whatever was to come, I accepted it truly for the first time. My future and the future of my children was assured; I was home.

CHAPTER THIRTY-ONE

Present time New Zealand 2019

It was early morning and the sun in a cloudless sky climbed slowly above the horizon. Yesterday's southerly blow had moved north and today felt fresh and full of promise of things to come. I slipped out of bed in anticipation as I felt excitement rising for the next stage of my research. Tui was as usual at the head of the queue for the shower, as she was the first away to work. My job was to sort out the kids; they had to be washed, fed and out the door in time for school, and then I had to rush over to Mum's to drop off Shane. Tui kissed me and the kids goodbye as she headed out the door in her crisp nurse's uniform. An hour later, I had completed my assigned duties and was keen to tell Mum of my research breakthrough. I called out as I entered my old home, loving the familiarity of it. I was lucky that Shane always enjoyed his time there and when I had enquired of Mum to watch him for me, she had said that it let me get some serious research done. Then she had smiled and told me she loved his company and was more than happy to care for him each day. This morning she was thrilled to hear what I had to report, knowing I had slogged over it for a long time. 'That's incredible news Bob; I know Sam's parents will be tickled pink.' I kissed my wee fella and headed out the door. 'See you this arvo,' I called and waved to them both, as I pulled out of the drive and returned home to continue my research.

I booted up my computer and made myself a drink before opening my program. I was slightly nervous to say the least, but there in the inbox was new mail with an attachment pinned to it. I gingerly clicked on the file and a marriage certificate filled the screen; it was the one I'd been waiting for of Sam and Bella Selkirk. Even though it was what I had hoped for, I stared at it for a few seconds stunned, as it had surprised me to actually see their names written on it. Then a big smile spread across my face. Bloody hell Sam, you were a hard bastard to find, but I've got you, mate. Boy have I got you. I read the information written on the document and was amazed that it was legible, as more often than not, it isn't: 'July the 20th 1863, Bride, Lady Isabella Downett Gale, age 24, born Shrewsbury, Shropshire. Father of the Bride, The Earl of Shadymore, Bernard Edward Gale. Mother of the bride, The Countess of Shadymore, Margaret Isabella Gale nee Wrightson. Bride Groom, Samuel Selkirk (Mack) age 30. The minister, The Reverend Duncan Macintosh. Witnesses, Dorothy Temple and Lieutenant Angus MacDonald. The Church, Saint Andrew and Saint George.' My friend had added her own comments in the email. Naturally, everything about Sam was unknown and it looked like Bella had taken her mother's maiden name to stay incognito when she left the estate to go nursing. Of course; it was all falling into place. I now had the confirmation I wanted; finally, the brick wall had fallen, and I felt elated. Oh, I still had plenty to find out about their lives, but the beginning was out in the open. Frankly, I was over the bloody moon. They were married in Scotland and evidently, both travelled back to her home in Shrewsbury. I sat there with a grin on my face. I turned and spoke to his photo on the mantelpiece 'Sam mate, I'm stoked for you and also for your parents and your sister Mary. You are not lost to us anymore, and mate, I'm ecstatic that I found you after all of these years. You know I can hardly wait to learn more about you and your life; I'll make a point of it you can be sure of that.' The memory of his rifle crossed my mind; I wondered what happened to it. Could it have survived, along with all of the other gear he took from the 21st century? I put myself in check, realising that I was off on a tangent again. As I found out more about Sam, I was sure that riddle would be solved. My mind told me to savour the moment and be content that I had made it this far. I realised it was time to listen to what it was saying.

I sat down and started to transfer what I'd discovered into a Word file for safekeeping. This included all the information from the various electronic documents I had found over the last couple of days. I knew his family would be thrilled to hear the news, so I spent the next hour duplicating the material into an email to the three of them, and included a copy of the marriage certificate as an attachment. After I sent it off, I Skyped them and Mary answered. Trying to contain my excitement, I announced, 'Mary, I've just sent to you an email. Grab Wayne, both of you read the info I've sent, then Skype me back. It'll give you a chance to digest everything I've written so we're all on the same page.' An hour later, they all came online. As I'd expected, both women's eyes were filled with tears, and I could see Wayne was struggling. I could well understand, as now we had tangible evidence that Sam had survived and had gotten married. But when I mentioned he must have had children, poor old Mary couldn't hold it back any longer and blubbed. Trying to talk through her tears was hard work, but when the sobbing eased, I explained what I was getting at. 'Look, we might be able to find his descendants of today who will be your 3rd great-grandchildren. That's the same scenario as Tui has to Shane's parents, and you know how they treat them as if they were their regular grandparents.' 'Well as far as I'm concerned, I'm thrilled that you've got this far,' Wayne broke in. 'We have found him at last, thank you Bob. Judging by all the information you have learned, it looks like he was well and happy, so all I can say is thank goodness for that. It looks like that young lady he married sure had her head screwed on right, don't you think? Anyway, I know that if we can find his family lineage, that would be an added bonus for us. If not, we have the reassurance that he had a good life. There is one thing that's been troubling me, now you know we are proud of our boy, but what I really can't get my head around is that he was knighted. What on earth could he have done to deserve that; do you have any idea?'

We spent the rest of the morning discussing our opinions on all the scenarios as to how this could have happened. Then we followed on to surmise about what his life could have been like back in the middle of the nineteenth century. The hours flashed by before we finally said our goodbyes. Afterwards, the euphoria I'd experienced talking to them was gone and it had left me drained, so I sat quietly thinking over what we'd discussed. I really needed to refresh myself and clear my head, so I took my cuppa outside and sat on my knoll, letting the breeze and the tranquillity refresh me, till it was time for lunch. Later in the afternoon, with time enough before picking up the kids, I thought it was time I went deeper, to consolidate all the information I could find on those weeks he'd spent in Scotland. And then when I had done that, I would move on down to Shropshire. But where to start? With Google of course; what would we do without it? I searched the minister's name to start with to see what I could pick up. As it happened, I had no trouble finding him, along with his church, as it looked as though he never moved at all and was still there up to his death in 1894, at the age of eighty-one years. I trolled through a lot of stuff that was irrelevant to me until I found a site with his photocopied diary recording his personal thoughts and records on the day-to-day running of his parish. The pages were tightly handwritten, but the book was a gold mine! Luckily,

I could magnify each page to make sense of what was written. After some time, I managed to find the relevant page for 20th July 1863. It was a blessing that this minister was methodical. He had not only documented the day, but he'd recorded at a later date, on that very page, any relevant information he'd heard related to the wedding. The final words he wrote on Sam's wedding day caught my eye. This is what was written:

'I have the greatest respect for Samuel Selkirk, or Sam, as he keeps insisting that I call him. He is a gentleman. He has a pleasing personality, a pleasant disposition and is an intelligent man, even if he cannot recall his past life. I cannot place his accent and his way of speech is slightly different to what is spoken in these Isles, but it never grated on my nerves. The couple in my mind are dedicated to each other for life, as their love for each other is apparent for all to see. I understand Lady Isabella was concerned her father might head north and disrupt their intentions to marry, so it was of chief importance to her that the wedding was arranged sooner than expected. Their best man was Angus MacDonald, a lieutenant in the Scottish regiment and an architect by profession. He had met Sam on board the HMS Esk on their trip back from the New Zealand Maori wars, and had lost part of his arm in the conflict. On the day of the wedding, I was thrilled when I saw some of the unusual guests that came to the ceremony. All at the invitation of Sam of course, but a respectable percentage of the Jewish community attended, most of them shopkeepers from Portobello; apparently, Sam had business dealings with the store owner. It did surely turn a few heads, but this is God's house and everyone is welcome, and the roof did not cave in as some were predicting. The son of the store owner, Aaron Hayman, gave me his card on leaving and suggested that there was a special discount on all clothing for Sam's friends. I must confess I did take up the offer and found the Selkirks establishment is most admirable to deal with. Colonel Mcrea gave the bride away, and the bridesmaid was Dorothy Temple, another nurse who worked with Lady Isabella back in New Zealand. I was honoured to be included as a guest at the wedding breakfast banquet at the Waterloo Hotel.' On the corner of the page were two footnotes:

'Samuel was knighted by Queen Victoria in November 1863. Angus married Lady Amelia Gale in 1865 at St Chad Church Shrewsbury.'

There it was again, the mention of a knighthood right there in black and white, so it must be true. His parents were blown away by it all when I'd told them, so for their sake I'd definitely have to find out the details; still, I was chuffed about my mate's achievement. I gazed at the page wondering once again how the hell it had come about and why. It baffled me; after all, he had only been in the UK not quite six months. How had it been possible to be knighted by the Queen in such a short time period? When you think about it, who in our lifetime has ever received a knighthood? it's only awarded to people with money, or folk in business, or maybe some top sports people. Joe public never gets a look in, so Sam must have done something extraordinary to receive such an honour. I looked over the minister's diary once again. What a godsend to find these sorts of details! I was elated that I had found it, as he described the day with such clarity. I noted down the facts it included. I now had the names of both Bella's sister and Sam's best man. It looked like they married each other a couple of years later, which resulted in Angus becoming Sam's brother-in-law. I emailed the latest information I'd gathered to Sam's folks, and ten minutes later they Skyped me again. I could see Wayne was stressed, and insisted, 'You'll have to find out about that knighthood, Bob, a bloody knighthood for heaven's sake; we can't just leave it there and not know how it came about.' 'Look, don't worry Wayne; I'm on to it. I won't let this slip by; you can betcha life that when I get stuck in, I'll find the truth.' We chatted for a while, going over everything once again, and he relaxed. I then added, to ease his mind further, 'Also, tomorrow I plan to start researching Sammy's life in Shrewsbury. I want to examine the births around that time to see if they had any children. At the very least, this will give me his immediate family, then I'll hunt further till I hit a wall. We could be talking three generations here, so there will be a lot of decedents that I'll have to identify. But before all that, my plan is first the knighthood, then the births.' We said our goodbyes and I closed Skype. I glanced at my watch once again and I was out of my seat like a shot heck, Libby's school day would be over already. I kicked the door shut as I raced out to the wagon.

As I raced to pick up the kids, I thought about Sam and his title. Then it hit me this might not be as hard as I had first thought, as there would surely be records of all knighthoods. So because of that, he wouldn't be able to hide the paper trail of his life even if he had wanted to. Though I don't think he would intentionally hide himself away, things can happen and records sometimes do get lost. Still, that doesn't mean it would be a problem in Sam's case; well I hope not anyway.

CHAPTER THIRTY-TWO

Present time New Zealand 2019

By the time Tui arrived home, I had made dinner, and we all sat down to eat. I told Tui about my research, and she was thrilled. Our youngest Shane who starts school next year turned to me, asking, 'Have you found Uncle Sam, is he coming to stay?' 'I wish Shane,' I muttered then perked up a bit and tried to clarify, 'No mate, he is a long way away. I have found him and, one day, fingers crossed, if we are very lucky we might find some of his family.' It's pretty hard to explain to a four-year-old about what I was going through, but he did grasp a few things. Tui got up and grabbed a bottle of wine from the fridge and a lemonade for the kids. 'As we have found Sam and Bella, let me propose a toast.' She smiled and filled everyone's glasses. 'I think we should toast to their health, life and family.' We raised our glasses and clinked them. 'To Sam and Bella.' I went quiet for a moment, feeling a bit forlorn as I thought about them. But Tui didn't want me to dwell on it and insisted, 'Ok now, let's not let this lovely meal of your dad's go cold.'

I didn't have a chance to go back to the computer the next day as my little bloke was crook, and he needed my attention. So it wasn't until a week later that I sat down properly and restarted my search. My strategy was to work on his knighthood so I Googled, 'knighthoods plus England plus London plus newspapers plus 1863.' A few of the tabloids came up: South London Press,

258

London Daily, and a couple of others, but it surprised me that The Times wasn't on the list. I narrowed the search even further to include Samuel Selkirk this time, and bang, big headlines.

'Mr. Samuel Selkirk saves Queen Victoria from assassins'

Bloody hell! I went to the page, and the full story was there in black and white. The article fairly shouted from its pages about how he had stopped three men from shooting the Queen and Princess Beatrice. 'Windsor Railway Station was the scene of an assassination attempt on our Majesty the Queen's person after she had travelled on the new underground. Mr Selkirk put his life on the line for our Queen. As three men rushed the Royal Coach, Mr Selkirk realised what was happening and with no regard for his own life, charged straight in and took on two of the villains, throwing them to ground. Mr Selkirk, accompanied by his wife Lady Isabella and their housekeeper, had a good view of the proceedings from the steps of the station along with a large crowd gathered to observe her Majesty. The Queen spoke with Mr Selkirk after the incident and then ordered both Mr Selkirk and Lady Isabella to be collected the next day from his father-in-law's The Earl of Shadymore's summer home and to be chauffeured to Windsor Castle. Mr Selkirk was knighted that day at a ceremony in recognition for his bravery. Government dignitaries gathered at Windsor Castle to witness the accolade.' There was more, all written in the flowery words of the 19th century, and it even included a description of how Bella was dressed. I was proud of the big bloke, as he was always prepared to protect the underdog. It looked like he hadn't lost his principals or his values even if she were the Queen of England. I smiled. My mate was still Sam even if he was in a different century, and I bet his parents will be proud of this as well. The article referred to his memory loss and his marriage to Bella in Scotland and also his rounding up of a poaching ring on the earl's property in Shrewsbury. I had to smile at that one; that's my old mate in his element, doing what he loved the most protecting the environment. He had undoubtedly made a name for himself, that's for sure.

I copied down all the additional information. It was a promising start, but my days seemed to fly working on the computer, so I had to keep an eye on the time. Now to take a gander for any of their children. I made myself a cuppa whilst thinking over this step and, with a coffee by my side, began to search for births in 1864 in the name of Selkirk. This was getting easier, as their names came up immediately. In the April quarter of that year, two Selkirk children were born, a boy, Bernard Samuel, and a girl, Mary Isabella Margaret. As both were born in the same quarter, I guessed they were twins. I marvelled at his use of Mary for his daughters name, as it was both his mum's and sister's name. Could he have remembered something about his past? Because if he had, surely he would have got a message back home to his parents as we did in Auckland back in 1863, when we placed letters in the BNZ bank vault. The letters had arrived in our time as we'd hoped. If he had remembered, wouldn't he have done something similar? However I was getting ahead of myself, as I first had to be sure that these were actually Sam and Bella's children. Their names were there, but I couldn't confirm it without the mother's maiden name. As none of the websites included that information, I had to buy the original birth certificates to get my proof. Anyway, I believed I was on the right track, as besides including Mary, they had used all of Bella's family names. So I'll send away for the document and hopefully it won't take long to get validation. If I'm right, Sam's parents, David and Mary, will have been the grandparents of twins. Mind you, these kids would have died about seventy-odd years ago; it's so confusing when you think about it. Anyway I'm going to dread having to pass this on to them, as once again I'm pretty sure it'll tear them apart. Boy, this was an emotional roller coaster for us all. I'll contact them tomorrow if I get the proof, but in my heart I know these children are who we were looking for. Now there's a thought; I wonder if they had any more. I glanced at the clock. Time was ticking by and I had to pick up my kids from school soon. I really should have waited until I had plenty of time, but I couldn't help myself; I needed to know if they had had more offspring.

I quickly searched the birth records again from 1865 right through to 1890. Sam would have been sixty by then, so if they'd had children after that, then he was nuts. As the first two had been registered in Shrewsbury, I looked for the Selkirk name coupled with any of the family names in that area. Bingo. I had a hit in 1866 December quarter, a Margaret Amelia Isabella Selkirk, and once again in 1869 January quarter, Samuel Angus Selkirk. With those names, they had to be both Sam and Bella's, it all tied up. I found no related births from 1869 onwards. So I sent an email away to my Welsh friend, asking her to buy these four certificates for me. I sat back relieved that that was out of the way, tomorrow I would know, and then I'd sort out what's next. I still had to check the census from 1871 onwards, so that could probably be my next port of call. I checked the clock. I still had a few minutes left so I did another search, for something that had been playing on my mind for some time. I searched for death certificates of both Sam and Bella. I checked from 1869 right through to 1930. That would have made Sam one hundred years and Bella would have been in her nineties, but I never came across one. Bugger that's strange; what the hell was he up to, I'm sure he's done this on purpose. I had this gut feeling that I'd find the last stage of their lives just as hard as I found the beginning. Well, I thought, that's for another day; right now I must focus on the kids.

With a fresh start in the morning, I booted up the computer, and four birth certificates were in my inbox. As I'd hoped, they confirmed that the four children were Sam and Bella's. Bella's maiden name was given as Gale, and Sam's occupation, a gentleman. I had to laugh at that. I wonder how he coped with that handle, as it was a big step up for him. I composed and sent off an email with all the information including the newspaper story to Sam's parents, then sat back and waited for the inevitable Skype call with all the tears. An hour later, David, Mary and Sam's sister Mary came online. It was heartbreaking to hear them talk of the grandchildren they'll never meet. I kept trying to interrupt, but they were pretty distressed. In the end, their daughter assumed control, so I managed to tell her what I had been trying to express. 'Look, Mary,' I proclaimed, 'we have a good chance of finding descendants of all those grandchildren who are alive and well today. If we are lucky, your parents will be able to treat them as their own grandchildren.' This seemed to settle them down a bit and I continued with encouraging options of what we could do.

After the tears had quietened, Mary told me what she had called to mind. 'Bob, do you recall the little kiwi broach I gave Sam before he left? I wonder if when he found it in his pack, even if he couldn't remember receiving it, he must have known that there had to be his own family somewhere. The broach had been wrapped in a waterproof cover and it had my name written on it, along with my note. He must have discovered it, after all, he gave his own daughter his mum and my name,' she ended in a whisper as the memory made her eyes fill with tears once again. 'That's a good point, Mary,' I acknowledged, hoping to cheer her up. 'That might be the reason, as he never used any of your family's names again.' We talked on for a wee while longer until I saw that their emotions had settled down. As we said our goodbyes, I added, 'Don't worry, I'll be in touch again later with another update,' and I closed off the call. The call had left me feeling shagged, so I sat on my wee knoll again overlooking the bay. It had been tough on them and on me too for that matter. They had thought they were over it, but finding grandchildren had changed everything.

As I looked out over the water towards a distant Stewart Island, I wondered if it was time to call a halt to my quest. Oh, I still intended to find Sam's descendants as I'd promised, but apart from that, I was happy with my research to date. But it couldn't go on indefinitely, could it? There were a couple of things I had wanted to explore, but I supposed it honestly didn't really matter. I still couldn't locate where Sam and Bella had died, but after all this time it was just one of those things that maybe I'd come across down the line. Of course, as it's over one hundred and fifty years now, they would have passed on somewhere, and I suppose knowing where that was didn't change anything. It had been while I hunted for Sam and Bella's death notices that I had come across the death of Bernard, the Earl of Shadymore in 1889. The notice mentioned that the service was held in their small chapel at Brittermore. I clicked on the arrow at the bottom of the page to continue overleaf, and up came a full-page photo of Sam and Bella, the new Earl and Countess of Shadymore. It went on to say that the earldom, by decree of Queen Victoria, was to pass on to Sam and Bella. It took a while for that to sink in and then I realised, my God, Sam was an Earl as well. Usually if there were no sons, the title becomes defunct, so I had rung David and Mary straight away to tell them the latest. They were as dumbfounded as I was at this change in protocol; I guess the Queen must have seen that Sam was an extraordinary man to have passed on the title to him. What a way to finish this journey; my mate was an Earl! I had looked at his photo on the mantelpiece once again and bowed, then said, 'Your Lordship,' as I grinned at him.

Then in my mind, I heard his voice call out to me, 'Just call me Sam, you twit.'

So was my mission now over? I finally had answers to most of our questions to date. Sam had been found, and his parents knew he was okay and had enjoyed a good life, but that didn't stop me from wishing I could see him again, to watch his smile cross his face. I still missed both my mates, Sam and Shane. Mostly friends drift apart when we marry and each of us gets caught up in our own lives, but in my case, this wasn't the situation, as one minute we were together and the next they were gone. My problem was I knew where they were and that they were alive back then, but I couldn't communicate with them as we were centuries apart. I felt that a large part of me had shrivelled up and died. We had been the best of mates, brothers in fact. I was tickled pink to have my research and time vindicated, but I would have rather sat down with them both and have a couple of beers. I'm sure there was still a story or two about their lives we could yarn about, something that hadn't been told before.

I had to remain positive; after all, you never know in life. Sometimes things change when you least expect it, and I hoped it would do so with Sam. He might even turn up on my doorstep tomorrow; we can only hope. In the meantime, all I can say is I did what I needed to do. I found Sam and his family, which was a blessing for his family of today, and now I'd even discovered his earldom. I'd given all the information I'd found on Sam's life to his mum and dad, and now I'll let them decide if they'd like me to take it any further. Maybe in the future, I will look at it again, but for now, we need to sit back and just enjoy the moment. I went back into the kitchen, opened the fridge and took out three beers. I placed them on the table next to the photos of my mates. I sat down and looked at them. Sam, Shane, I'm sorry we never got back together but I'm pleased you both have had happy and interesting lives. I'm proud of you my friends, and to be able to call you good mates. I lifted my can, saying, 'Cheers to you blokes.' Then I turned to Shane's photo and lifted his beer. Taking a sip, I heard his voice in my head: 'Tui and I will catch up again mate, or die trying.' I smiled. Then I moved around to lift Sam's can to my lips, and in my head, his voice was loud and clear: 'Follow our old pathways, Bob, get back up into the mountains. I'll be there with you, mate. Look for the mist at Ruapehu, because you never know, I might get through.' I sat up with a jolt, and a shiver went down my spine. Can you hear voices between the centuries? Nah, it's all in my imagination. 'I'll catch you both later,' I muttered, feeling spooked as I sipped at his beer and headed for the front door. Then I heard a slight movement behind me, and I turned back to notice Sam's photo had blown to the floor. My eyes flew open in shock and I started to shake as I looked down at it. How could that be, I had put his beer can on the edge of the photo and there's no breeze, it's a still day, so how did it end up on the floor? 'Come on,' I said out loud to reassure myself, 'this is creeping me out.' I took a deep breath, shrugged my shoulders and walked out to the Ute. It was time to pick up the kids, and about time I should think, to get back to a normal life.

EPILOGUE

A few years later when I was back working as a teacher at Southland Boys High, a black Mercedes pulled up outside our house. I had just arrived home from work and even though it was a warm summer's day, chills ran down my spine when I saw the black sunglasses brigade knocking at the door. What the hell was this all this about? That's when the realisation hit me that my problems with the government had returned. I had no idea how to answer their myriad of questions, but they did set me thinking. Sam had been dead for years in our time, hadn't he? So what were they concerned about? 'It has nothing to do with me,' I denied with more confidence than I felt, 'all I've done is enquire about him for the sake of his family and friends.' They didn't listen of course and went to great lengths not to give much away, but I gathered that somewhere down the line there was evidence in the UK purporting that Sam had been trying to get back to our time. How or why they knew, they wouldn't say, as these buggers had their own conspiracy theories. I was warned once again that they were watching me and that the area of Ruapehu was still out of bounds. I felt like I was up to my neck in it again. Over the last few years, I had continued my research for Sam's descendants as his parents had requested. Now that the secret service had re-entered my life, they interfered and held me back wherever I turned, so I had to call a halt to it for a while. Well, quite a while in fact. I quietly waited and hoped they would eventually lose interest. However, it still troubled me that they never revealed the reason why they had suddenly turned up at my place. Then out of the blue in 2025, I received a parcel from Sam. My face turned white with shock as I stood looking at it, and my breath shallowed. The courier told me when I'd recovered a little that apparently it'd been in a safety deposit box for years at the BNZ bank in Auckland. I couldn't believe that after all this time, he had at last made contact. I accepted the package with shaking hands and placed it on the table. I made myself a cuppa and stared down at it; I wanted to see its contents, but then again I didn't. The house was quiet as the kids were at swimming lessons and I didn't expect them to phone till around five-ish to let me know when to pick them up. So I had an hour or two alone to go over what was inside. I inspected the packet closely, guessing by its size that it was more likely to be a manuscript than a letter. I took the package out to my knoll and plonked myself down on the grass. I sipped my tea then gingerly opened the envelope. Inside was a covering letter and a hard-covered journal with pages that had yellowed slightly with age, but the printing was as clear as if it was written yesterday. The diary was written back in 1895 when Sam was sixty-four. It was a methodically recorded story of his life. It even gave the reason why I couldn't find records of Bella's deaths in the UK. Apparently the packet had been placed in the bank vault to be delivered to me around 2015, but it seems the bank had messed up and it arrived at my door ten years late.

I opened the covering letter and it read:

'Bob, my memory has returned to me finally, after I have been left in a kind of void for the last thirty years. Anyway I'm going to do my best to make it back home. Please don't tell anyone just in case it goes belly up. If I'm not home within two years of you opening this letter, please let Mum and Dad know that they have always been in my heart even though I really wasn't aware of who they were. If they're still alive, show them this manuscript, and to my wee sister

Mary, too. I have often thought of her through her note she left in my pack all these years, wondering who she was, what she looked like. We have a lot to talk about my friend; after all, I've thirty years to catch up on with both you and Shane. My son and I are both going to attempt to get back through the mist; he thinks his old man is losing his mind and insisted he be included. There will also be a woman travelling with us whom many are hunting, so she is in extreme danger. I'm doing what I can to protect her, and this is the only way I can think of to keep her safe, so she will be part of our group. Also, Abe is coming with us. Do you remember him from the Auckland Rough Riders? So please look out for us. Anyway, read the manuscript; it will tell you what you need to know.' I then opened his journal and these words from the first line jumped out at me:

'I was born on 18th of May 1863, at the age of thirty years old or thereabouts.' I quickly flicked through the manuscript. I felt overwhelmed to think I finally had his story in my hands after all this time. I set the book back on the table, intending to work through it properly later on when I was better able to focus. My thoughts were in turmoil my God, Sam are you really going to endeavour to get home, and if you do, when? I was uncertain of my best course of action, especially with the SIS sniffing around. I guessed all I could do was wait, whatever the outcome. I intended to be here to welcome him home, or not, as the case may be. Of course, I'd keep his parents in the loop, as they needed that hope after the emotional turmoil they have gone through in the years since we all first disappeared. I guess it's in the lap of the gods now. I turned and headed out the door, shutting it quietly. I couldn't muck around; I needed to pick up my children at the baths. I started the car, backed out the driveway and accelerated down the road.

CLEARING OF THE MIST

The third book in the trilogy

Thirty years have passed, and Sam's memory has not returned, until a disastrous trip to Rhodesia with his wife Bella changes his life once again. Heading home to the UK, slowly his memory returns where he is summoned by Queen Victoria to meet a Maori delegation. At this meeting he is further requested to meet with the Prince Regent. The story that comes out of this meeting will send dangerous consequences around the Empire. Government agents don't want him or his party to arrive at their destination. Sam and his party need all their wits to stay safe. Sam's priority, find the cave at Pukekawa and wait for the mist that transported him into the past all those years ago and slip back to his own century and safety.

OTHER BOOKS AND CONTACTS

Look out for Clearing of the Mist, the last book in the trilogy of the Whispers series

Web: www.owencloughbooks.com
Whispers of the Past: The first book in the trilogy.
Facebook: https://www.facebook.com/Book1WhispersofthePast/
Shadows of the Mind: The second book in the series.
Facebook: https://www.facebook.com/Book2ShadowsoftheMind/
Clearing of the Mist: The third book: COMING SOON
Facebook: https://www.facebook.com/clearingofthemist/
Liquid Gold: New Zealand one hundred years in the future
Facebook: https://www.facebook.com/Liquidgoldnovel/
Email: owen.cloughbooks@gmail.com
Phone, cell from overseas: +64 27 649 6687
Phone, cell New Zealand 027 649 6687

www.ingramcontent.com/pod-product-compliance
Lightning Source LLC
Chambersburg PA
CBHW030157200626
46812CB00017B/2251